Thanks to my mum and dad for deciding to have a sixth child.

Thanks to my kids for keeping me young at heart.

Most of all, thank you to Dawn, who rescued me one winters night

and continues to save me on a regular basis x

Chapter 1 – Archie needs the toilet.

It was yet another uninspiring day.

Nick could see drizzle slowly falling through the half-opened window as he stood in the shower, staring pointlessly into the distance. The sensation of watching rainfall, as warm water cascaded over his body, gave him a slight sense of peace and well-being.

He remained stationary in this sodden statuesque state for a while, allowing the shower to unsuccessfully massage his shoulders. Simultaneously, and with the sole aim of capturing his eye sockets, shampoo suds began commando crawling down his forehead, sporadically bursting out of the hair line in some kind of facial, frenzied raid. They continued their menacing journey down his temple, pausing only to regroup at the bridge of his nose, before launching into their final, chemically driven, kamikaze type assault.

Nick rubbed the foam from his eyes just in time, as he gathered without this intervention, the suddy sting was only moments away. This wiping action also woke him from his meandering daydream, and he began contemplated the possibility of not going into work, which was a thought he had most days if he was being honest.

The daily shower routine was one of the times where his creative thinking came to the forefront, although, it was argued, that the only person who agreed with that modest opinion, was the owner himself. As normal, he tried in vain to convince himself that he could be the entrepreneur he always felt he should have been. The only factors that had stopped him in fulfilling this impresario dream, was commitment, drive, and the severe allergy to arduous work. It had to be said that this attitude had developed into full on decay over the years, rather than just a slight teething problem.

Brake lights on the front of cars, as well as the rear, were his most recent creation. The number of accidents that were caused by drivers inadvertently leaving their indicators flashing, leading to unbeknown motorists pulling out, causing accidents a plenty, was his most recent project. The idea was that if the brake lights were not glowing on the car indicating, there was a good chance that they were not turning, prompting the driver on the verge of pulling out to just think twice about making the move. This theory was slightly floored if Lewis Hamilton was the person behind the wheel, taking the racing line, but in general, the concept held its ground.

His recent innovation was that good, he was going to patent it, changing the motoring world forever, whilst dramatically improving his bank balance at the same time. However, had this notion been backed up with factual evidence, collated after meticulously trowelling through hundreds of files found on the DVLA internet site? Had he spent hour upon hour, painstakingly unearthing historical data on road traffic incidents?.

Of course not. Nicks entrepreneurial drive had yet again given up at the first hurdle, after unsuccessfully searching the website for relevant information on day one. The idea was therefore as likely to get off the ground with as much success as an Ostrich, carrying a baby elephant tucked inside a rucksack.

His rambling pipedreams were interrupted as Archie, his eight-year-old son, came barging into the bathroom.

"Sorry Dad.....Need a wee" he announced ..... Just about allowing enough time to do what he needed to do.

"When is that downstairs loo getting built Arch, we can't survive with this one toilet malarkey?"

Announced Nick, turning his body towards the tiled wall in the process. Although he wasn't embarrassed, something about displaying his privates proudly whilst his son urinated, surprisingly just didn't sit right.

"I don't know dad.....do you want me to build it out of Lego or something" replied Archie, feeling the need to put his father well and truly in his place in relation to his last pointless question.

"Don't bother...it would probably fall over anyway" mumbled his dad, knowing full well his son would rise to the bait.

"That's a bit harsh" snapped Archie, who had recently started copying his dad's phrases.

"Alright, don't bang on ...... can I continue with my shower now mate if that's alright with you?."

"Jog on" declared Archie, borrowing yet another of his father's phrases.

"Hands!!" Shouted Nick, as his son went to open the bathroom door.

Archie smirked and mooched his way over to the sink.

The water pressure eased off slightly in the shower as Archie turned the tap. He rubbed his hands vigorously for two to three seconds before turning the tap off again.

"Have you thought about inviting soap to the party?" questioned his dad.

Archie let out a massive sigh before repeating the action, this time squirting an ample amount of soap into his palms. The introduction of hand gel quadrupled the time it took to wash them, mainly thanks to the bubbly slime he had manufactured and the subsequent time it took to break it all down again.

"Love you mate" declared Nick, as his son began drying his hands, in a fashion of course, before opening the door.

"Bummmmmmmmmm" shouted Archie as he walked out, giggling and describing the fact that he had just seen his dads massive bottom to his smiling sister, who was mulling over the prospect of getting ready for school. By this, it meant she was lying on her bed mesmerised by her mobile phone.

Nick smiled, continued rinsing his thinning hair and washing the suds off his body, before mulling over the letter that had uninvitingly plummeted on the door mat the day before. He had established upon opening the envelope that he was now of the age where you get invited for an NHS health check, a MOT on his aging bodywork if you like.

This was no twenty quid, back street garage, pretending to do an oil change scenario, no, no, no, this was a full-on, specialised, thorough service, including height/weight measurements, blood pressure and blood tests. So thorough, it was also offering the additional chance of having his prostate checked.

"Joy to the world" he thought, as he briefly checked his testicles, something he had unwittingly started doing whilst showering. This by the way, wasn't a conscious part of his daily grooming and the meeting between hand and testis, was more of a reluctant handshake with a homeless tramp than a warm embrace with a long lost loved one. Nevertheless, an introduction it was and a meaningful relationship it was to be.

Chapter 2 – Doc Martin versus Doc Martha ?

He just could not shake the thought of his pending visit to the doctors.

"You are now of the age where you can have a stranger shove his finger up your arse……….hmmm, lucky, lucky me. Why haven't I had the opportunity before?," he reflected cynically.

"And what is better, a male or female doctor? Surely if you have a man, that is bordering on being a bit fruity isn't it. Having a bloke's finger, or worst still, fingers up your bum, institutes a certain level of sexuality, doesn't it? No, it is a medical procedure you weirdo! Why would you even consider it to be sexual." Nicks internal discussion was now turning into a full-on debate.

"Granted if the doctor starts kissing your neck and invites you to slide your hand down the front of his Farrah's, then yes, that will constitute a certain amount of sexual connotation.

What if you like it???   What if you get a full-on erection mid-way through the examination? Does that mean you might start asking the other half to do the same thing during sex? People do that anyway, maybe its normal, maybe I gently suggest it to Beck next time the opportunity presents itself ?".

"So, a lady doctor it is then …No, that is not right either! That would be like your mum, talking to you about your Auntie Joan's hip replacement and then silently slipping her lubricated finger up your anus…. No that's it …..I'm fine….I don't need to go….prostate cancer wouldn't happen to me anyway……………it's not like it's in my family's history now is it……or is it……you just don't know ? Maybe my Great, Great grandfather had a problem with his prostate….maybe he didn't even know about it. Maybe he was already "prostated to buggery" as he went over the top in the first world war, only to be shot in the neck by some petrified young German lad. The Boche actually did him a favour in hindsight, saving him from all that pain and worry, Maybe I will leave it for now………. I will go in a few weeks…there is no rush now is there."

His mind took a well-earned breather from the ongoing debate that, he would certainly win and lose, all at the same time.

"Grow a pair" dismissed Becky, as she slid past him on the stairs, ruffling the letter that Nick was now frowning at.

Becky or Beck was Nicks younger and safe to say, more attractive wife. It was not unusual for people to feel the impulse to tell him, in no uncertain terms by the way, that he was "punching way above his weight." The most embarrassing time in this particular arena was when a co-worker, upon seeing a picture of the pair on their wedding day announced "Rrrr.... what a lovely picture.....How old is your daughter?"

Becky liked that story. She also liked telling him every time the lady at Sainsbury's asked for her ID. He couldn't remember the last time he got ID' d.... he wasn't sure if he ever had that honour in fact. Ultimately, anytime she could remind him of the age difference, she would, albeit in a playful manner. Becky was thirty-nine...but looked twenty-three. Nick was forty-seven.... and looked 47, but he quite liked these facts.

The pair had met years earlier, when they had worked together at a large Call Centre on the outskirts of the city. Back in the day, Contact Centres were called Call Centres as you simply called in for everything. Only in recent years had "Call Centres" become "Contact centres" mainly due to the development of different communication channels such as email, web ordering and web chat. In the early nineties, people did something that the youth of today would struggle to comprehend, they actually spoke to someone using their vocal cords, brrrrrrr, shudder the thought.

To place an order, make a complaint, ask for help or raise a return were done over the phone. To ask to speak to Drew Peacock when drunk after an afternoon drinking session, was also done over the telephone. The fact that back in the day, most of the bigger companies had free phone telephone numbers, made it a cost-effective way of taking the micky out of the poor unfortunates on the other end of the line. In fact, that is not completely accurate as there was another, much maligned, method of communication back then. For those born after 1975, there was a thing called the Facsimile, or Fax Machine as it was more affectionately known. This piece of machinery was designed to send documents electronically, instead of trotting off to the post office and waiting for a week for them to get where they needed to get too. The frequent issue with this method was that the receiving party would be greeted with a blurred piece of paper, which meant they had to call the sender anyway to verify the information.

Apart from those blank transactions, the only other memorable thing about the facsimile was that it would burst your ear drums if you were on the receiving end of someone misdialling when using the contraption. On these all too regular occasions, you were welcomed by some wailing banshee, screeched down the phone some electronic gobbledegook that you would only ever expect to experience if you had been captured, and were undergoing torture techniques in some training camp in the Afghanistan desert.

When they met, Nick was already married and was the father of two children, a boy, and a girl, although that marriage was wrong from the world go. He had made the mistake of settling for a relationship which was destined to be as unfulfilled as a poorly made jam donut. Hindsight would not only have saved him several years of heartache, but also thousands of pounds in counselling fees too. As normal though, retrospection is a smug old bastard and only turns up wearing his "told you so" tee- shirt when the damage is well and truly splattered all over the floor.

The early stages of their relationship hadn't been easy for both Beck and Nick. Reluctance to accept that his life was crap, twinned with the duty's fatherhood had brought, meant that the split with his then wife, wasn't quite as stress-free as both he, and Beck, would have liked. She had to endure his constant toing and froing and in the end their relationship had more off an ons than a Belisha beacon. It was safe to say the song "smooth operator" wasn't written for Nick, and If Sade had penned a tune at the time, dedicated to his exploits, it would have most probably been called "shitty let down". However, Top of the Pops would have surely found it challenging playing that little ditty on a Thursday evening, and it's doubtful that that the video would have been up to much cop either.

"All I am saying is that you have to do these things" declared Becky, this time displaying a slice of empathy and understanding that Nick, like most men, didn't embrace a visit to the doctors.

It's safe to say that men find it difficult admitting something is wrong at the best of times so dropping their trousers and having a strange man (or woman as we have established) rummage around in the old back passage, doesn't get many reaching for a pen enthusiastically shouting .... "Sign me up captain!!!"

"What is a prostate anyway?" thought Nick.

A few hundred years ago, you never heard of some peasant dying of prostate cancer. In all fairness, most people died of other horrific diseases by the age of thirty-four, so the old prostate was way down the pecking order in relation to illnesses that kept Edwardian gentry awake at night.

"What's that new blood test you can have" shouted Nick, who was now upstairs unsuccessfully gelling is hair.

"The one in the penis?" questioned Becky calmly.

"In the whatsis??" Responded Nick.

Becky poked her head round the bedroom door smiling.

"Just book in to the see the doctors for heaven's sake" she advised, before closing the door again.

"See you later…"" shouted Beck, as she ran down the stairs.

"And don't worry, they will be able to put their finger on it…or up it."

"Funny" yelled Nick as the front door slammed shut.

He stood in front of the mirror, raised the handset to his mouth and took a deep breath.

"Hello……..Can I book an appointment to see a doctor please…….. Can I request a male doctor as well if that is not too much trouble"?

Chapter 3 - Connie Lingers.

As luck would have it, two days later he found out that you could take a blood test that indicates how likely you are to get prostate cancer. He jumped at this option faster than a religious man leaping towards his faith. The thoughts of having some old man "fingering" his bum hole wasn't, excusing the appalling posterior pun, sitting right. The icing on the "what a coincidence cake" came almost simultaneously, when his workplace announced that they were taken on an external well-being organisation, that would introduce various health initiatives. Onsite blood tests, mental health awareness, breast and skin cancer examinations were all on the menu, as was prostate cancer screening. He didn't hang around. One cancellation call to the doctor's surgery and one slightly embarrassed email to the local HR team later, he was all booked in.

A colleague of Nicks also put his name down and although that specific conversation was brief, there was an element of solidarity in that their prostates would be checked around the same time. That's what he thought anyway, until the day of the deed arrived.

"You are kidding me" he expressed in a slightly camp but aggressive manner, a mix of Alan Carr and Phil Mitchel if you like.

"You're not actually old enough to have your rectum inspected" he continued. "Who came up with that ruling…. The bum police ?"

"Looks that way "quipped Chris, a rather annoying co-worker, who as well as being Nicks prostate buddy, was also a bit of a dick and had a knack of saying the wrong thing most of the time. He was a fusion of Jedward and Joe Pasquale….. either way ….. he was bloody irritating.

"So ...just to confirm .....you can't see the nurse today because of your age... is that right?" Nick giving the conversation a slight interrogation feel to it.

"It looks that way Jose" he smiled, hitting his target of annoying the shit out of his colleague again with his casual response. Chris had just discovered that apparently, you need to be over forty-five to have the "prostate check" and seeing that he had only just turned forty, it was yet another reason why Nick wanted to repeatedly smash him around his head with his keyboard.

"Unbelievable" he announced, taking one last sup of his tea before heading off in the direction of the warehouse, mumbling as he stomped off down the stairs.

The warehouse wasn't a place he normally frequented. He was an office boy and Becky often reminded him of this work-based fact. She was very generous in this area and would be more than willing to share this information with people who she befriended. On this occasion though, visiting the warehouse wasn't on his agenda. The occupational health officer's office, sick bay as most of the business knew it, sat on the outskirts of the warehouse, and that was the direction in which Nick was heading for his prostate blood test.

Normally, staff would be sent to see the Occupational Health Officer, or Occy Health as it was affectionately known, when they had legitimate health problems and the business needed to ensure they were doing all they could to support. As well as the "genuines," another group of people would find themselves lethargically being forced to make a visit. They were known as the "sickies," and they were the ones who pretended to be ill too many times. It is amazing how many people are "poorly" every third Monday..... and how the same people are unable to work for at least one week every summer due to recurring bowel problems.

Today was the first well-being event and the company being proud of its aim at becoming an employer of choice, was all over this special occasion and to not put a finer point on it ..... had basically promoted the crap out of it. Maybe that is an overstatement as there wasn't bunting garnishing the walkways and a local celebrity hadn't popped in to "pronounce the blood tests well and truly open." No, they essentially had advertised the fact that this beneficial health check was available. You couldn't accuse them of scrimping on the promotion as TV screens, emails and posters had all been advertising the event for a good month. There was even a poster in the lady's toilets promoting the benefits of checking your testicles on a regular basis.........maybe the HR team could have been blamed for being overzealous with that particular flyer.

Now, there are three types of people who normally attending these types of business-driven sessions. There were those, Nick included, who had genuine concerns and had therefore decided to plump for the less intrusive blood test rather than opting for the more traditional "legs a akimbo, fingers erect, in we go" approach. There were others that self-diagnosed their multiple ailments daily and therefore would never miss the opportunity to share their concerns with some poor unsuspecting health officer. Connie from the post room was one of these. Her name was Fiona but was given the name "Connie" when it became all too apparent that she was a close friend and supporter of the condition Hypochondria. She was one of those people who would give you a full and detailed response to the question..."good morning, and how are you today?." There are certain rules in life and most people know that the response to this question is always "fine thanks...how are you?." Maybe If things are really bad, perhaps if you've lost a limb, are unable to breath or even had died the week before, you might just get away with "Could be better." There is however no acceptable situation when you are actually allowed to tell someone your problems, none whatsoever. Connie was the exception to the rule, she was also the exception to washing herself , brushing her teeth and having friends.

The third and final type of person is the slacker. They sign up for everything. These are the people that will do anything to get out of work, regardless of the event. Run a parcel to another department...tick........ Go to the shops to pick up a retirement card for Doris....tick............Sign up for a smear test even though you are a bloke ......tick. The magical thing about the slacker is they have a real knack of extending time. A job, task or appointment that takes thirty minutes is no match for the slacker. They can double the time it takes and on occasions triple it, such is their skill level. The easiest scenario to relate it to when describing a slacker, is being back at school, when you were young. You will have encountered the moment when you were so keen to volunteer you raised your hand to everything.

Who would like some sweets ?.....hand up

Who would like to go for a break? .....hand up

Who wants to help clean the shit up that Henry has just done behind the bookshelf? ....hand up.... Oh no....hand down.

Now this is the slacker....... they just haven't stopped putting their hand up.

Transatlantic Direct, Nicks employer, had to be applauded for their approach to embracing "health in the workplace." It was quite refreshing, although his father mentioned on several occasions that they didn't have any of that "namby pamby nonsense" when he was young. "You got paid for an honest day's work" was something that would often find its way into a conversation when vocation was discussed. Nick was often tempted to remind his father that in the "good old days," they never wore a safety helmet when they were on the building site, always drove without the aid of a seat belt and back in the seventies, regularly chewed asbestos like it was hubba-bubba. However, seeing that he lived to a ripe old age , checking for prostate cancer in the workplace did seem a bit of a luxury and for that alone, Nick never argued the point further.

He arrived at the Occy Health office and knocked twice. He toyed with doing a "rat a tat tat" on the door but thought better of it, seeing that the reason for him being there had a serious element to it.

Morning" said the Nurse cheerfully as he entered the room. She was the proud owner of two rosy cheeks, so Nick briefly tried to establish if this was due to the room being too hot, the nurse being slightly overweight or if she was simply just rosy cheeked. He decided without doubt it was the middle option and refocused on the matter in hand.

"Morning" he replied. "How is your day going?" he enquired politely, fully expecting the standard response of "fine thank you…. and you"

"Fine thank you…. and you" responded the nurse.

"Good… good" he responded in an upbeat but dishonest manner.

"Can you just confirm your name, date of birth, first name of your address and postcode please" she asked, turning her back on Nick as she busily prepared the needle for the forthcoming injection.

"Nick Dean……6.6.70, 13 Winstanley Drive, LE4 4BB" he announced confidently.

"Thank you" said the nurse, appearing not to pay too much attention to the information provided.

He now wished he had provided different personal information, just because he felt that Rosy was on autopilot and wasn't listening to his response. He knew that ultimately the fact that he lived on Winstanley Drive made no difference to the forthcoming procedure, but he felt if you are going to ask for specifics, you should jolly well check them, or at least look as if you verified the information.

"Can you roll up your right sleeve please Mr Dean" asked the nurse calmly. He undid his shirt button at the wrist and gently rolled the sleeve above his elbow.

"Thank you" announced Rosy, tapping away on his arm in a vain attempt too, well find a vein. "Slight Scratch" she added.

Nick looked away as he wasn't too sure if he had a problem with needles and decided at that moment in time, to play safe and not to chance it. Unfortunately for him, the phrase "slight scratch" was one that would become all too familiar over the forthcoming months.

Chapter 4 – Bez and Erectile Dysfunction.

"When do you hear about your prostrate then?" enquired Chris, sitting back in the chair, bouncing to and fro ever so slightly.

"I reckon you get the results back within a week" replied Nick, staring at the screen, and trying his best not to enter into an in-depth conversation with his interested, yet still tiring colleague.

"And its prostate, not prostrate you tart" he added, still gazing at the screen.

"Prostate, Prostrate, Frustrate, front gate" replied Chris, still doing sod all and increasing the rocking motion ever so slightly. "It's all the same really" he added.

"What the hell are you banging on about" muttered Nick, glancing over in Chris's direction, who was now tapping on his keyboard, but not actually typing anything.

"I'm just saying" Chris chirped…… as he leant forward and picked up the handset on the telephone.

"Yeah…as normal…saying a lot….a lot of Shite that is" exclaimed Nick, shaking his head before redirecting it back in the direction of his computer screen.

"Good morning, can I speak to Bob" enquired Chris, putting on his professional telephone voice but still managing to sound like a Grade A penis.

Nick refocused on his outlook inbox that was showing 137 emails. He opened the oldest email entitled "missing goods," which was from the day before. He had recently realised that managing his email inbox had become his main directive, something with which he wasn't overjoyed with. An increase in workflow within his department and a decrease in staffing levels meant that more and more of his day was taken up responding to customer queries. Previously, his team would be the ungrateful recipients of this workload but seeing that several had left the department and finding replacements had become trickier than Paul Daniels performing a magic trick whilst trick or treating, he found that his delegating opportunities had become severely limited.

He began typing a response to his oldest email. The transport manager, Warren Blunt, who he knew fairly well, was the intended target on this occasion. They had worked together on a project a few years back, so their relationship enabled him to add a brief dig about his unkempt appearance, especially in relation to his new hairstyle. It was normal for Warren, or Blunty as he was known, to be on the receiving end of Nicks endearing banter. In all fairness to Blunty, he worked with the driving fleet so wasn't out of his depths by any means when it came to earthy chitchat. If truth be told, the "bants" that arrived from Nicks direction bordered on saint like, especially in comparison to some of the more hard-hitting comments that came Blunty's way. A good example would be Dougie, a 63-year-old Scottish van driver who tended to start and finish most of his conversations with a swear word.

Nick paused for a moment, reasonably content with the fact that he had managed to crowbar the comment "looking like Bez from the Happy Mondays" into the correspondence he had just sent. He knew full well that Bez had shorter hair and Shaun Ryder would have been a better fit, but "Bez" worked better from a comedy aspect and Blunty would have appreciated the nineties dig all the same.

PROSTATE CANCER…. appeared in the google search box as Nick switched attention from his emails and instead, began typing into the internet search field. He was somewhat annoyed that it was in capital letters but seeing as the search functioned worked in upper or lower case, he let it go, albeit switching the caps lock key off in the process. The information instantaneously appeared on the screen, and he began scanning for the one option that had the word "symptoms" within it.

This wasn't the first time he had visited this page; in fact, he had probably reviewed this subject several times in the last three weeks. Frequent urination and blood in the urine were two of the big symptoms. There had been no apparent signs of blood in his wee, although four years earlier, when he had eaten pickled beetroot, well, let's just say that was a bit of an eye opener. NHS 111 were the lucky recipients of that conversation. Maybe in hindsight they needed to promote the question "have you eaten beetroot" up the pecking order. Fifteen minutes of intense medical questioning could have been avoided if that little pearl of wisdom were thrown into the mix earlier in the conversation.

Frequent urination? five, ten, twenty, fifty times a day, "What is frequent?" he thought, mulling over the toilet regularity inquiry. He felt the urge to go to the privy just reading the subject matter, so instantly, doubt made an appearance and Doctor "Online" Dean had yet again completed his thorough examination, and his prostate, was obviously riddled. He took comfort from the fact he rarely woke up during the night to pass water, so this gave him slight reassurance, although looking for positive outcomes when analysing ailments on the web is not part of the game.

Erectile dysfunction was another area he could rule out. The only time that this had been an issue was when Red, Red Wine stayed a little too close to him and he had discovered that this beautiful poison would bring the phallic Berlin wall crashing down, with no hope of it being rebuilt until the morning. Becky may have disputed Nicks over confidence within this specific area as she would have been able to recount other, non-wine related occasions, when Newtons gravitational theory of "what goes up must come down" had fallen at the first hurdle. If a power point presentation were available, it is safe to say she would be reviewing past performance data thoroughly.

The only other concern in relation to his toilet rituals was the need to go toilet after drinking cold beer. It was well known within his circle of friends that he would need to go to the loo at least three times, in fifteen minutes, if he was going to have any chance of making the journey home. There were numerous times when a friend or taxi driver would be forced to pull over, and Nick would have no option but to do the necessary at the side of the road. It was a blessing that Nick lived on the outskirts of the city, as most of the routes home involved unlit country roads,   otherwise section 235 of the Local Government Act 1972, more commonly known as going for a wee in public, would have surely crossed his path with an "allo, allo, what do we have here then!".

He also took further reassurance that this particular cold beer trait appeared to run in the family. His brothers and father all had the same relationship with chilled lager, something they had discovered when they found themselves standing next to each other at the urinal at a close friend's wedding. Of course, there is nothing out of the ordinary with this scenario, but to find the exact same line up ten minutes later, did literally take the piss somewhat.

Chapter 5 – The best of Chesney Hawkes.

"All clear" he announced as he lumbered through the front door, his laptop bag bashing against the door frame as it tended to do from time to time.

"Told you there was nothing to worry about didn't I?" shouted Becky, busily preparing food in the kitchen, whilst sucking up an unhealthy mouthful of vodka and tonic through a novelty straw.

"One slight issue though" replied Nick, in a raised voice.

"Go on" she questioned.

"It states that the blood test results, combined with the questionnaire information, indicates that the risk level is low" he queried, ensuring that his voice could be heard from the hallway.

"And….." she quizzed, getting a little bored with the unnecessary drama being created.

"Well………… I didn't complete a questionnaire, so how do they know?" he revealed, fully aware that he simply needed to fill in a questionnaire to get the full result.

"Well just fill in a bloody questionnaire then!" declared Beck, walking through the kitchen door, making a clinking noise as she frantically stirred the ice with one of the kid's minion straws.

"I know …I know…… its positive though isn't it…. the blood result I mean?" he said, seeking some kind of reassurance. "Surely if there was a problem, the bloods would have shown something on their own wouldn't they Becky…surely they would?."

"Definitely" she proclaimed confidently, picking up on Nick's insecurity but also starting to feel the benefits of her second vodka of the evening. "It will just be a formality I would have thought" she added, walking up to him, gingerly standing on tip toes to kiss his cheek.

"Yeah…. It will be fine wont it….it's positive news …and I didn't have to have anyone fiddling with me nether regions" he joked, adding a slight accent to the end of the comment in a pitiful attempt to sound a bit northern.

"I just have to have my bloods checked in four years to ensure the levels are the same……..did you pick up wine by the way?" shifting his attention to the bags that were scattered on the kitchen floor and making a half-hearted attempt to look through them, pushing a few of the empty ones to one side with his right foot.

"It's still in the boot" declared Beck, gliding past him nonchalantly, before refilling her glass for the third time.

"Hey, how did it go with the planning department by the way? he chirped, picking up a celery stick from one of the kid's plates and munching on it like a drug induced rabbit.

"No news yet…..someone's apparently calling me back tomorrow" sighed Beck, raising her eyebrows slightly, stirring her drink with a dash of frustration.

What she didn't know was that the application to build a two-story extension that she had submitted two weeks earlier, had already been declined. The information finally meandered its way to her a few days later, and it was safe to say that "being slightly miffed" was a dramatic understatement. It wasn't as if they actually needed more space as the three-bedroom detached house was more that big enough for the four of them. Nicks children from his previous relationship hardly ever came around anymore either, so it wasn't for that reason that they needed extra bedroom space either.

The reason why his older kids didn't visit was a combination of reason. The first, was their age. Both were in their mid to late teens and however "street" and down with the kids he thought he was, he wasn't. The fact that the last album Nick purchased was "The best of Chesney Hawkes" leaves no further need for discussion on this specific matter. The second reason was that it simply wasn't safe for him to collect them. Over the years, several issues, all instigated by their mother, had meant that trouble would be waiting for him on arrival. This would range from the customary verbal abuse all the way through to physical violence, where she would have family members, boyfriends or just acquaintances on standby to give him a jolly good kicking if the opportunity presented itself.

Eventually, she shacked up with a rather simple creature, a traditional foul mouthed, overweight, beer drinking goon, who if he had been blessed with a brain cell, would still have been one level below an amoeba on the evolution front. He was far from the catch of the day and although many had rightfully thrown him back, he had finally managed to find a woman who matched his own magnetism.

Ultimately, collecting his children had become challenging to say the least and the fact that his ex had moved into the cave of this beautiful specimen, didn't help the cause, and increased the difficulty a thousand-fold. There was no reasoning with the troglodyte who she decided to co habit with either. He had already shown his leopard fur colours by unnecessarily messaging him mild to moderate threats, so this meant that he had little option but to avoid collecting his children from that particular dwelling also.

So, as well as kids just growing up and the aforementioned safety concerns, the last and most pertinent reason for the breakdown in the relationship with his older children was of course, the person who gave birth to them. It was safe to say that Nick had grown to dislike this person more than anyone else he had ever met. The loathing seeds were sowed during the time they were together, but this grew significantly when they eventually split, and she started playing mind games with the kids.

It was he who left to be with Becky, so his initial feelings of guilt, empathy and regret vanished quicker than the invisible man playing hide and seek when "the games" began. In all fairness to his ex, she should have put on an opening ceremony with dancers and acrobats to justify what lay ahead, such was her Olympian status of game playing. It wasn't the text messaging, the threats or even the physical violence that broke Nick, it was the manipulation of his children and using them as weapons of choice that finally took their crumbling relationship tumbling over Beachy Head with no point of return.

As time went by, many a family member or close friend would offer their unwanted thoughts in the matter too. "You need to talk to each other for the sake of the children" or "you should let bygones be bygones," were the most popular pieces of unsolicited advice. Most of these people hadn't been through a breakup, many hadn't even had children, so where did they gather their knowledge?

The only feasible answer must have been that these people were first in line when the "dishing out good advice without having any experience whatsoever" queue was formed. These magical beings had also missed a trick in the workplace when you consider the power they had been blessed with. Surely, they just need to free-lance themselves.

Consider it, their day could start early by rocking up at the construction site to advise that they have overdone the porosity of the cement mix. Two hours later after a quick trip up the M6, they could be at the hospital pointing out to the neurosurgeon the best central and peripheral treatment of the nervous system for Betty, a middle-aged lady who had been in a coma for the past six weeks. Finally, there would just be enough time to nip outside to make a quick call to UKs leading nuclear scientist to offer support on the best way to harvest energy from an atomic nuclei…..Job done…..invoices in the post…back in time for bargain hunt.

These chuffers offered their unwanted, unfounded advice at the drop of a hat, so with a bit of extra belief, they just needed to spread their enormous angelic wings and share their knowledge on a wider scale…… making a living to boot …………everyone's a winner!

Anyhow, returning to the unsavoury mother of his elder children. The saying "you can take the girl out the estate, but you can't take the estate out of the girl" was appropriate. Also appropriate in Nicks case was "Don't have kids with vindictive women", but unfortunately, no one had come up with that old wife's proverb through the years. The hard and indisputable facts were that Nick disliked his ex and nothing would ever change that.

Chapter 6 – Annie and the Reapster.

"You are joking...let me speak to your manager" insisted Becky, her face turning a subtle shade of plum.

"What do you mean they are unavailable?"

As was the modern way, no supervisor was available. The next line manager wasn't in either and Beck had about as much chance of finding a four leaved clover in a haystack than there was of her being put through to a director.

"I expect a call back within the hour" and with that Becky tapped the screen and the call was gone. She quickly scanned her phone and dialled a familiar number, which turned out to be her husband's work telephone line.

"It's been declined...it's been shitting declined" announced Becky calmly, although the colour in her cheeks indicated that calm was about to leave the building.

"Why?" asked Nick, moving the handset so it cradled awkwardly between his cheek and his neck.

"I don't bloody well know!" barked Becky, moving aside to let calm make its hasty exit out the room.

"They are calling me back in the hour...well they had better call back in the hour...... if they don't call back in the hour..... Well, I will give them ....."

"Another call back?" he interrupted, risking it a bit but knowing it was an opportunity not to be missed.

"Well, you can call them if they don't call me back" she snapped and with that, she tapped the red button for the second time in 30 seconds and he was left with a redundant handset that was gently edging towards his chest.

Becky had assumed that a neighbour had disputed the plans for the extension and had already decided that she would be giving everyone who walked past the house "the stare" from that day forward. In the end though, it turned out to have nothing to do with any vindictive individual and was more to do with circumstance. It worked in the Deans favour down the line ….although they were not so blissfully aware at that point.

The house, or bungalow next door had recently been vacated by a lovable old lady who had basically …well…..just grown too old really. Her son lived the other side of the city, so it was a bit of a trek for him to keep popping over. She lived alone and had recently had a couple of minor falls, so he wanted to have her nearer to home. Relocating his mother to a care home in his village cut the travel time down by a good ninety minutes so everything stacked up for her to make the move.

However, the planning office were unaware that Annie had moved. Why should they…they weren't the care home coppers. They also weren't aware that the people that had bought the premises had decided to renovate the property and had therefore knocked through the living room to make it an open planned room. So, several not-so-simple calls later and one brief visit from a planning officer, confirmation that the changes had indeed been made were logged, documented and the Dean application was revisited and subsequently approved. This is where luck was on the Deans side.

If Annie had continued to live next door, the application would never have got approved, unless of course she decided to go all Laurence Lleweyn-Bowen and decided to renovate her house dramatically. This was highly unlikely, seeing that the décor was that dated, there were authentic cave paintings on the wall. The issue that led to the refusal of the application surrounded the lack of natural light that would have shone into her kitchen. This meant that the application would automatically get refused, regardless of the fact no one had objected.

Annie's relocation was swift too. She was quite an independent individual and the Deans had never even considered that she would leave the house that she moved into thirty years previously. It was only in the last year that she started to go downhill health wise, but even with her ailments, they felt she would have been there for quite a few more years to come. Maybe "a few more years" was a slight overstatement if truth be told. The grim reaper had caught wind of Annie's falls and had recently set up home in her garden shed. He would gleefully shine his scythe in the early hours of the morning, listening out for further tumbles. In hindsight, maybe it was more of a waiting game for all involved really.

 Nick liked Annie and although she would keep him talking over the garden fence longer than he ideally wanted, he was sad to see her go. Many a time Nick had looked out of the landing window to see her, in a well-lit kitchen, making a cup of tea, in a rather stained nightie. Now there are moments in life when something slightly sexual appears out of the blue, highly unexpected and catches you completely by surprise………..this wasn't one of those moments. This was as sexual as picking your nose in a church…. and if anyone finds anything sexy about that, firstly you need help and secondly, Annie can be found in her new abode somewhere on the outskirts of Leicestershire ……that's only if the reapster didn't cadge a lift in the removal van and get to her first.

Back to the question regards why the extension was being built in the first place. Becky knew exactly why…...Nick didn't have a Scooby. His lack of drive had materialised in several areas of his life and therefore he was happy to stick rather than twist on most situations. Funny enough, he actually discovered some of the reasons for this safe outlook during his yearlong counselling stint. The findings were a little bit too Freudian, with the parents bearing the brunt for most of his downfalls, albeit nothing more than confidence issues and mild addictive traits.

Becky, however, wasn't one for resting on her laurels and was real hardy in many ways. She had recently transferred from an office-based role and was now working from home. Although difficult, this had ticked the work/life balance box and being there for her children after school was something she had always wanted to do. In addition to this, she was good at what she did. She was blonde, looked blonde and occasionally when the situation required, behaved blonde. Nick loved Becky for this. In her early days he felt she didn't quite manage the image as well as she could have, but as she had grown older, wiser and more people savvy, she got the balance just right…most of the time anyway. Becky knew that she had a battle with perception and working within the construction industry didn't make the job any easier as most of the men would much rather get into her underwear than get into the failings of the building trade.

So, simply, Becky wanted a nice house that she could be proud of. She wanted a home that reflected the effort and hard work she had put in over the years. She wanted a safe place for the children to grow and create memories that they would cherish and that would stay with them forever.

It also needed to be noted that she wanted a massive bedroom with a walk-in wardrobe.

Chapter 7 – Cocky Pigeons.

He could see the sun peering over the roof tops as he stepped out into his back garden. His size eleven shoe left a dewy footprint in the grass as he stepped off the decking that he had proudly put together the year before. Birds, that moments earlier had been in deep debate, had mostly all vanished, that is apart from one cocky pigeon that was fronting it out to impress its podgy mate, who had decided to settle on the fence two houses down.

Nick appeared anxious….he gave the impression of being anxious…. he looked anxious….. the simple fact of the matter, he was anxious. That morning was the first day of the build and the anticipation of what was to come was starting to take its toll. He had spent the entire day before, moving wall units and boxes from the utility room, as that part of the house was on the "to be demolished" list. The day before that was spent moving cartons, bags, toys, golf clubs, bikes, wood, tiles, tools, motor oil, cement, old car seats, a damaged exercise bike, baby equipment, an old mattress, more bikes, garden equipment and several mice ravaged cuddly toys out of the garage, as that was to be the first casualty of the build.

There was so much stuff in there that he was surprised he didn't find Uncle Tom Cobley sitting under a pile of blankets. Funnily enough, the only thing that wasn't in the garage was the one thing that should have been…his car. Saying that, he did reverse it in as soon as everything had been moved out and took a photo. This was mainly for comedic reasons, but he also felt that the garage deserved to be utilised one last time, for the purpose it was built. It was like its final meal before its execution. In this instance though, the meal was a battered Ford Fiesta and a bloke called Jeff and his trusty lump hammer, would be taking on the role of chief executioner.

He wiped the cold away from his nose and headed towards the open door that led back into the now, partially empty, utility room. Suddenly, without warning, he turned and clapped his hands together and the cocky pigeon leapt into the air, making a whistling sound with its wings, as they were suddenly asked to mirror the speed of its heartbeat. A satisfied Nick, pleased with the fact that his mere fifteen stones had managed to scare a bird weighing no more than a couple of kilogrammes, entered self-assuredly into the unlit room.

He switched on the light and the undressed bulb unashamedly glowed, instantly lighting the room in one last proud and defiant stand. Fully knowing that the space only had hours left to live and the focus would be on dismantling the utility after the garage was down, he bent down to unscrew the pipe that led to the back of the dishwasher. He was against the clock to get everything out before the builders arrived and to add to the stress levels, his knee made a creaking sound, which was accompanied by a wincing "oooo" noise from his mouth, as he stooped and knelt on the floor.

A few family members and friends had questioned why the dishwasher was hiding in the utility room anyway, as they felt it should be next to the sink in the main part of the kitchen. Seeing that the pipework was already there when the Deans had moved in, they simply conformed and had decided that trapesing across the kitchen to load and unload pots, was something they could comfortably live with.

The new build would mean that the washing machine and the dishwasher would be out of action for a couple of weeks. Neither of them was fond of washing up, so the thought of being without a dishwasher was like looking forward to a dental appointment. The kids had not yet entered into the "pocket money zone," so they had limited, bordering on zero, inclination to help. His parents had never embraced dishwashers either, which had always puzzled him. Even when he had offered to give them his old one, they refused. His mum had often joked that she had her own dishwasher called Johnusi...... a line she overused, so as the years passed, took it from being just a lame jest, to a full-on wheelchair bound pun.

He started to dance the disconnected dishwasher into the kitchen in a rigid ballroom style manner. He gently placed the unit on the tiled floor but forgot about the pipe that was lagging behind the unit. Dirty water vomited itself out the tube, leaving a pungent puddle in the middle of the kitchen.

"Shit" squirmed Nick, contemplating leaving it for Becky to clear up, who he could now hear making her way down the stairs.

He thought better of it as she wasn't the best in the mornings, and he couldn't be doing with her grumpy grumblings early in the day. He grabbed several sheets of kitchen roll off the holder and bent down to mope up the machines mess. Three sheets would have done the job, but he didn't want to run the risk of the sick pond seeping its way onto his fingers, so doubled up on the quantity. He moved his head to one side as the smell leapt into the air and greeted his nose with a massive nasal hug.

"Shit" he announced again, this time through gritted teeth.

"What you shitting about now?" asked Beck, as she switched the kettle on, snubbing the opportunity to check the water level.

"Nothing" he responded, shaking his head whilst discarding the paper towels in the bin.

"Well keep your voice down as the kids are still asleep and they don't need to be woken by you and your potty mouth" she whispered, reaching into the fridge, pulling out a half empty milk carton.

"How can they hear me up there!" he snapped.... Already frustrated with the fact he had been lumbered with moving machinery early in the morning and finding that it wasn't quite as straight forward as he had hoped.

"You know what I'm saying, so stop your moaning" she responded, yawning towards the end of the sentence so the final word actually came out as "onin"

By now, Nick had heading back into the utility room and again, his knee made a slight creaking noise as it made its way to the floor.

"We have a problem with the washing machine you know" he called out, as he started to wrestle with the pipework at the back.

"The pipe is stuck, and I can't get any grip to loosen it" he muttered, partly telling Becky but also talking directly to the machine in the hope that it might loosen its grip.

"Can't you use a hammer or something" she asked ……. pouring the water into her favourite cup and gentle whisking the contents together.

"Hammer….. What's that gonna do?" he said through gritted teeth …… now in the midst of a losing battle with the pipe.

"Do you mean a spanner or plyers" he shouted, now sitting with his back against the wall, annoyed that the machine just won round one with ease.

"Yep…. same thing" announced Becky …… sipping her coffee and cradling her mug like it was an abandoned baby bird.

He shook his head and went back in for round two.

"I don't know where they are anyway, so it's all a bit pointless" came a harassed voice from the back of the machine, as the second round started and began to take on identical traits to the previous one.

"Why don't you just cut the pipe?" announced Becky…..looking out the kitchen window, still protecting her coffee from potential predators.

"Cut it …..Bloody cut it!" cried Nick, now standing at the back of the machine, frustrated to the maximum and fully aware that he was now two clear rounds down in the bout.

"Yeah cut it…." She said calmly "we don't need the pipe and as soon as it's been cut, it might be easier to manoeuvre and take off. They are coming at 7.30 you know, so the machine has to be moved by then …..Alexa, what time is it?"

"The time is 6.47 am" proclaimed Alexa confidently.

"Thank you Alexa" replied Becky politely, before heading off upstairs to get ready.

Nick scratched at the one-week growth underneath his chin and mulled over her previous comment. Moments later, he reluctantly conceded that her idea was probably the only way forward, especially with the fact he was already two falls and two submissions down and his trainer was in the process of throwing the proverbial towel in the ring. With his renewed strategy in place, he began tracing the pipe work back to where it used to sit within the cupboards. To a bystander, it would appear that this man was in control. To anyone who knew him however, they would have known that it was the complete opposite as he wasn't all that good when it came to DIY. Put it this way, if his "do it yourself" skills were graded against a random group of a one hundred people, and they were asked to put themselves in order of capability, Nick would be found battling it out with some one-handed elderly lady for the rights to claim the ninety eighth spot.

The stopcock valve for the dishwasher, which had been successfully disconnected the day before, had been turned horizontal and this appeared to have done the trick with regards the flow of water. Therefore, in a simple process of common sense, he turned the valve for the washing machine the same way, so that it now sat in an identical position. With that in-depth and thorough prework completed, he leant over and grabbed the scissors that were snoozing on the sideboard. Cutting through the polyvinyl piping proved harder than he thought, and it appeared the sheers were still waking from there slumber as he began the compressing action between thumb and forefinger. He felt a sense of uneasiness sweep over him as he continued the squeezing action, his left eye involuntarily squinting as he began to pre-empt the potential disaster that was now only seconds away. It was safe to say at this point that he was now fully questioning the wisdom of Becky's suggestion that he had welcomed moments earlier.

A spray of water shot out, first escaping to the wall a few feet away before quickly refocusing its attention on Nick, or more to the point his face. He quickly turned the stopcock one way and then the other. Nothing. He turned it again and it came off in his hand. Water was now escaping like the crowds running from the bulls of Pamplona. The once dry utility room was quickly becoming a snazzy new wet room.

"Becky..Beckkkkkkkkkkkk" he bellowed, no longer caring if he woke the dead, let alone the two sleeping children upstairs.

"What's wrong?" shouted the incoming Becky, fearing the worst.

"Shitting...shit shit shit" he replied, displaying about as much cool as a melted choc ice.

"It's ok... calm down" she announced, going into work mode, and starting to think logically about the water puzzle that had just presented itself.

"OK…. Shitting ok…..it's far from OK" shouted Nick, now looking as if he been for a refreshing swim in his clothes.

"Pete….call Pete" he claimed in a brief eureka moment, still unsuccessfully trying to stop the deluge.

"No" she replied instantly, "We can sort this."

Becky was a real private individual who didn't like to put on to her friends. This materialised many a time, especially in relation to DIY. Nick was completely the opposite. He felt that the adage "that's what friends are for" was one of the many benefits of having close friendships. Two of his friends lived in DIY land so they would instantly know the answer to this countdown conundrum. The fact that he couldn't easily return the favour was a bit of a pain. It was more of skill than will factor, but if any of his mates ever needed to know the average call length of an incoming customer service telephone call, then he would be on the spot in a flash to provide that type of information.

"Let's get the pipe out the back door first" declared Beck, moving into the sodden utility room, waddling the machine side to side and nearer to the exit to help with her pipe diversion plan.

With his right hand, Nick picked up the pipe that was erratically pirouetting on the floor and stretched it out the back door. In his other hand, he held his phone aloft in some weird kind of Excalibur pose, mainly in an attempt to keep it dry, but also to give him the best chance of getting a signal. He had completely overruled Beck's request to keep it "in house" and was now attempting to connect to his friends mobile. The water, that had started as a fine spray seconds earlier was now gushing out the back door as Pete's cheerful voice came over the load speaker.

"Hey up fella" he said gleefully.

"Thank god you're there Peter" announced a relieved and slightly desperate Nick…… an overwhelming sense of relief flowing over him like the water he had encountered minutes earlier.

"What's up chap" he added, noting a sense of panic in his voice.

"Everything's fine" shouted Becky from the Utility room doorway, annoyed that the call had been made and now, for reasons that only she could explain, was standing in the middle of the disaster area holding on to the washing machine.

"We just need to find the main stop cock" she shouted out again in despair, but also in the direction of the phone that was still being held aloft in a "Power of Grayskull" manner.

"Everything is shitting not alright …." He announced, directing the comment to the pair of them.

"We have a flood Pete….." added Nick. "We've cut the water pipe to the washing machine and water is currently pouring into the garden" he announced frantically.

"What did you cut the pipe for?" Questioned Pete…… unable to and unwilling to disguise the fact he was laughing.

"Well, we …. Look it doesn't matter mate…. what do we do to stop it" he replied, starting to grow a bit impatient with the questions that were starting to come his way.

"Becky's right chap….. You need to find the main stop cock" "It's normally under the sink or in the kitchen somewhere" added Pete.

"We need to find the stopcock" shouted a sodden Nick from the utility room.

"I'm not deaf…..I can hear him …and I told you so" said Becky, who had given up hugging the machine and now had her head under the kitchen sink, moving all the bottles of cleaning fluid to get a better look.

"It's not here" she said ………………… "owwww!!!!!!!!!" added Beck, bumping her head slightly as she came back up.

"Not under the sink" announced Nick….aiming the question squarely at the feet of Pete.

"There should be a main one outside …near the house" he declared "I would come around but I'm on my way to a meeting" he added, realising that Nick was not handling the situation as well as he would have.

"Found it!" shrieked Becky….. "It's down there" pointing to a hole in the wall that had been left by some builders a few years earlier.

"Put your hand in then Beck" screamed Nick from the other side of the room.

Becky hesitated. It was a hole. It was a bit on the sinister side. It was a definite hiding place for spiders, mice, and any other animal that she wasn't comfortable with. She turned to Nick, shook her head, and gave him a look along the lines of "you owe me big time" and put her hand in. She turned the handle and Nick could hear the gushing noise decrease outside.

"Think she's done it" he cried out....... now sitting in a small puddle and beginning to realise that Pete would be repeating this story at a later date, also acknowledging that he would be painted in an extremely comedic, but disappointing light.

"Well done Becky".... Hollered Pete "It's a good job there's at least one man in the house!"

"Hmm good one" said Nick "thanks mate...owe you."

"Thanks Peter....sorry for bothering you" shouted Becky from across the room.

"Laters" said Pete , who was still laughing and disappeared from the scene.

"Shit-ting hell" declared a disgruntled Nick, shaking his lower arms a couple of times in a woeful attempt to remove the excess water from his soaked hoodie. "The build hasn't even started yet and I'm well and truly sick of it already" he moaned, dragging himself off the floor.

"I'm getting showered and going to work" he muttered, and trudged past Becky who was shaking her head and checking how much water was in the kettle.

As he slowly traipsed upstairs, dreading the forthcoming build that lay ahead, he stopped in his tracks as Becky shouted up.

"Good luck with the shower ….you know we don't have a water supply now don't you!"

Chapter 8 - ♪Der der der der der ♪...Inspect-your Gadget.

Weeks had passed since the utility "H20-no" incident, and Nick, again whilst showering, found himself looking out the opened bathroom window. This time he began mulling over cutting some of the stray branches that were restricting his distant view of the school fields. Although this would involve being about twelve foot off the ground, he considered the pros and cons involved in clearing the branches with a ladder and a chainsaw.

He had recently purchased one to assist him in his seemingly never-ending pursuit of getting firewood for the wood burner and was still very much a novice when it came to his lumber jack experience. On the plus side, removing the branches with the chainsaw would be a massive time saver, as it would zip through the branches in a matter of seconds. The negative aspect, which he quickly conceded was a major stumbling block, was the potential loss of life, as he began imagining himself overbalancing and neatly slicing through his left leg as he tumbled backwards onto the lawn below. This image alone satisfied Nick that the view from the bathroom window was just fine and that it didn't need human intervention after all.

To the left of the open window and through the frosted pain, he could see the outline of the scaffolding that had been in place for the past four weeks. The build had been going well, better than expected if truth be told. Apart from the water mishap and a weekend of limited electrical supply, (due to the builder cutting through a cable) he was pleased that the build hadn't inconvenienced him, or the family, that much. The lack of a dishwasher had taken its toll and the drawer which held the takeaway menus had not just been overused, it had been seriously abused. If Ester Rantzen had created a "menu line," a helpline for all mistreated takeaway leaflets to contact in a safe and confidential environment, then the Happy Palace and Crown of India would have almost certainly been in touch.

The menus themselves were a pointless piece of literature anyway. Both Nick and Beck would examine them, every time, deliberating and asking if they should "give something else a try" this week. On every single occasion, without fail, they would look at each other and say, "shall we just have the same as last time" and shove the disappointed menus back in the drawer and await the next occasion where they would prove to be equally useless, yet again. The only thing they brought to the party was the fact that you didn't need to search the internet for a telephone number, which realistically, was the only reason why they kept the pamphlets in the first place.

The only other problem that the Deans had encountered with regards the build, was the lack of a washing machine. There was no nearby laundrette and even if there was, neither would have really considered watching their pants spin right round, baby right round, in public. Friends and family all seemed to offer their help, something Becky again found difficult to embrace. The fact that she didn't want to ask for support when Lake Deanermere was very nearly created in the old utility room meant that there was absolutely no chance she would allow her underwear, or other delicate items for that matter, to be distributed within the village. Instead, she had got into a routine of hand washing and would fill the bath up every Saturday, and sometimes Sunday, with dirty and soiled washing. Unfortunately, all the scrubbing and all the softener in the world just couldn't quite mask that unwashed feel.

The water pressure in the shower eased significantly as someone turned the cold tap on downstairs. Nick moved forward out of the flow that now mirrored a trickle from a broken gutter instead of the surging waterfall that cascaded moments earlier. Due to a build-up of steam and the fact he was near the window, he leant forward to open the small, long frosted pain that sat above the main glass frame. The aim was two-fold, one was to release some of the mist that had built up, and the other was just for something to do as he waited for the bathroom shower drought to end.

One gentle push against the window and steam immediately rushed out like school kids at term time. Just for good measure, he pushed a little more, but the frame came to an abrupt halt as it hit the scaffolding outside. The opening act in itself had served its purpose though, so rather than leaving it half open, he decided to close it again, hoping that the other open window would now be able to manage the remaining steam on its own.

He began to now think that the shower was holding its breath on purpose. He had heard the slight clunking of the pipe work downstairs, which normally indicated that the flow had stopped elsewhere , and that the current should now reappear. Sure enough, the shower suddenly let out a relieved breath and the water gushed happily onto the vacant bath below. Nick moved steadily backwards into the pathway of the free-flowing water, firstly, with his left arm gently feeling its way and then only when he was confident that the temperature had returned to the original setting, he gradually moved the rest of his now shivering body into the cascading stream. He felt the warmth instantly re-enter his body and continued with his grooming programme. It was always the same routine, first the body, then then the hair, then the teeth.

Many dentists appeared to advise against brushing teeth in the shower. Apparently, it has something to do with the damp brush being a breeding ground for bacteria. Nick knew this, as it was something he had googled once, mainly due to an element of intrigue as to why it was an issue. He initially thought it was something to do with using warm water or getting a combination of toothpaste and shampoo in your mouth, however, he decided to rebel against the second-rate online revelation, as the reasoning appeared petty to say the least. All he felt was required to remove potential clamminess was a few brisk Zorro-like swishes of the brush and then placing it out of the way on the windowsill after use.

It was also a no brainer from the aspect of time, as he could brush his teeth, whilst showering, and continue his other grooming activities, such as shampooing, which had taken on a starring role in recent years. This was mainly due to the thinning nature of his hair and had therefore been encouraged by Becky to use a specialised shampoo. The instructions were basic when it came to this specific hair cleaning product, with all the usual lathering and massaging required but with the additional, crucial step, of leaving the shampoo on for at least four minutes , even longer for enhanced results. In all fairness, he would have had to keep the shampoo on for about a week for it to do its stuff! The reality of the "magic" was that you paid six times as much, had a longer wait for the shampoo "to do its thing" and in the end, it was all down to believing your hair wasn't thinning when you left the shower. It was as magical as faulty Christmas lights.

You couldn't get two further differing concepts for washing your hair when it came to his previous shampoo either. That one encouraged him to wash and then go…. literally. This new wonder product told him to manipulate his scalp, leave it to work …leave a bit longer…… just a few more minutes more …then wash…..then massage in some specialised oil…… then you can go. So, this new hair washing regime, or more to the point, hair waiting regime, meant he had time to kill whilst in the shower and this is where the brushing his teeth concept was born. However, as he brushed with his right hand, his left hand became somewhat redundant. This meant that every now and again, unknowingly, he found himself checking his testicles. He wasn't that sure what he was really looking for but was confident that if there was anything out of the ordinary, it would jump out like a mugger in an unlit alleyway. In this instance, this particular assailant would be a bit sticky and sweaty, have saggy skin and would be splattered with the odd hair or two…..on reflection, pretty much like your standard thief really.

As normal, nothing exciting was going on down there during this specific exploration. Same saggy scrotum and same toughened jelly filled bean bag that slipped in-between his fingers when manoeuvred. Whilst daydreaming and over brushing his back-wisdom teeth, he moved seamlessly onto the right sided testicle. Again, same saggy scrotum, although now with an additional minty fresh foam covering, which had been unwittingly transferred over when he switched the brush to his left hand, allowing the right hand to continue with the examination/fondling.

Whilst the toothpaste unsuccessfully attempted to hang on to its unfamiliar surroundings, Nick persevered with his one-man self-molesting strategy. Completely out of the blue, a sharp pain shot into his stomach. It wasn't on the same level as the time Tom McDonald kicked him square on in the testimonials when he was twelve, as that was on a different playing field, literally. The pain he had just felt was more of a level two, maybe at a push, halfway up the ramp to the next floor. Tom's conversion style kick was more like the 10th floor.........everybody off, end of the journey, open air parking only.

Nick flinched slightly but carried on fumbling, although now with less enthusiasm as before. He felt it must have been the over vigorous handling that led to the momentary pain and the testicle felt normal...as far as testicles go. It wasn't that he had a sound knowledge or studied them during his college days and his previous job didn't involve cupping gentlemen's balls and grading them from one to ten on the three S's.... size, smell, and sag. In fact, the more he thought about it, he realised that he didn't have the faintest idea what normal actually meant or felt like, although he was aware of the anecdotal stories of a pea shaped size lumps, so that seemed a good starting point as any.

The sharp pain that he had felt moments earlier had however, quickly pushed its way to the front of his thoughts and subconsciously, he had now completely taken his foot off the pedal with regards his fiddling on the roof.

"No, there was nothing there anyway, or was there. No... nothing" Nick thought and twisted to turn the shower off.

On stepping out the bath, he briefly glanced out the window and got a glimpse of the goalposts that looked just like staples on the horizon. They were quickly hidden by a branch that blew back covering the window, wagging its leaves in a "pee po" type manner. He climbed out the shower, stood in front of the mirror, wiped the condensation from the glass and noticed the mass of soap suds that were still partying on top of his head.

"Piss on it" he said under his breath and let out a sigh.

"At least it got an extra minute to do its thing" he thought, as he climbed back into the bath, turned the shower back on and began frantically rinsing the shampoo out of his hair.

Chapter 9 – Don't you just love an acronym.

"Call the doctors Nick for god's sake" instructed Lorraine, hovering over his desk, and giving him one of her "I mean it" looks.

Lorraine was Nicks boss and had a knack of getting people to do what she wanted. It was a combination of fear, respect and basic hounding until the issue was resolved that made it a winning formula. She had joined the company a year before and they got on well, although he was apprehensive before her arrival. A new manager meant fresh ways of looking at things and although he was confident in his own ability, experience had shown him that changes were inevitable. Different strokes for different folks were an adage that became more relevant in the workplace, in this particular instance, he had a stern looking Lorraine saying, "seek medical help Nick" rather than a boy-ish Gary Coleman saying, "What you talking about Willis."

It became apparent quite early on that she liked a laugh which suited him. His previous manager, who was also a woman, was as cheerful as a professional mourner, so it was quite refreshing to have a new buoyant approach to the workplace. He realised that most of his career he had worked for women, it didn't bother him in the slightest and if he was being honest, he preferred it. Call Centres were female dominated, so it made sense that women would take on senior roles within those environments. Strangely though, Transatlantic Direct had just initiated another one of their workgroups that this time, focused on women at work. (WAW)

The idea was simple. The aim was to empower women to have the confidence to promote themselves within the work environment. It did, however, seem as if they were teaching grandmother, not grandfather, to suck eggs on this occasion, as virtually all the managers were female. When the promotion began, Nick had to double check that he hadn't been transported back a hundred or so years and that the news headlines for the day wasn't that of Emily Davison making the ultimate sacrifice for womankind during the Epsom Derby, such was the apparent contradiction.

The concept on a wider scale was good, it made sense, it just felt that the initiative was 40 years behind the times, and he struggled to understand the target audience. He also thought that if some brave soul had created a "Male in the workplace" workgroup, it would have got off the ground with about as much success as a penguin wearing a tuxedo made of cement. The apparent mindset did make him consider what other archaic workgroups where in the pipeline. "Witches Here Often Receive Execution" (WHORE) and "Stop Hanging Innocent Treason supporters"(SHITS) must have been on the short list, if the recent proposal had anything to go by.

The HR manager, a lady (obviously) called Jackie, was promoting the new women at work idea across the site. Nick had childishly reinvented the group and called them "Woman Also Need Careers……. WANC to give it its acronym. He had desperately tried to get the letter K at the end, but spelling the word career with a K just took the credibility away from the gag, so decided to settle for the letter C instead, as it ultimately read the same.

He didn't believe he was sexist, quite the opposite, and although he didn't fully understand the thought process and found the whole thing quite bizarre, he was more than happy to show his face when the management team had been asked to turn up to promote the open day. Along he went with Lorraine, his boss, Rachel, the manager from sales, Helen, the finance manager, Nicola, the purchasing manager and Jane, the warehouse manager. There were a lot of successful women promoting the event and to say it was all a lot of WANC would have been harsh.

In fact, the two previous occasions he had found himself working for a man hadn't really worked out, mainly because he could see through them and their bull crap. If he were being totally honest with himself, he also felt that he could do a better job than them in both cases too. In his early career, Nick was possibly considered as overconfident, some would say he bordered on cocky. He was simply comfortable in his skin and felt that he hadn't met anyone who he felt was better than him. Yes, they may have been more successful in their careers; they may have had more money, more possessions. They may even have had a more of a fulfilled social life, but none of this made them a better person. As a young lad, he thought that there would be an epiphany, when one day he would metamorphosis into adulthood and have a different view on life. Forty-seven years on, Nick was still waiting for that moment when he would wriggle out of that cocoon and start to stretch his adult butterfly wings.

"Go on then...ring them!" instructed Lorraine sternly, his pitiful attempt to appear busy was as successful as a playing catch with a handless man.

Her management style was similar to his. They both felt that if you could get your staff to work for you because they wanted to, rather than because they had to, then results would follow. This method appeared to have stood them both in good stead throughout their working lives and another of the reasons why he had picked up the phone that morning and called the doctors.

"They got me in on the 25th at 4.30" he replied.

"I managed to get a late appointment so it wouldn't affect my workload that much" advised Nick optimistically, knowing that the response coming back wasn't going to be favourable, especially seeing that today's date was the 6th of October.

"So that's nearly three weeks then?" she said, glancing at her calendar but doing the maths in her head anyway.

"You know what it's like Lorraine............and anyway, it doesn't feel as bad today."

The slight shooting pain that he had felt in the shower on the Sunday had happened again a couple of times at work that week. Initially he had put it down to tight boxers, and to clarify, that's the snug fitting pants rather than a group of fighters who are loathed to part with their money. Blaming them would be pointless and would almost certainly lead to a tricky confrontation followed by a severe beating.

In addition to accusing his undergarments for the discomfort he was feeling, he also thought it might have had something to do with the oversized box he picked up on Saturday evening, as he felt a slight twinge in his groin at that time. He found himself happily clutching at those specific straws in a severely uneducated attempt to self-diagnose the spasms and because he briefly mentioned the pain the day before, Lorraine had now taken it upon herself to ensure he got it checked out.

"You really should get seen earlier you know, she announced, deciding to let this one slide, partially because she had a meeting to attend and also because she knew that getting an urgent appointment at the doctors was like getting a straight answer from a politician.

Over the next few days, he dedicated a few extra minutes in his grooming programme just for his testicular friends, knowing that in theory, the more time he spent examining them, the more he could rule out any major issues. Of course, there was the fact that his hair would reap the rewards too.

There continued to be a severe lack of lumpage or bumpage and no signs of any pimples or dimples, although this may have been due to the gentle approach he had now adopted, as he was keen to avoid the shooting pain he had instigated a few days earlier. Whilst there may well have been a distinct lack of obvious swelling, something just didn't feel right.

Was it all in the mind, maybe it was, but the thought had squatted itself and its rights not to be moved were becoming established. The following day and another night of mulling things over, the "something wasn't right" message was getting louder and louder. The trespasser that had moved into his mind the day before had turned out to be extremely unsociable and had done an outstanding job of keeping its occupant awake for most of the night. Unlike most nuisance neighbours who insist on playing "fire starter" on full pelt over and over again at 2.15 am, this unwanted tenant just kept mentioning to Nick every time he closed his eyes "something is wrong, and you know it."

He eventually decided that the three-week delay to see a doctor wasn't ideal and that he had no option but to take part in the "play your call right" game at the doctors. This consisted of waiting until 8:29 and 55 seconds before dialling the surgery's number in the futile hope of getting a same day appointment.

He had shared with Becky his concerns over the first cup of tea of the day and she supported the decision one hundred percent. To assist, she decided to play along with the farcical game and at 8.25am, the pair of them sat on the sofa, looking at each other knowingly, before synchronising mobiles. This was more strategic than any world chess tournament and they both were fully focused on the job in hand.

"Eight Twenty-Nine and thirty seconds" Nick announced, staring at his mobile with over-the-top intensity.

"Hold on...are we both calling at 55 seconds?" questioned Becky.

"What …..Err ….yes? Replied Nick, clearly realising they hadn't reviewed the pros and cons of the game as well as they thought they had.

"I just thought we might have a better chance staggering it" responded Becky, now matching her husband on the intensity scale.

"Muuuuuum" shouted Maddison, who was busy annoying Archie upstairs.

"**NOT NOW**" shouted the pair in unison.

"Call the number" said Nick, pointing needlessly at Becky's phone.

"Now?" questioned Becky as she hit the green button on the display pad in a slightly dazed manner.

"Yes now " he instructed, as he watched the clock tick and began miming to himself ...... "Fifty-one, fifty-two, fifty-three."

"It's ringing!" exclaimed Becky as Nick tapped the telephone icon on his screen to begin the call.

"No way?" he exclaimed ..... how lucky is that !

"Damn, No, it's the answer machine" she said frustratingly, cancelling the call before hitting redial.

"Call now he says" mumbled Becky sarcastically as the phone waited again to reconnect.

"Shit" said Nick....." thought we had cracked it then as well" .

A few seconds past before .... "Deet,... Deet, ...Deet" went Nicks phone as the engaged tone rang out.

"Shiiiiiitttt" he declared again, cancelling the call and redialling frantically.

Becky stood motionless; one arm outstretched in Nicks direction. "Hold on" she said.

........"deet....deet....deet" "Engaged ... Damn" announced a frustrated Becky, hitting redial instantly.

"Dial again!" he prompted.

"Do you think I'm stupid?" snapped Beck, giving him one of her finest "you are such a tosser" looks.

"Good morning surgery" echoed a voice .

Just like a couple of meerkats that had caught site of a bird in the corner of their eye, the pair of them lifted their heads in unison. He was in the motion of cutting the call off and ready to redial, such was the expectancy of him not getting through and only managed to avert a schoolboy error of dramatic proportion with a last-minute intervention from brain to hand.

"Hello..Hello" he said, still in a hazy state of shock.

"Good morning, you are through to Little Glen Surgery" repeated the voice again, this time adding the surgery name for good measure.

"Good morning…Is it possible to see a male doctor today " he added, as a relieved Becky walked by, putting her hand on his shoulder, before disappearing up the stairs. This was sharply followed by a "What are you two up to?" comment aimed in the direction of her daughter.

"Can I ask what it is in relation too?" enquired the receptionist.

Nick at this point was in two minds. Should he go for the safe, classified "I would rather not say as it's of a private matter" or instead plump for the, let's get it out in the open "I'm a bit worried about my old cock and saggy bollocks" statement.

Feeling that the "it's a bit too private" statement may not help him in his aim of a getting a priority appointment, he decided to quickly choose the more honest "bollock statement" but deciding to go down more of a medical terminology route, to give it, and him, an element of decorum.

"Let me have a look to see what we can do for you" said the receptionist, showing a distinct lack of interest in relation to his faltering private parts.

"We have an appointment at 9.30 this morning if that helps?"

Boldness beats bashfulness he noted to himself in the medical game of paper, scissors stone.

"That would be great" he said, still a little surprised that he was talking to a person rather than still playing the frantic dialling and redialling game.

"Can I take your date of birth please" said the receptionist, now getting into the nitty gritty of the job in hand.

He duly obliged.

"Is that Nick Dean?" she enquired.

"Yes, it is!" established Nick, slightly taken back that no one else in the district shared the same birthdate.

"Thank you ...all booked in...see you shortly" she said, to which he thanked her and disconnected the call.

 To be honest, he felt he had already shared enough information with the lady on the other end of the phone, so it was the right thing to let her go. The fact he didn't even know her name either made it feel like it was some seedy conversation with a premium chat line, although without any significant benefits for either party. Briefly it crossed his mind to murmur the words "good game ..good game" in celebration of being todays "Play your call right" winner, but decided against it and instead rushed upstairs, now with the sole aim of getting ready for the appointment.

As he got dressed, he began to realise the enormity of what was about to happen. It was highly likely that he would need to remove his trousers and have his testicles inspected and for a man who struggled to open his mouth to let the doctor inspect his tonsils, dropping his Y fronts and confidently telling the doctor to "check them bad boys out" wasn't filling him with much gusto. He held a glimmer of hope that the doctor would take one look at him, announce that it was "obvious from your stance that this is a classic case of tightpantitis" and that he would be able to gleefully skip out of the surgery, slightly embarrassed, but relieved that he didn't have to reveal all.

His mind was now working overtime and he started to convince himself that there was an outside chance that the doctor may want to have a look at the old prostate while he was there. Oh yes, I am sure that is exactly what the doctor would want first thing in the morning. Not only could he have a "good old play" with a couple of saggy nut sacks, but he also had the once in a lifetime opportunity to have a little fiddle of a middle-aged man's bum hole at 9.40am on a dull Thursday in September.

Although his thoughts bordered on pure nonsense, he couldn't get over the fact that all the work he had done months before in avoiding the doc inspecting his back passage, was now potentially all in vain. Ultimately the fact remained that in the next 55 minutes, a man would be squeezing his testicles whilst making polite conversation. This was an appointment that Nick did not want…. but he also knew the option to stand by and do nothing, had now left the building and was sitting in the back of a cab, heading to the zoo to find an ostrich to bury its head with.

Chapter 10 – The removal man versus the cloakroom.

The reflection off a nearby solar roof panel briefly dazzled him as he hesitantly curved his car into the surgery car park. It was the first time he had been to this health centre, so was a little cautious in his approach. It didn't help that the entrance to the car park was shared with the local, "Kidz R Us" nursery, which was situated to the rear of the clinic. The last thing he would have wanted was to go into that building and ask which room he needed to drop his trousers in.

The diamonds were still shimmering in his eye line as he parked up in the only vacant spot left available, although factually, there were six more vacant bays. Two of these had been designated to the practitioners and the other four were available for the disabled. Seeing as he didn't fit into either category, he had to make do with the one and only space left open to him. It was a slight surprise that they hadn't added a couple of parent and toddler bays as well, leaving the able and childless patients to fight between themselves for just two spaces. On this occasion however, it appeared someone in the planning department had actually catered for Jo average, which wasn't always the case.

His door thudded against the parked car next to him, as he badly misjudged the distance between the two. The planner, who moments earlier had been applauded for creating parking opportunities was now being well and truly slated for only allowing malnourished cars and motor bikes to safely use the spaces provided. Nick began limbo-ing out of his door, which was now knocking against the other car in a dull rhythmic fashion. The only thing missing at this point was some Caribbean music and a Pina Colada to go along with the snake like positions he was creating, in an awkward attempt to get his six-foot two frame out of the car.

Several inept moves later, he succeeded, kind of, in standing up, and began shimmying his way along the side of the stranger's car. He stopped after a few shuffles and hooked his foot round the base of the door to close it shut. He would have slammed it, such was the frustration that was building, but due to the close proximity of the cars, he was unable to generate the appropriate force, so it just closed gradually with a generous amount of apathy.

He crabbed the remaining few steps before dusting off the muck off his coat, which had been collated after making the enforced decision to slide down the side of the unknown car for the past 10 seconds. He gave his bottom one last brush in a manner that wouldn't have gone amiss in "Carry on crap parking," before entering the surgery.

Surprisingly, it was empty inside, apart from the receptionist who was busy looking in a downward direction. He quickly concluded that all the cars outside must have belonged to patients who had optimistically driven to the surgery but had never made it back home due to the seriousness of their illness. It was also safe to say that positivity hadn't come along for the ride that morning and wasn't man cuddling Nick as he stood alone in the entrance of the surgery.

He stood briefly, faced with the first doctor's appointment dilemma of the day…. receptionist or VDU screen? He glanced over in the direction of the receptionist, who was still way too busy ignoring him, so decided to make his way to the computer screen. He was just about to type "Dean" in the surname box when the receptionist reluctantly beckoned him over.

"Can I help?" she said, knowing that the answer would more than likely lead to extra work, but was asking anyway out of loathing sense of duty. I think it's safe to say no one has ever responded, in that specific environment, to the "can I help?" question, with a "no, you are ok thanks…I'm just browsing!"

"I'm here to see Dr Agarwal" replied Nick, not sure whether to share the reasons why he was there or not.

The receptionist saved the day in this instance as she was way too busy moving paperwork for idle chit chat. She had already ignored the ringing phone twice, and as he had also experienced, was doing her utmost to ignore incoming patients too. Pretending to care about Nicks potential ailments was way down on her list of things not to do, so his secret would be safe for the time being.

"Take a seat" she said, the lack of warmth in her tone shining through.

He was now faced with the second dilemma of the day and began mulling over the choice of seating available. This was a ridiculous concept, seeing that no one else was actually in the waiting room. Nonetheless, he thought about sitting on the end seat, he considered sitting in the middle seat and deliberated about sitting in a row of three seats versus a row of four seats. All of these had pitfalls, especially if some strange, contaminated leper came bumbling in, coughing and a spluttering to their diseased hearts content. He had to ensure that no one could sit next to him but couldn't make it obvious. This was a game of mastery and was long overdue as an event that should be on show at the modern Olympics.

Option 1. The "removal man." This consisted of moving the furniture slightly, ensuring there was a sufficient enough gap to make any conversation awkward. Although this obviously depended on the style of chair. If they were connected to each other, he was as buggered as a ladybug being bugged by a bedbug. If, however, they were single chairs, like the old-fashioned school ones, then he could discreetly move them, ensuring he avoided the unwanted screeching noise those chairs tended to make when they were abused in that manner.

This specific chair type was something that Nick had coincidentally encountered only days earlier on his last parents evening fiasco. He found himself staring submissively up at the teacher of his 8-year-old son, sitting, or more to the point, a third of his bum cheek was sitting on a rather hard, plastic chair. He had questioned why schools didn't have a few "normal" sized chairs that they could wheel, or drag out of the corner, especially for this type of event. It wasn't as if parent's evenings were one off occasions either, as several times a year, he would be forced to sit, with his knees tucked under his chin, looking up like a scolded puppy, as the teacher began to pull young Archie to pieces in front of his very eyes. Maybe that was the reason why they have small chairs...... as by

58

the time you have managed to get out of one to give the self-important tutor a clip round the ear, they had packed their satchel, pulled out the car park and the janitor was already halfway back to his shed after locking the gates.

Option 2. The "lounger." This option was quickly dismissed as putting his feet up on one of the chairs was a non-runner, mainly due to the slovenly impression it would have given. Even if he pretended that he had a poorly leg, which of course was extremely viable considering where he was, he would have had to continue the roll play all the way in and back out of the doctor's room, which just seemed an awful lot of work. This would have also encouraged further questioning from the doctor as to the reason for the limp and his plan was to be in and out, like an over excited stud, so option 2 was ruled out instantly.

Option 3. The "cloakroom." This was more plausible and was the option he plumped for as he could simply leave his coat on the chair next to him. Not the most ingenious choice and as it worked out, not very well executed either, as the coat, with the weight of his car keys, simply slid off the shiny chair and sat in an embarrassed heap on the floor.

"Mr Dean" shouted the doctor as he appeared from behind a door, just like the magical shop keeper out of Mr Benn. Nick briefly assessed how necessary the big introduction was, seeing as the only other person in the room was the secretary, and she was way too busy telling some poor sod on the end of the telephone, that there were no appointments available for at least a fortnight.

He picked up his coat, producing a humble moaning effect as he reached down. The doctor gave him a smile that was either out of pure pity or politeness. Either way, he had successfully made himself look like a bit of a tit with the whole option 3 scenario.

The walk through to Doctor Aggarwals room was brief, it was no more than 8 steps from waiting room to the medic's private space. The door was open when he arrived, and he could see there was an examination table at the far end of the room. A sense of destiny came over Nick that the two of them would become better acquainted in the very near future.

"Take a seat" said the Doctor amiably "What seems to be the problem?" he added.

Nick shuffled in his seat slightly before starting his ramble.

"Well, I've been experiencing some pain……… not a great deal but some……….more discomfort I would say………… every now and again…………………… so it's not all the time……………………… but a few times a week…………………… well when I say a few times, it's probably more a couple of times a week……………… or maybe not that much when I think about it…………………….down in the area surrounding ……. Well, when I say around…… near to……. or it feels approximate to ………. or around that vicinity …. the groin…… or maybe close to …. or possibly in …………… or close to the testicle area."

He paused slightly, took a breath, and set off again.

"….. and I think I might have pulled something………………………….. when lifting………………… because we have been moving quite a lot of stuff around…………………… loads of things with the extension we are going through…………………… and I'm aware of the correct lifting procedure…………………… bending the knees and all that …………………………… but I can recall one specific time when I picked a box up and I thought to myself that my groin was tight………………………… so I'm not sure if I have simply lifted something the wrong way…………………….which has led to the pain ………………………or more discomfort I have been feeling rather than pain………………………… every now and again…….. which as I said…"

"Well let's take a look shall we" interrupted the doctor, fearing that if he didn't speak, Nick would have dragged the conversation on for another five minutes.

"If you undress from the waist up, we will see what's going on" announced the doctor, opening his drawer and pulling out a pair of surgical gloves.

Nicks heart sank faster than a discarded sack of house bricks thrown off a bridge. Even though he knew that this would be the outcome, he had continued to hope, from somewhere in the cabinet at the back of his mind entitled "misplaced optimism," the doctor was going to state something along the lines of.

"I can see from here that you are a splendid example of a man, and just by your stance and posture alone, I can diagnose that you do have an acute case of manliness, especially in the nether regions….. Now get out of my office you fine specimen, as I have patients aplenty who need my help."

"From the waist up??" questioned Nick, deciding to re-join the real world.

Was this a new way of checking for serious genital disease? He knew that there were several new initiatives within the medical world, but this seemed a little strange to say the least. A blood test to indicate prostate cancer, a breathalyser to reveal dangerous bacteria in the stomach. Could they really tweak a nipple to establish first signs of testicular cancer?

"Apologies Mr Dean, I meant from the waist down" smiled the doctor, looking momentarily as if he wanted to add a punchline, but deciding against it, has it probably would have been out of place, unprofessional and inappropriate.

 Nick began to unbuckle his belt. The overwhelming desire to start waffling took hold of him again.

"It's quite funny when you think about it…….. well not exactly funny…… strange, really ……… that I have been through my entire life………………… without having these type of issues…. You would have thought that at some point………. along the way …… I would pick up some kind of ……"

"Relax Mr Dean…" advised the doctor, mainly so that he could concentrate on his examination but also because his constant waffling was now beginning to get on his nerves.

By now, he was now lying prostrate on the doctor's examination table, his trousers and pants looking up at him longingly from around his ankles. He stared directly up at the ceiling light that dazzled him slightly, making him blink in the process.

"Let me just turn the light down a bit" said the doctor, noticing the squint from Nick.

As the light faded, Nicks embarrassment took a turn for the worst as he regrettably chirped up with

"All we need is some mood music!"

Now call it nerves, the lack of sleep or just the whole situation, but in hindsight, saying this to a doctor, who from his mannerism and whole demeanour potentially may have "batted for the other team". Nick was that confident in the Docs sexual preference that that he thought there was a good chance he probably bowled and kept wicket for them as well. Due to this, he felt it wasn't the wisest of comments that had ever flowed from his vocal cords and to make an uncomfortable situation slightly worse, Doctor Aggarwal didn't even respond.

As the silence decided to loiter a little longer than Nick would have liked, he analysed the comment further. Obviously, it wasn't meant as a sexual come on and was confident that the doctor thought likewise. It was a comedy moment, and although one to avoid, unfortunately he was incapable of stopping it dribbling out his mouth. He wasn't naïve enough to think that a gay man would find him attractive just because he was of the preferred gender. The fact he was there, with his rather disappointing penis on show, that incidentally, was now getting smaller the longer it was exposed, didn't have any bearing on the issue either...or did it?

Dr Aggarwal was a professional man who was in the middle of a procedure that involved an examination of his sexual organs. Nick assumed that from time to time, Mr Agarwal would or had, taken part in fellatio or other sexual activities involving the penis and other surrounding points of interest. Due to this, he questioned if this would have any bearing on the predicament he currently found himself in? NO, of course it didn't, definitely not. At the same time as this pointless internal conversation was taking place, his manhood had shrunk to the point that it looked like a small bald dormouse and even the most sex starved homosexual would have found that about as exciting as a brown paper envelope.

Whilst he was on this subject, he had always wondered how straight gynaecologists managed to maintain a healthy sex life. Looking at vaginas every day may seem like winning the jackpot when you are teenager, but after a long day at the office, and years of looking at nothing but vajayjays, surely the last thing you would want to cast your eyes on when walking through the front door is another minge, albeit of the person you loved. Not so much a busman's holiday, more of a vaginal vacation.

Back in the surgery, the examination was still going strong and although Nick had no direct comparison to refer to, it did feel as if the current inspection bordered on something that would be classed as "thorough." He had noticed the odd fleeting expression from the doctor that you would see when someone was trying to get the answer to a question on a crossword, or when you desperately try to remember the name of the person you had just bumped into in the supermarket.

"Get dressed please Mr Dean" said Dr Aggarwal softly yet abruptly.

He didn't need a second invite and his pants and trousers were pulled up before you could say the words "wee willie winkie." He had just tugged his belt clip onto the last notch when the doctor advised:

"I'm going to just refer you for a scan. I am sure everything is fine, but I would just like to get that done to rule out other issues."

"What kind of things?" enquired Nick, looping his belt into the first loophole on his jeans and pulling it through.

"It's just precautionary but I will ask the receptionist to push this appointment for you."

"Do you think it will be within the next 10 days as I am going away in a couple of weeks." He quizzed.

"Yes, I would have thought so, but I can't make any promises."

And with that, he hurriedly said his thank you' s, before shuffling his way out of the office and then the building. He did notice on the way out that things had picked up somewhat and there had been an avalanche of people who had come pouring into the surgery. Maybe it was more of a snow flurry than a full-on landslide, as there were just the three people now in the waiting room.

One gentleman had already adopted "the cloakroom" approach and had his coat strategically plonked on the chair next to him. Some poor individual, who had taken the brave, or stupid option, not to address the whole waiting room etiquette was now being talked at by a rather withered and safe to say, unhealthy looking lady.

Massively relieved and although still in the dark regards the odd shooting pain, he was pleased that the appointment was over, and remained generally unconcerned regards the whole situation. He slid back alongside his car and squeezed himself through the half-opened door, nearly bursting an appendix in the process. Once inside, he dialled Beck and didn't even wait for any niceties.

"Well, let's just say that wasn't very embarrassing at all ….and we will leave it at that!"

Chapter 11 – The pirate the witch and no wardrobe.

Like any good person who decides to bury their head in the sand, Nick took the decision to forget about his current health issue and instead focused on a different type of beach and his forthcoming family holiday to Cornwall. He had made a call to the doctors to chase up the appointment a few days before he left, but seeing as the receptionists didn't know anything about it and that she would have to speak to Dr Aggarwal to confirm the detail, he got the distinct impression "well it can't be that important if they aren't that bothered."

So, with that feeling neatly folded and packed away in the suitcase, off they set on the mammoth journey to Kernow. On a good day it was at least a 5-hour trek, so the Deans had implemented an overnight stop over. He was more thankful this year than others with the half-way house booking, as sitting in one position, in a pair of tight jeans, did seem to bring back an uncomfortable feeling in his boxer shorts.

The holiday itself was pleasantly uneventful, for almost the entire week. The views were as stunning as ever, the beaches were not over-crowded, and the weather was good for mid-autumn. The on-site swimming pool actually appeared to help him, and he found himself regularly doing some aqua aerobics in the water. The squatting and bending motions, gave him reassurance that his self-diagnosis of a pulled groin, caused through poor health and safety in relation to box lifting, was the cause of his recent twinges.

This mindset continued throughout the week, until that is, the penultimate night. The holidaying couple had spent a lovely autumn's day, strolling the quaint back streets of St Ives, admiring the picturesque landscape that surrounded them. On return to the lodge, they decided to partake in not only a few bottles of wine, but also engaged in a moment of holiday passion. The issue itself reared its ugly head, for want of a better expression, at the point of climax, when a pain shot through his stomach that even he couldn't ignore. Beck, although used to the odd sexual cock up, or not in some cases, instantly knew something wasn't right.

"What's wrong" she said with a genuine level of concern.

"Something is definitely not right" he uttered, still grimacing slightly.

"I'm going to chase up that appointment when I get back as that's just not normal" he added, slumping onto his back in dejection. Nothing more was said on the matter over the next few days, but this was the first time he began to realise that maybe, just maybe, something was amiss.

The long journey back was broken up by a stop off at Wookey Hole. This was a bit of a relief all round, as not only did it give everyone a chance to stretch their legs, but it also split the five-hour, testicular scrunch contest, in half. Beck, who on seeing the pamphlet for the attraction that promised witches, fairies, and all things magical, was probably more enthusiastic than she should have been. The excitement and expectation of Somerset's very own Harry Potter World disappeared quicker than Ron Weasley borrowing his best mates' cloak of invisibility. The journey from the M5 motorway didn't help, as the anticipated 15-minute detour got more than a little tiresome, forty-five minutes later.

The main feature at the Hole of Wookster was a series of ancient caves, so in all fairness, it made sense that this would be off the beaten track somewhat, although Nick had overlooked this palpable point when taking travel time into consideration. The frustration just kept on building as they went from one tight countryside lane to another.

On arrival, the car park didn't give away any secrets of the experience that lay in wait, but all was about to be revealed as they set off up the pathway to the caverns. The decorations and ornaments that festooned the foot path instantly gave the game away, as they were in desperate need of a lick of paint or if being brutal, a one way visit to the storeroom. After thirty-five minutes, which included a ten-minute queue time, the whole family agreed that the caves themselves were worth a visit, even though when they got to the witch's house, which is buried deep inside the cave, she had gone to lunch.

In her place was Pirate Poncho, who had obviously drawn the short straw and was doing a shift in her absence. Maddison and Archie even questioned the link between a sorceress and a rogue sailor, but seeing as they got a gift, they quickly forgave everyone involved. The present itself was an Easter egg, and although appreciated, fooled none of the adults and if truth be told, the majority of the older kids too. It was clear that the marketing team had "over egged" the foot fall coming through the gates six months earlier and were now in desperate need to off load them, before they got accused of dispensing out of date smarties eggs.

The witch incidentally passed them by as they left the caves which again, lost some of the magic. The management team at the event needed to think about potentially building an alternative route into the caves, so that she could discreetly pop out for a sarnie without losing the mystic feel. To her credit, she wasn't munching on a big mac and did her best to make her way back prudently, although a 5 ft 9 inch, fully dressed witch, marching through the tunnels, wasn't easy to miss.

Outside the caves and chocolate treats aside, the place just couldn't hide the fact that the rest of the attractions were as run down as two-day old roadkill. Although the Deans all tried their very best to see through the fatigued and weary charms the place had to offer, they decided to call it a day two hours earlier than they had originally expected. Becky struggled to hide her disappointment as she always liked to find a way to extend a holiday and hoped that this particular stop off would be something memorable. It was unforgettable for all the wrong reasons, but Nick did give his wife utmost respect, when she got in the car, put on her seatbelt, and whispered in his ear "they need to change the name to Wankey Hole."

On arriving back home three hours later, Beck stood outside examining the roof that had been worked on whilst they were away. Nick would have preferred it if she had taken a couple of bags in from the car, rather than standing admiring the house in near darkness. However, he knew that a five-hour journey, twinned with the disappointment of the stop off, meant for once, he kept his comments to himself.

Ten minutes later after he had finished dumping the bags, pillows, and suitcases in the hallway, he moved into the lounge, where sprawled across the sofa was his wife, kids, and some post that Beck had sifted through and left for him. He pushed Maddison's legs to one side and sat down whilst scanning the letters. One was from Barclaycard, one was a normal envelope which had been handwritten and one was a flyer from a furnishing company where he had brought a bed side table, or more to the point, Becky had brought a table, and used his information 8 months earlier. As often is the case in these situations, the name was ever so slightly incorrect and was addressed to a "Mick Dena."

He placed this on the coffee table to be reviewed later. By reviewed, he meant thrown away in the recycled bin, but due to the increase in cybercrime, he always tore out the name and address and threw that in the normal bin. In hindsight, it was a bit pointless, as anyone could find out this information with ease, but as it made him feel slightly safer, he continued to do it.

He opened the letter that was in a normal white envelope, expecting that this would be the ultrasound date, but in the back of his mind, there was a chance it was from his ex-wife, complaining about something, more than likely the fact she wanted extra money. The fact that he was hoping it was letter from the hospital , rather than a communication from his former partner, just about summed up how much he despised that woman. He leant over to Becky and advised "the scans on Tuesday at the Royal". She looked at him sharply and shook her head slightly, to gesticulate that the kids could hear. It was however too late.

"What's that for Dad?" asked Maddison, who in the last year had become increasingly nosier when it came to adult conversations.

"Oh, it's just for my…….. back" he responded, hesitating slightly mid-sentence as he wasn't sure whether to plump for back or knee.

Maddison was a sensitive wee thing and was going through the transition of child to teenager. This meant that issues of health, death and worry had started to creep slowly into her perfect little world. Actually telling her the truth was not only embarrassing due to the nature of where the issue was, but it would also generate multiple questions along the lines of "but are you ok Dad?", that would be repeated over and over and over and over again.

"Are you Ok Dad?" Maddison asked, a slight concern beginning to show on her face. Archie was oblivious to the conversation and was staring at the TV in a half asleep, half zombie state due to the journey. It was also because he was a kid watching TV, and that's part of the contract for an 8-year-old boy.

"Yes, moodle" said Nick, "I am fine."

This, along with "Maddy Moo" was his favourite nick name for her. "Moodle" was often followed by "Poodle & Doodle" or any other word that rhymed with "oodle".

"I have just got to get it checked out Maddy Moo…. nothing to worry about" he added.

She thought for a split second about questioning the statement but the fact the programme had just reached an interesting point, she decided against it and joined her brother in a living dead state.

Becky raised her eyebrows in his direction yet again and shook her head slightly once more. He blew out his cheeks and headed in the direction of the kitchen.

"Cup of tea?" he asked, picking up the flyers and ripped out the address section.

"Coffee please" responded Becky, as he flicked the kettle switch.

Whilst it boiled, he focused his mind on other important matters such as, had any of the goldfish died whilst he had been away and who was responsible for leaving the cup on the sideboard, with an inch of tea, that had happily been growing fungus to its hearts content whilst they had been away. Realising it was him, he decided it was best to remove all evidence before his wife found out, and discarded the leftovers down the sink, leaving him with the unpleasant task of then having to remove the mould from the drainage plug. He picked up the appointment letter and began reading again, looking for any signs that they may suspect a problem.   Of course, there wasn't, what did he expect it to say ? We recommend you get dropped off, as you aren't going to be able to talk let alone drive, when we tell you what ailment you really have !!

Unsurprisingly, Tuesday soon came around. He had found that as the years passed, days, weeks and months appeared to arrive and disappear way faster than when he was a kid. He could recall as a child those summers that seemed to go on forever, birthdays that actually lasted 24 hours and the build up to Christmas that seemed to start in October. However, as he got older, summers were over before they had even begun, birthdays came and went with limited celebration and Christmas never lived up to the magic it held as a child.

He set off early to the appointment, which was far from normal for him. His overused motto of "why should I turn up early just so that I can wait" had been a mantra he had adhered to for most of his adult life. Granted it had caused the odd warning at work, as lateness is somewhat frowned upon within a 9.00 – 5.00 environment. He often wondered why Dolly couldn't have helped his cause by warbling ……."Working 9.03 – till 5.05, what a way to make a living", but as Tardy Parton was a stickler for time keeping, he had to endure the backlash of management with regards his flexible approach to the time he turned up.

On arrival, he discovered a car park that although was an extra five minutes away, was a better option than driving around a busy hospital carpark, desperately trying to find that "one space" that was available. He parked up, paid the man sitting behind the counter that could only be described as a shed, (which incidentally has to be beneath cleaning toilets on the list of crappy careers you wouldn't want your kids finding themselves in), and set off in the direction of the infirmary.

On the short walk, he recalled the times he had been to this specific hospital. This was the hospital where all his children had been born. He had visited his mum and dad when they were admitted for ailments connected to just getting old and maybe the worst time he could recall was when his oldest son underwent emergency surgery when he was only 1 years of age. He remembered that particular event every time he visited and the memories of watching his baby boy being wheeled away, after he had signed a form allowing them to do so, was still vivid. The recollections were growing grainier each time, but the feeling of helplessness always swept over him like a despairing tidal wave when he relived that moment.

He was also proud that during his 48 years on the planet, he had never spent any significant time himself in any hospital. The closest he had come to booking in time at any Premier Inn-firmary, was when in jest, he jumped on the back of one of his mates on the way home from school. Instead of his friend carrying him off into the distance in a Bob Champion/Aldaniti type moment, it quickly turned into more of a baby donkey, carrying a twenty stone cabbage on his back scenario as the humble mule had little option but to let its legs buckle under the weight and sadly for Nick, his ankle took the brunt of poor Neddys collapse.

This resulted in him being carted off to the local hospital, sobbing the entire 5-mile journey whilst his mum repeated "well it was a stupid thing to do wasn't it Nicholas". Thankfully, on that occasion, he was released the same night with just severe spraining. This was a result all round, as another friend had got him a ticket to watch the local Leicester City v Manchester United game the following day. The downside after the mishap, was that he had to be carried into the stadium by his friend's mum and her sister, sporting a rather fetching support sock. As expected with compassionate football supporters, there was the odd comment being thrown around, as these two, dwarf like ladies, struggled to carry a gangly 5-foot 4-inch, pre-pubescent lad, into a busy stadium.

The weather was as dejected as Nick as he made the five-minute walk from "potting shed" car park to the hospital. Instead of going through the main entrance and weaving his way through the labyrinth of corridors, he noticed a sign outside that indicated there was a short cut to the scanning department. It turned out not to be a short cut after all and more of a "run the gauntlet" against the electric cleaning buggies that were whizzing up and down outside the building. In addition, to the dangerous, dodge the cart game, he had to then hurry past the three smokers that appeared to be competing with China on the air pollution front, as they stood puffing away outside the entrance. One of them was obviously accompanied by a mobile oxygen tank, but Nick made the decision not to mull over the irony and simply entered the building instead.

He felt fine physically…. why shouldn't he? He hadn't experienced any further pains since his holiday but psychologically, he was beginning to harbour doubts. In addition to all of that, he also acknowledged that he would, yet again, be enduring the drama of showing his penis and balls to yet another complete stranger.

Chapter 12 – Swafega.

As he strode down the corridor, his positivity returned slightly and was semi confident that everything would be fine and that within half an hour, he would soon be outside again, heading back to his car, after been given the all clear. He was also suitably impressed with the ease in which he was finding the correct department. The only time that he began to doubt that he was in the right place was when he entered the waiting room to find a crowd of patients, but no receptionist. Either they had already been booked in and Rebecca the Receptionist had decided to do one for the day, or the people who were sat in the chairs weren't awaiting a scan and had simply decided to take a breather on their journey through the warren like corridors.

After doing a double take by checking the departmental sign and receiving the necessary confirmation that he was indeed in the scanning department, he was again faced with doing the groundwork for the upcoming waiting room etiquette game. It became very apparent that all the main options were off the table. There was no chance of moving the chairs, and to be honest, he didn't fancy touching the seats more than was necessarily required. Putting his feet up was an absolute no no and deploying the old coat trick would have probably instigated an unneeded interaction with a total stranger in relation to "is this chair free?." This left him with the dreaded, unspoken option no. 4, otherwise known as "the best of a bad bunch ". This simply meant that you had to choose someone to sit next to and the aim of the game was to choose, well the best of a bad bunch really! The opportunity hadn't showed its ugly face on the visit to the doctors a few weeks earlier, thanks mainly due to a lack of patients. However, this scenario was often the only viable option in hospital waiting rooms, something that he hadn't had to experience due to his lack of visits to those establishments. Like any good folktale, hospital waiting room stories were handed down from generation to generation. They basically consisted of poorly worded anecdotes, remembering that time when the "old fella" basically passed away on my shoulder or recalling the young lad who had an Air fix model plane stuck to his forehead. The concern that Nick had with these stories was that it almost sounded as if his forefathers enjoyed these interactions, something he could never see himself embracing.

Back in the busy waiting room, the assessment was in full flow. The vacant seat next to the gentleman wearing Bermuda shorts, a bandaged head and food stains down his top, was ruled out instantly for obvious reasons. The seat to the left of the couple, where the lady hadn't stopped talking at the poor chap next to her, was quickly crossed off the list over fears that the poor sod might just choose to drop dead to escape the constant ear lashing and that she may then turn the interrogation onto himself. The unoccupied seat next to the lady who hadn't done her hair...ever... was a no....and the young lad in the tracksuit, who he was just starting to get a smell of, had quickly slid down the pecking order, so much so, Teenage Mutant Stinky Tracksuit guy was even behind scary stainy funky short man on the list of potential suitors. This left him with the last man standing, or more to the point, sitting. He had no choice but to park himself to the right of the twitching man near the window.

He puffed out his cheeks longer than needed and began squeezing himself through the slalom of poorly placed chairs. He smiled out of politeness at the gentleman who sat next to the window and took his seat. The man smiled back briefly, either that or it was the natural tic that was forcing his mouth to move in an upwards direction. Nick made the mistake of glancing again and discovered that it was his tic, as he was now looking across the room with the same smile, however this time his eyelid was jerking simultaneously as well. The receptionist appeared a minute or so later, so he jumped at the chance of getting away from tic-meister general, albeit only for the time that it would take to confirm his name and postcode. After providing the limited but essential information, he turned around, half hoping that someone had taken his seat. Regrettably, it was still there with its arms open wide, yearning for his return. However, whilst he was confirming his details and in a delicious twist to the waiting room etiquette game, the woman with the wild hair got up and walked out. This left him with the unexpected, but highly tempting wild card option of moving seats.

Without a second thought, he made a step in the direction of the recently evacuated chair, only for a bald man to boldly, obviously, stomp into the department and plonk himself, unceremoniously, in the recently vacated seat. This selfish deed forced Nick to do an awkward step and turn movement, half realising that he had to quickly make a move back to the chair he had previously vacated before someone else took it. He also needed to give the impression that he was always going that way anyway and it was just a misunderstanding between his brain and his legs with regards the direction he was heading. It failed, he looked like a proper loon and the ticmeister himself would have been proud of the stupidity he had just created.

His appointment time came and then went agonisingly slowly. Bermuda boy, stinky sod and Mrs Chatterboxes husband had all been and gone and Nick was now regretting his decision to sit next to twitchy magoo, especially as seats had become almost instantly available as soon as he had sat back down. Not only was the guy twitching and jerking to his heart's content, but he also found out that he was mumbling to himself as well. Initially, Nick responded, as he thought the question was directed to him. Only when tick tock laughed to himself and answered the question he had just asked; did he realise he was madder than the mad hatter listing to a Suggs album.

"Mr Dean" shouted a smartly dressed individual who appeared out of one of the rooms.

Nick abruptly rose, overjoyed with the fact that he had done his time; he was finally getting out of Twitchtonville. He had briefly forgotten that he was about to display his manhood to yet another person, but that realisation was about to come crashing to the floor faster than a pair of loose trousers filled with pound coins. As he entered the room, just to add a soupcon to the embarrassment factor, there was an unexpected bloke sat at the far end of the room.

"M..Morning" Nick said, slightly taken aback by the guy sitting motionless in the corner.

He smiled back but said nothing.

"For god's sake" he thought. "it's bad enough having a bloke rummage around without his sad voyeur friend watching."

"Okay Mr Dean… just lie on the bed and remove your trousers and underpants please" requested the smartly dressed chap who he had followed into the room.

Nick reluctantly obliged but as he did, he glanced over at the bloke, still sat motionless in the corner. He appeared to be filling in some kind of documentation, although Nick wasn't confident that it wasn't his own private questionnaire…… overall appearance…4….. Dress sense …..3 penis size… disappointing!

"So, you have been advised by your doctor that he has found a small pea sized lump in your right testis is that right?" Announced Dev, who was the smartly dressed one rather than the pervert sitting in the distance.

KAAAAAAAAAA……BOOOOOOOOOOOOOOOOOOOOOOOOOOOOOOOOO OOOOOOOOOOOOOOOOOOOOOOOOOOOOOOOOOOOOOM……

For a moment Nick's life became incoherent and the room mirrored a scene from Mission Impossible, as everything went into slow motion. However, instead of Tom Cruise dramatically vaulting to safety, it was a small bespectacled chap glanced up, blinking twice, before gently returning to the file in front of him.

"No…. that's not the case "exclaimed Nick nervously "that is the first I have heard of any lumps….. I was advised it was just precautionary."

"Oh…" responded Dev, sounding slightly surprised but clearly showing the desire to not get invested in a conversation on the matter.

"Well let's just take a look anyway shall we?" he announced cheerfully, desperately, and unsuccessfully attempting to smother his previous bombshell.

With that, he smeared a substance that in appearance, was a mixture of gloy glue and Swarfega onto both testicles. He then began scanning with a device which didn't look too dissimilar to the tool you use to scan your shopping at Tesco's. It may well have been for all they knew, and no one would have been the wiser if the consultant had wiped the memory of cat food, Jacob's crackers, and broccoli against his bollocks. Nicks attention had now clearly switched from the perverted onlooker to the consultant himself and he watched fiercely for any expression as he pressed and depressed the scanner against his balls. Although paranoia had instantly taken up residence on Nicks shoulder, the look of concern that kept appearing on the face of the consultant gave justification for its attendance.

"Everything ok down there? "questioned Nick, trying to sound light-hearted but failing miserably.

"Wellll"...the consultant said in an elongated manner, focussing on the job in hand, concentrating solely on the bald appendage in front of him. "I just need to double check the area on the right testicle in more detail" he added.

By now Nick was beginning to experience some uneasiness in his private region. Paranoia immediately jumped out of the deck chair that was nestled on his owner's collar bone and whispered in his ear "that's cus they've found something!" Although concerned and fully understanding paranoias sentiment, Nick had to remind his thoughts that rubbing a scanner across your testicles, over and over again, would inevitably cause some kind of discomfort and therefore would he mind "doing one" for the time being.

"Ok Mr Dean, all done, please get your self-dressed" announced Dev, wiping the lubricant off the scanner which would make it easier to return to the local shopping centre.

He passed Nick a disposable towel advising he might want to "wipe himself" and walked over to his perverted friend who in all honesty, Nick had forgotten was in the room. The pair of them were now reviewing the pictures of the scan on the small screen like a couple of perverts with a dirty magazine.

"Is everything ok?" enquired Nick, this time displaying a hint of concern in his tone.

"Well, there does appear to be something" said the consultant "but we won't know fully until we have been able to complete a full investigation."

"Oh" was all that Nick could muster, as he turned his back on the pair and spent a few seconds wiping the excess gloyfega off his balls.

"The results will be back with your doctor in a day or so Mr Dean and he will go through them in more detail with you" Dev stated, giving him a reassuring smile in the process.

"Oh ...ok" was again all that Nick could assemble, although it was a 100% improvement on his previous effort.

He zipped up his trouser zip, thanked the consultant for his time and walked out of the room, awkwardly giving a smile to the other chap as he walked by. He didn't even notice be-twitched, who was still sat in the same spot as he strolled out the department. It wasn't as if he would have gone and said his goodbyes, but such was the uneasiness that was now swirling around his head, he didn't even give him a second glance.

He began the long walk through the white corridors, that now seemed to be taking twice as long as they did on the way in. The exit signs appeared to be playing some type of Alice in Wonderland game and were showing left, right, straight on, backwards, up, down, and even diagonal. He was just about to ask a member of staff for assistance when he noticed the hospital shop in the distance and as he knew that this was adjacent to the exit, he got his head down and upped the pace somewhat. Outside, he took a massive gulp of air that was laced with fresh nicotine and diesel fumes, removed his mobile phone from his trouser pocket and dialled a familiar number.

He'd waited until he got outside to dial as he wasn't sure on the rules around mobile telephones/medical technology, and although he was under the impression that it was now deemed ok to use mobile phones within the hospital itself, he aired on the side of caution as he didn't want to be the one responsible for switched off Gladys life support machine as he slid past her room. In addition, he was feeling quite delicate and the last thing he wanted at that point, was a member of staff having a go about telephone usage as he meandered through the hospital.

The only other significant time Nick had questioned the "no use of mobile phone" scenario was in Petrol stations. After probing several friends for their thoughts on the matter and all of them responding with "it's a fire hazard," he decided to google the information for clarity. It turned out that the main reason was the risk of distraction whilst dispensing petrol. Fire hazard did get a brief mention further down in the report, however he felt this was just thrown in there to give some justification for a rule that had now outlived its great great grandparents.

"Hi its Becky… I can't take your call now but do leave me a message and I will call you right back…. Byyyyyyye! Said the voice on the end of the phone.

"Err Hi Beck……it's me. Not the greatest of news…they have found something…. Not sure what…..err… will need to see the doctor in a couple of days…..call me back…. erm….when you can…see you later." Nick pressed the red button and stared longingly at his phone for a few seconds.

He looked up, breathed in another breath of musty air, and set off in the direction of the car park. The gloom had lifted, and the sun was playing peekaboo through the buildings, although he wasn't in any mood to play. He really wanted to talk to someone and by someone he meant Beck.

Chapter 13 – The call.

"Hiya... Let me just connect you to the car" announced Nick as he fumbled with his phone, one eye on the lights in front, one on the Bluetooth sync button.

"Just got your message...." replied Becky "Bloody hell..... You ok?" she added.

"Yeah, I'm ok" he said sheepishly.

This meant he wasn't ok. A flippant response along the lines of "why shouldn't I be.....why what do you thinks wrong with me" was normally a good indicator on how he was feeling. Fewer words normally meant there was a problem.

"Try not to worry Nick......someone at work had the exact same issue.... remember me telling you about Paul. He had the same thing...... it took them ages to find out what the problem was, and in the end, there wasn't a problem. It was a cyst or something along those lines. I can't quite remember what it was, but it was definitely ok and nothing to worry about in the end.....I'm sure I told you about it...yeah, Paul ...I told you... remember....anyway, I am sure there is nothing for you to worry about."

Becky was the complete opposite to Nick in these situations. When she waffled, it normally meant there was a problem or that she wasn't comfortable with the situation. Normally, those moments of yakking on, would swiftly be followed by another stream of one-way chatter. In addition to this, she would more often than not, then analyse the comments she had made mid conversation, which would always lead to further ramblings. The problem she then had was that she would then analyse the analysation, again during the conversation, which meant she would be forever analysing the analysis. This inevitably led to more verbal nonsense, which would go on and on, until she ran out of breath anyway.

"I suppose so" responded Nick. "I just didn't think they would find anything..." he added.

"It might be nothing" interrupted Beck. "Please try not to worry...... I'm sure it's really nothing overly serious. I know I'm going on about it but Paul at work was worried sick for weeks. At the end of it all it was nothing, so he worried himself ... for nothing, and when I say nothing, I mean nothing. No further appointments, no surgery, I don't think he even had medication, so when I say it was nothing, I really do mean it was nothing.... "

"It's easier said than done though Beck" interrupted Nick, justifiably feeling more than a bit sorry for himself and getting the point that Beck was making about it being nothing in Paul's case.

"How long do you have to wait for the results?" she asked, realising it was probably time to calm it on the "nothing" front.

"Not quite sure when they will be back to be honest...they said a couple of days.....I assume they will send me an appointment letter" he added.

"Look, I know you will worry Nick because that's a Dean trait, but let's wait to see what it is before we start jumping off that cliff eh?."

Beck was right. It was a Dean trait. The whole Dean family had a penchant to milk a situation more than any device used on cattle. It may have been because there were five boys in the family and blokes, in general, are not the best when it comes to illness. Even his dad, Father Dean, who Nick had regarded as a strong, no-nonsense kind of guy as a kid, found out in later life that he was actually, Prince of the Hypochondriac tribe. He could have been King if he hadn't have felt so poorly all the time.

"Yeah, I know you are right Beck….. I will call you later, on the way home."

"Ok…. love you …. and try not to worry."

"Alright…" he sombrely replied and disconnected the call.

Work that day was strange. Every now and again he would get engrossed in his work and completely forget about the situation, although, as soon he switched back to his personal life, the tides of worry crashed against his mind's defences and breached them time and time again with ease. Just after lunchtime, he took the decision to tell Lorraine. He felt that he needed to talk to someone and as she had some involvement and was pretty good at providing support in times of need, it seemed a no win no fee scenario.

She did a pretty good job of holding back the words "I told you so" as she quickly gathered from his demeanour that it wasn't neither the place, nor the time. She was the only one who had mentioned the sinister "C" word from the very beginning and although there was no confirmation at this point, the chance of it being that diagnoses had increased considerably from the day before.

Chris, Nicks annoying colleague was on holiday, which turned out to be the only shining light of the day. Not having to answer his questions on where he had been that morning and why he was acting all miserable, was a blessing. Although he meant no harm, the last thing he needed at that point was an arrogant, jumped-up colleague coming out with the standard clichés of "keeping his chin up" and "focusing on the positives." In addition to the unrequited platitudes, there would inevitably be a story that followed about an uncle or some distant relative that was diagnosed with the worst possible illness, only for them to recover, skateboard up Mount Fuji, wearing nothing more than a pair of speedos or something equally unbelievable. He decided therefore, not to tell anyone else and made the unconscious decision to keep the concern carousel going around in his own mind instead.

On the journey home, the much-delayed introduction of positivity finally made its entrance. Beck had called and had confirmed that her work colleague had undergone the exact same scan and was advised, after several days of waiting, that it was a cyst. Although she had confirmed that a small operation was needed, he was back to work within a few weeks, none the worst, just with a better falsetto singing voice. She even made a comment that he could potentially be off work for a couple of weeks which wouldn't be a bad thing with all the house build going on. Typical Beck, always thinking of killing two bollocks with one brick.

He was greeted by Archie as he arrived home and it was safe to say that he was relieved to be back in the comfortable surroundings of 13 Winstanley Drive. Although the welcome was brief, basically it was a" Hi" swiftly followed by a "Bye," it was just what he needed. Nick responded with a "Hi Archie" but the last syllable faded slightly as the youngster disappeared up the stairs like a crazed chimpanzee and wasn't prepared to enter into a whole conversation with his boring old dad.

Beck's welcoming wasn't much better, as her greeting was disrupted by her mobile phone ringing halfway through the "How are you feeling?" inquiry. He was just about to enter into a heartfelt dialogue about feeling really low but unknown to him, it was just about to get lower than Warwick Davis commando crawling. Beck shouted with more than a smidgen of urgency "Nick, I need you upstairs."

The telephone call wasn't for Becky. It was the doctor's surgery or more to the point, the doctor himself. It transpired that they didn't have Nick's new number on file and had done some Inspector Morse shit in the background and had found Becks number. The fact he had upgraded his telephone number three years before indicated that not only was he not a regular visitor to the doctors but also that their patient data process left a lot to be desired. It was understandable if it was the receptionist job to update patient files. Her overall manner and winning smile were obviously a glowing factor for people not willingly offering their personal information to the sour faced handbag.

Now there are certain things in life that you don't want to be greeted with. A burglar in mid burgle, catching your parents in the middle of a passionate sexual encounter, coming face to face with a wild animal after the zookeeper forgets to close the enclosure. All of these are highly improbable, some more unlikely than others, but having the doctor ring you at home, on the same day you have had a scan, makes staring Tony the Tiger directly into his eyes, not such a bad proposition after all.

Nick walked into their bedroom, Beck passed the telephone and closed the door behind them, just standing close enough to listen to the doctor's conversation.

"Hello" said Nick.

"Good evening Mr Dean" responded Dr Aggarwal in a polite yet daunting manner.

"I apologise for calling so late. We didn't have your correct telephone number on file but managed to find your wife's number in our records. Are you ok to talk?"

Nick wanted to say "no" and pass the phone back to Becky. Of all the things that he wanted to do in his life, taking the telephone call and hearing what the doctor had to tell him was definitely way down on the pecking order. It sat in-between pulling his fingernails out with plyers and listening to the full Jive Bunny album.

Yes, I can talk" replied Nick quietly.

"So, I have the results back from this morning's ultrasound scan and there is something there that I need to discuss with you tomorrow. Can you come to the surgery first thing?"

Nick wasn't far off from what he thought the doctor was going to say, but hearing the words turned a small seedling of a doubt that had been gently flourishing in the sunlight, into an enormous, daunting, storm damaged oak tree.

"Err … err… Yes, I can…." He replied, flustered in relation to the whole conversation.

Becky looked into Nicks eyes and mouthed "Do they know what it is?"

"Do they know what it is?" asked Nick, abandoning his filter mechanism and now just repeating what Beck was asking him. It was a good job she didn't whisper "Tell him to go fudge himself" as there was a strong chance Nick would have told the doctor exactly that.

"Do they think its cancer?" he continued, knowing that the answer coming back wasn't the two-letter word he had heard a million times before.

"I can't say over the telephone, but I do need you to come in and see me" said the doctor calmly.

"So, they think it is" pushed Nick.

"Look, I can't say over the telephone but there is a strong chance it is. I just need to see you so we can talk through the situation. What time can you get here?" he asked.

"Er…er…. erm" spluttered Nick.

"Whatever time they want us there, as early as possible" declared Becky, who had now given up on the Marcel Marceau impression and was now audible so that Nick and the doctor could both hear.

"Shall we say 9.15?" suggested Dr Aggarwal.

"Yes, that should be fine" replied a dumbstruck Nick, "see you tomorrow" and he passed the phone to Becky.

They stood silent for a few seconds before she interrupted the awkward stillness.

"Shit" she said simply. Nick said nothing.

"Right, we go together and see what the situation is" she added. "He didn't say it was cancer did he…he just said there is a chance…. that's right isn't it."

"No, he didn't, but why would he call if it wasn't?" he muttered, looking out the window into the unlit back garden.

The pair stood again for a few moments feeling that there was so much to say but realising that words, at that moment, were about as relevant as a pair of goggles to a drowning man.

"Muuuuum" shouted Archie, breaking the disconcerted silence. "Is dinner ready...I'm Marvin" he bawled from his bedroom.

Beck let a few more moments pass before she stood up.

"Right, we go, we listen to what he has to say, and we then see what we need to do" declared Becky, trying to bring an element of positivity to the situation. "I've got to go and get Archie's dinner.... you stay here and I will be back in a minute... we will sort this Nick ..."

Nick nodded his head in acknowledgement but said nothing. She gently closed the door behind her, making sure it was fully closed, before heading downstairs. He could hear Archie sarcastically mention the fact that he was "wasting away," blissfully unaware of the life changing news that had presented itself to his mum and dad only moments earlier.

The cogs were now in full flow as his mind sprang into action. Fears, worries, and concerns where being flung around his head like a fairground Wurlitzer and although Nick wanted to scream at the top of his voice , he definitely didn't want to go any faster. He slumped onto the bed and brushed away the tears that had begun falling down his unshaven face.

"Shit, shit, shit, shit, shit, shit, shit, shit" he muttered to himself.

Nick sat alone, sobbing into his cupped hands for what felt like the longest five hundred seconds ever, each one dragging him a step closer to the unavoidable end. The realisation was starting to sink in. The sedate, driving miss daisy type excursion he had been on for the past 48 years had suddenly been interrupted and the handbrake had been well and truly deployed. He found himself spinning out of control, with no influence on where or when the journey would come to an end.

Chapter 14 – Justin Hawkins.

Twelve twenty-three, that was the time being displayed on Nicks mobile phone. There was a chance it was a minute out, so in all probability it was actually twenty-four minutes after midnight.

Upon waking and for the splitest of seconds, he questioned what was happening in his life. Was it midweek? Did he have to get up for work? Was that a noise he thought he heard outside? The truth in the form of the conversation he had with Dr Aggarwal six hours earlier, instantly began caving in on him like ghostly debris falling in the darkness. He took a deep breath in through his nose and stared desperately into the blackness. Light gradually began to form and he started to see the outline of the bedroom door. Due to it being ajar, he began to see the glow from Archie's night light on the landing. This had been moved into a vacant socket a month earlier and was designed to help the kids, and Nick, find their way to the toilet at night. At this moment in time though, it was doing a reasonable job of providing much needed brightness in an extremely dark situation.

"You ok?" questioned Becky, waking to the sound of his phone being replaced on the unit next to the bed.

She, like Nick, also hadn't really fell into a deep sleep due to the news and the fact that she was awake, and actually talking, indicated the seriousness of the situation. Typically, Becky talking after she had gone to bed meant one thing and one thing only. She was drunk. The differences in these circumstances were astounding as normally, any type of noise after lights out would be greeted by disgruntled shuffling. However, after she had been on the vodka and tonic, you couldn't shut her up. Her conversations would always be of the highest importance, to her anyway, and it was par for the course for her to wake him with a telephone call on her way home from a night out on the town. Most of the time it was drunken drivel, such as "hiiiiiyaaaaaa…. I'm on my way back

90

hooooooooommme" or " wahoooooo..... What's wrong...were you asleep?."

Every now and again there would be a serious issue, which was often accompanied by the dramatic statement "I need to talk to you when I get back!." On these occasions, it basically meant that he had to meet her at the door and then sit in the lounge, for the next twenty minutes, listening to her banging on about her friend (who he had probably met once), being on the verge of a nervous breakdown. This was usually something to do with her manager picking on her, her kids having behavioural issues or her partner not appreciating her and basically taking her for granted.

These early morning tete-a-tetes, were always complimented by regular slurring and her munching on a pack of mini cheddars or essentially anything she could find that didn't need cooking. Although it may have been a distressing and difficult situation for Beck's friend, that incidentally seemed to have been heightened significantly with the aid of alcohol, it was never on the apocalyptic scale and hardly needed discussion at 3.30 am. Something that was often backed up the following day when Becky didn't even think it was worth talking about!

"I'm really scared Beck" came Nicks voice from the gloom.

"I know you are" she whispered back, shuffling over the bed to give him a cuddle in the process.

"What if they can't cure it?" he questioned.

"You don't know what it is yet, the Doctor didn't actually say it was cancer did he" she responded, mixing sternness with a hint of empathy.

"He couldn't, could he, that's why we are going tomorrow to get the news officially" he replied.

Beck thought hard about a response but found nothing. Instead, she transformed briefly into a petit, blonde, boa constrictor, and squeezed him tightly for a few seconds. She finally settled with the slightly cliched "we will get through this you know" and whispered these words whilst giving him one last crush. She let her grip loosen for a few moments, turned to the side and within minutes, was purring like a piglet.

Nick was not even close to sleeping and continued to stare into the darkness. Without hesitation, the darkness stared back. This contest continued for the next fifty minutes or so, mainly in total silence, the only exception being Babe, who was lying next to him, shuffling, and snuffling every now and again. His mind was whirling which helped focus his gaze, giving the gloom an absolute run for its money, and for a while, matching its unerring power. He inevitably conceded defeat in the game as his eyes reluctantly closed and darknesses one hundred percent record stayed intact.

He woke what seemed minutes later, to find it was, essentially minutes later. He checked the time and replaced the mobile phone on the side unit again. This time however, Beck remained committed to her sleep and continued with the soft growling that came with every in-breath. Nick again, entered into a staring rematch but almost immediately admitted defeat as his competitor's strength and commitment level were on another level. Instead, he chose to try and switch his mind off everything through the power of television. The light from the TV lit up the room which instantly woke Becky from her slumber. Normally this selfish act would be greeted with "what on earth are you doing?," but as there was a sleep amnesty going on and his "sorry, I just need to watch something for a while", was greeted with an obliging "not a problem...wake me if you want to talk?". Although the acceptance was fully expected in the circumstances, it was also appreciated as he knew that the governing body in Beckyland, insisted that TV and sleep went together like banana and gravy.

"Try and get some sleep ..... and sorry", replied Nick, taking full advantage of the temporary armistice, and increasing the volume so that he could just about hear something.

"Just wake me if you need me" remarked Beck again, stroking Nick's side lazily with the back of her hand, so much so it became more of an effort and due to this, stopped as soon as it had started.

As he was finding it difficult to concentrate, he again found himself reopened the staring contest, this time in the form of the bright glare of the Television screen. After a few oblivious moments though, he realised that this was just adding tension to his already pummelled eyesight, so instead, began searching the TV guide to find a channel that he hoped would send him to sleep, or at least take his mind off the situation.

Before long, he found himself scrolling down past channel 150 and only paused once to consider watching a repeat episode of "who wants to be a millionaire". Finding something to watch was proving harder than he initially assumed and eventually, he reluctantly plumped for some kind of "traffic cops" episode, as somewhere in the depth of his mind he was hoping the subject matter may make him feel slightly better about the predicament he currently found himself in. It didn't. He just found himself watching, not taking any notice, and the fact that the man was found crouching in the undergrowth was totally irrelevant in the great scheme of things. Even the impressive commentary from the helicopter pilot, leading the dog handler to the location via the infer red image, went unacknowledged.

All Nick could see was the drama in his own life. How would he cope with being ill? How much had the disease spread? Would Becky be happier with a new partner when he had gone? All these concerns paled into insignificance when it came to his biggest concern. The fear of not being there to see his children grow up. All the quiz shows, TV documentaries, comedy repeats and sporting re-runs couldn't shift that thought.

This trepidation accompanied him through most of the night and into the early morning. The sunlight that had started to haul its way over the horizon was a sight that although semi acknowledged previously, was not a display he had truly taken that much notice of before. However, it wasn't the grandeur, glory and splendour of the world announcing itself that filled him with gratitude, it was the simple fact that darkness had been replaced by light. Never had he experienced such need for sunlight and the wakening of a new day. Although exhausted due to the tears, the fears, the midnight staring contests and sleep deprivation, the light that was now playing peekaboo through the gaps in the curtain was a sight for his very sore and tired eyes.

Although the transition from night to day was in its infancy, he took this as an opportunity to get up and prepare for a day for which he was not prepared. The appointment had been made for 9.15am as Dr Aggarwal had offered the earliest appointment possible, which was foreboding on its own. Although getting the official diagnoses was an unwanted necessity, getting the children to school without them getting wind of any problem was first on the morning's things to do list. Both Nick and Becky needed no additional drama that morning, so Maddie and Archie eating their breakfast, getting dressed, having a wash, and brushing their teeth, with minimal fuss, was key in limiting the amount of stress before they even left the house.

Like a well-oiled machine, the children obliged. That is if the well-oiled machine was a manky, air polluting, battered old rust bucket that wouldn't have worked, even if you shoved a rocket up its exhaust system. Starting with breakfast, every cereal in the cupboard was now "trash," even though the week before they were the best thing since sliced Weetabix. During those seven days, obviously manufacturing of these breakfast cereals had changed dramatically and instead of wheat, barley and the odd additives being mixed on the production line, mouse droppings, belly fluff and toenail scrapings where being mashed together and moulded into a cheeky little briquette instead.

Maddie refused to get dressed because … .well, because it was Wednesday, and because she was tired, and because Archie hadn't got ready, and because her clothes weren't there, and because she didn't want too, and because she was watching TV, and because she hadn't had her trash breakfast, and just bloody because.

Archie was refusing to have a wash because he was a boy and washing hadn't entered his vocabulary yet. To round it all off, Maddie then had a further meltdown because the toothpaste wasn't the normal one. Therefore, she couldn't brush her teach because, well because, well you can guess the rest.

So, at 9.02, a full 5 minutes after the delightful duo should have left, they got ushered out the front door, one of them with only one shoe on and the other one unsuccessfully attempting to put their arm through a sleeve of their coat that was inside out. Becky shouted to Nick "back in a minute, be ready to go as soon as I get back." He was already ready. He had been ready from approx. 6.30 pm the previous night.

Chapter 15 – The life and times of Lance Armstrong.

They arrived at the surgery with a whole 1 minute to spare. This was impressive, seeing as the journey, which was normally a good ten minutes, was completed in a notable eight. Nick, who over the last 3 hours had been mentally preparing himself, was now equipped as he ever would be for the forthcoming news. He turned to Becky before leaving the car.

"Right, we confirm what it is and then move onto the next step...ok".

Becky nodded but appeared anxious.

Nick, for someone who worried quite a lot, did have a knack of focusing when it was needed.

He repeated his statement, recognising the agitation within her.

"So, we get confirmation Beck, we find out what we need to do, and we take it from there... yes?"

"Yep" nodded Beck, realising she was there to provide support and picking up that he was tuning into the fact that she was currently being as helpful as a deceased Samaritan.

"You do know he will tell us its cancer, don't you?"   he said calmly, as he opened the door and began climbing out.

"You don't know that for sure" responded Beck sharply, moving around the other side of the car before reaching out to hold his hand.

"There is nothing else it can be" he replied, opening the door to the surgery, advising the receptionist that he had arrived, completely dismissing the checking in screen in the process. Due to where they lived, there were three different surgeries that covered the surrounding area. Unlike the last time when he visited the new, plush clinic, this visit was to its run-down sibling, that in all fairness, hadn't done very well for the past few years with regards the allocation of refurbishment funds.

Nick, still focused on the job in hand, confirmed his details and sat down in the waiting room. Becky followed and the pair sat down, silently scanning the room, waiting for the doctor to call them in. Every poster, pamphlet or brochure seemed to be connected to Cancer and although he knew what was coming, he was not yet in the right frame of mind to start scanning those particular documents. To his relief, the doctor appeared from around the corner and beckoned them in.

The visit, however, was more comparable to a trip to the headmaster's office than it was an outing to the doctors. Both shuffled in silently and both had the fear of God painted all over their faces as they sheepishly deciding who should sit where. Nick decided he should sit in the seat opposite the doctor as it was the most sensible thing to do. Beck plumped for the chair that was neither here nor there, which made her look more like an observer taking notes than a participant.

"Ok Mr Dean, thank you for coming in so promptly. So, this is the situation....." Was Dr Aggarwal's opening gambit. In all fairness, there wasn't much that could be said. "Good morning ...how are you?" didn't fit the situation, neither did "whatsuuuuuuuuuuuuuuuuuuuuuuuuup bud". Furthermore, small talk about journey time or the weather was also inappropriate to the scenario, so retrospectively "Okay Mr Dean, so this is the situation" appeared to be as good a starting point as any.

He continued……

".. as discussed last night on the telephone, the ultra-scans have come back and there is a dark shading on your right testicle. Although it cannot be confirmed at this stage, the likelihood is that the mass is cancerous".

The faint hope that Nick was clinging onto had already got up, sneaked out of the door and was scurrying off down the high-street.

"Ok" confirmed Nick calmly, "How certain are you that it is cancer?"

"You can't tell until you have the testicle removed but in my professional opinion…it is cancerous, yes".

Nick held out his hand to his support, his rock, his soul mate. The, "we get confirmation and then find out what we need to do" conversation they had moments earlier, was now in its initial stages. As he turned, fully expecting Becks upper lip to be stiffer than stiffy the bullmastiff's morning erection, ready to ambush the conversation with a "so what's the next step" question, he was greeted with a distraught wife, in floods of tears, sobbing like a new born baby. So, it turned out she was more of a damp sponge than hard granite.

Dr Aggarwal quickly continued as Nick held her hand and gave her an unconvincing smile.

"The good news is that if you are going to get cancer, this is the one you want to get".

Gee …..What a result. All that was missing now was some party poppers, paper hats and a few of those blowers that go fffffllllllllleeeeeeeeeeeppppppp . It was good news according to Doc Doc Doc Doc Doctor upbeat. However, Affirmation Aggarwal hadn't finished with his positive spin on the news that was being provided.

"Have you heard of Lance Armstrong?" he questioned.

Great thought Nick, not only have I just discovered I have cancer, but I am now being forced to play a shit game of "guess who". He begrudgingly nodded, already pre-empting the direction in which "Dr Buoyant" was heading, as he remembered reading somewhere that Lance Armstrong was diagnosed with testicular cancer when he was in his mid-twenties. Although he had a good idea what was coming, he wasn't quite on the same track as the positive practitioner, who was ready to take the conversation up a level on the pessimistic front.

"Well Lance Armstrong was diagnosed with stage three cancer. This meant it had spread to his lungs, abdomen and even his brain" announced Dr Aggarwal.

"Aaaaaaa.......gaaaaaa do do do" ....Nick was thinking of starting a conga around the room, such was the cheerful and inspiring piece of trivia he had just received. The doc was now well and truly into sharing the "life and times of Lance Armstrong" and although he had focused purely on the headlines to this point, with what seemed a blatant disregard for how the message was being received, he was almost ready to provide them both with the reassurance they were craving for.

"The good news is that with testicular cancer, even though it can spread, it is treatable. In Lance Armstrong's case, he was treated, cured and as I am sure you know the rest, he went on to be a successful athlete". Dr Aggarwal chose not to mention Lance's steroid abuse that ultimately shattered his career, but as the message was all about curing cancer, he didn't feel the need to labour the fact that the former Olympian was stripped of all his medals years later.

It was all in vain anyway as Nick had stopped listening at the point when the words "Cancer of the Brain" entered the surgery. Whilst he could see the Doctors mouth moving, all he heard was his own mind telling him, "It has spread to your brain....and if not there, it's in your lungs.........you're a gonna!". Becky was even further behind the conversation after melting like the wicked witch of the west upon hearing the dreaded C word. All her mind was telling her was "he's got cancer, he's got cancer, he's got cancer".

Five minutes later, after Doctor Aggarwal finally picked up on their insecurities, ramping up the positive reinforcements and reiterating the words "it is a curable cancer", they walked out his room, and dragged themselves out of the surgery in a blurry haze, oblivious to the receptions polite smiling as they ambled by. They climbed into the car, hugged, and began to cry simultaneously. Words were meaningless and silence took complete control of the moment.

Chapter 16 – Dr Khan or Dr Can't.

Even though the journey home was short, the reality of the situation was starting to sink in and had pretty much hit the ocean floor by the time they got home Questions that didn't come anywhere near the surface whilst at the surgery, were now bobbing around like a collection of buoys in a quaint Devon harbour.

"So, I have an operation and get it removed?" questioned Nick, querying the statement towards the end.

"Yeah, I think that's what he said" acknowledged Beck, removing the leaflets from the large brown envelope that had been given to them back at the surgery.

He was reluctant to read the literature as there was a concern that it contained information that once digested, couldn't be unread. Ignorance wasn't quite bliss, but denial works for a while was an attitude that Nick often incorporated when he didn't want to face the truth. He decided instead to let Beck carefully pick through the pamphlet, in the hope she would frame the words in a better light.

"So, you are on a fast-track cancer programme", she confirmed "and will normally hear within two weeks of your doctor's appointment" she added.

Although two weeks seemed pretty impressive when it came to NHS service levels, he couldn't stop thinking that the disease, that was growing inside his right testicle, was spreading its unpleasant, tumour tainted tentacles, far and wide. For that reason and that reason alone, in a dragon's den stylie... he wanted it out. He momentarily reviewed the unrealistic option of self-removal, and although he knew it was impossible, still went through the motions of addressing the three major stumbling blocks.

One was the severe lack of experience in orchiectomy, the removal of one or more testicle. The second issue was the pain threshold. He expected that without the necessary antithetic, it might smart a tad and the likelihood of him being able to continue with the operation was thinner than a sheet of A4 paper, sliced depth wise in two. The third and final nail in the coffin was the prospect of him dying due to the self-inflicted wound he would create. This in itself won the battle of stupid thoughts and so had no option but to tune back into Radio Becky.

"Blah de blah …………. Operation procedure………..expected recovery time……….." Muttered Becky, as she scanned the leaflet for a scrap of positive information.

"So, it looks as if the first steps are they remove the testicle……………..Two weeks though to get that date through…… surely, they can do that in a few days' time, why wait for it to grow?" she quizzed, looking at the back of the document before flicking through it again, hoping to find something to help shift the despondent mood that had cadged a life back with them from the surgery.

"For the love of God, I don't want an operation Beck, but on the flip side, I don't want this shitting thing in me any longer than it needs to be. I have no choice but to wait".

"Have you got any private health care with your work?" asked Beck, still thumbing through the booklet, but clearly giving the impression that she was losing interest in its limited content.

"I think I have …. Not sure what's covered though…. Let me call work and find out" advised a glum looking Nick, still looking as if someone had just swapped his fifty-pound note for a fiver.

He called Lorraine, who probably was the only one who wasn't shocked with the news. If it wasn't such a delicate situation, she would have belted out arrogantly "told you so didn't I". However, the situation called for empathy and a fair old dollop of reassurance, so she duly obliged. As normal, she was ultra-positive about the situation and advised that she would speak to the HR team to see what they could find out. He thanked her sincerely, apologised for not being in work that day, and confirmed that he would keep her posted on developments. In return, she told him not to be daft, take as much time as needed, and although she knew it was inappropriate, was dying to make some detrimental comment about his nether regions. She thought better of it in the end, which although was the right action to take, still left her with that missed opportunity feeling. From Nicks point of view, he appreciated that she had maintained a compassionate stance throughout the call, but it had left him slightly saddened that she wasn't allowed to make a joke, simply due to his ill health and pending demise. It's always the way he thought, serious situations demand that humour takes on a submissive, spectator type role, regardless of how many top-quality gags and anecdotes are waiting in the wings.

"What did she say?" asked Beck, who was now scanning through the other leaflet that she had found stuck inside the brown paper envelope.

"She's having a word with HR, she was really good about it all", he confirmed.

No more than two minutes passed before his phone began vibrating. "Is that your phone" queried Beck, still reading the information she had just found. "Why on earth is it still on bloody silent" she added, with a twinge of distrust in her voice.

The story behind this was simple and if honest, pretty unspectacular. His phone, or more to the point, his mobile being on silent, had been a topic of conversation before. On several occasions, Beck had found that reaching him on his mobile, was extremely difficult. There was nothing sinister about the lack of response, it was due to the simple fact that he didn't know she was calling, solely because his mobile was on silent. From his aspect, there were three main reasons for this. The first and most pertinent was the fact that he had to put his phone in a silent state when at work. In addition to this, he regularly connected the telephone to the cars Bluetooth on the way to and from his workplace, so this took away any need to increase the volume on his ringtone when driving. Reason number three, and probably the most relevant, was that no one ever hardly called him!

That wasn't strictly true as his eldest son, Charlie, rang on a regular basis, but apart from him and Beck, that was about it. He had found that over time, he had drifted from friendships all too easily and acquaintances that he did have, all moved onto other messaging systems, such as WhatsApp, so calling had become a bit of a novelty. There was again, nothing menacing about his decision to move away from relationships, it was just that as he got older, finding time to meet up with people got more problematic, well that's what he told himself anyway. The reality was that Beck, his family and his home were his happy place and after a long day at work, or even a short day, he just wanted to spend time with them. From time to time though, when reflecting on the past, he was saddened that he had lost contact with former colleagues and teammates from his old football team. He also understood that is the way of the world, and friendships often just slip away like a frozen Jack Dawson, moments after his icy arms were detached from the floating debris.

Nick picked up the phone, muttered the words in becks direction "you know why" and looked at the number being displayed. He recognised immediately it was his workplace, although the number on show was the main switchboard rather than his departmental number. With this seemingly pointless bit of corporate knowledge, instead of gambling and greeting the caller with "Hi Lorraine", he decided he would play it safe just in case it was a member of the HR team, and go with a the harmless, albeit predictable, "Hello…. Nick speaking.

"Bit formal wasn't it, it's me you muppet!" announced Lorraine, deciding that treating him as she normally would was the way forward.

"Hi Lorraine" he replied, Beck stumbling over the sofa slightly as she attempted to move closer to the phone. "I wasn't sure if it was going to be you or someone from HR, so I decided ..... oh, it doesn't matter, how did you get on?".

"Good I think. If you give this number a call, they will be able to advise what's covered" she confirmed. "I can do it for you if you want?" she added.

" No that's fine, I will give them a call now, that sounds promising"" stated an appreciative Nick "thanks so much for your help".

"You take care of each other" she said, quickly followed by "and Let me know how you get on will you?".

As he was feeling extremely sorry for himself, he took the comment a little bit too literally, believing that on this occasion, she should have just said look after yourself. Although he got the sentiment in her comment and knew that the journey ahead needed them both to be strong, at that specific moment, he wanted all the sympathy pushed in his direction.

He contacted the number provided straight away and established to his extreme relief, that he was covered for anything that was required, although at this stage, he didn't know what that actually entailed. The male telephone representative, who was obviously experienced in dealing with anxious patients who have just been told that they have weeks to live, recommended, after spending several minutes searching his system, that he contacted the receptionist of a Dr Khan, who was not only in his local area but also a specialist in the testicular area. The thought of waiting for the NHS conveyor belt to trundle his way, wasn't filling him with the elations of autumn let alone the joys of spring. It was safe to say, the way that he felt, mirrored a dark, cold, winters day, somewhere in the middle of January, with the only thing worth looking forward too was, well the joys of spring really.

Again, he took no time in calling Dr Khan's receptionist, Joanne, and discovered that she wasn't as compassionate as Ben, the representative he had spoken to at Bupa. In all fairness, she wasn't even in the same sport, let alone league, when it came to empathy. He was really impressed with how he had handled the call, and even during the bleak episode he was currently starring in, Nick was appreciative, acknowledged the good customer service provided, and valued the way that he had approached the exchange between the two of them. He did briefly toy with the idea of greeting him with "Hi Bupa Ben" the next time he rang, as he thought it sounded like Ibuprofen, and that would have given him a modicum of self-amusement for a few fleeting moments. Although polite, Joanne digested his request for the "earliest possible appointment" without a smidgen of empathy, and unlike Ben who was very personable, Nick was greeted with a rather mechanical "I will see what is in Mr Khan's diary and call you back shortly".

Thankfully, punctuality was one of her stronger points as she called back 15 minutes later. Much to Nicks delight, he was advised that an initial consultation appointment was available the following day, if he was free to attend. Relief swept over him, albeit momentarily, as he was brought back down to earth with an almighty thud seconds later, when he realised he was relieved simply because he was getting someone to talk to him about his cancer diagnoses, that twenty-four hours earlier, he was blessedly unaware of.

The elephant, who had obviously snuck a lift back in the car alongside the despondent mood, was now in the room, and was making himself comfy, slurping a cup of tea and watching "Cash in the Attic". Nick sat down next to Beck, puffed out his cheeks and picked up the leaflet with the title, "what happens next".

"Do we need to talk about the "what if" scenario Beck? He murmured gently, staring at the pamphlet but looking right through it.

"No, we most certainly do not" said Beck sternly, taking his hand and squeezing it tightly.

And that was that. Jumbo carefully placed his cup on the side, clumped out the door and went off in search of another awkward situation where he could uncomfortably set up residence.

Nick began reading the leaflet that he had been holding for the past few minutes. The word cancer, that was previously connected to his sister, who heartbreakingly had been diagnosed with breast cancer in her early fifties, was now a word that appeared in every paragraph of the literature he was reviewing. Every time the word appeared, it seemed to initiate a short intake of breath. The more he read, the more reality sank in. He turned and announced calmly "Shitting hell Beck, I've got cancer!".

She did have to concede the fact that only twenty-four hours earlier, she thought that old Mr Worrychops was just being a bit of a soppy bollock. She was now in a position that she had to, and not to put a finer point on it, hold her hands up and confirm that it was indeed serious, and there was more of a case for it actually being one massive sloppy bollock rather than a soppy one.

"We will get through this Nick you know" she said, cuddling his arm briefly.

"We can't tell the kids though" she added "you know what Maddy is like, she just won't cope"?

Bringing the children into the conversation was the tipping point for him on what had been a difficult morning. He agreed with her, but soon after, made an excuse to leave the room. Moments later, he found himself in his bedroom, again staring at the fields in the distance through teary eyes.

Chapter 17 – Cilla Black at the Black Bull Pub.

"Yay, dads at home Maddy" shouted Archie as he chucked his bag on the floor, which was quickly followed by his coat and shoes.

"Why you not at work?" questioned Maddy, as she walked through the door and added to the recently created "school gear mountain" that was growing in the hallway.

"I've been to the doctors" he advised, giving her a massive cuddle in the process.

"Why? What's wrong? Are you ok? Queried a concerned Maddy, leaving no pause between each question.

"I'm fine maddymoo, it's my back again" he confirmed, rubbing the lower part of his vertebrae to convince her the reality of the story.

Nick did actually have an ongoing issue with his back, so it was a plausible fib which Maddy accepted with minimal questioning. She did add "are you SURE you are ok?", which was standard practice for her when it came to her dad. This mainly stemmed from the fact that he had always made-up stories for the kids, mainly for his own amusement.

Through her life, she was regularly told that parties had been cancelled hours before they were due to take place, holiday firms had allegedly called to say their vacation had been postponed and twice, Christmas had been moved to January 12th to give Santa more time to deal with the increase in volume. When she questioned once why the Easter bunny's handwriting was the same as her dads, he advised her, without hesitation,

108

that this was simply down to them going to the same school, and they obviously all got taught the same writing style.

Archie on the other hand wasn't as gullible. As a baby, he often felt that his son would look at him knowingly, with the expression "you are such a loser". The only difference as Archie grew older was that the looks were exchanged for words, and he started telling his dad how much of an idiot he really was.

As the hours passed and the gravity of the situation gathered momentum, Nick began to slide into his shell, although this was his typical reaction to anything traumatic. His loud, at times, outspoken personality, began the hibernation process that it had programmed itself to do all his life. Laughing, smiling, joking and sarcasm all packed themselves away in the nearest box, patiently waiting for the day when they would be allowed to re-join the mothership...or in this particular case, fathership. On previous occasions, these times were treated as a kind of mini break, with tom foolery often taking a Sudoku book to help him pass the time away. They always knew though, deep down, that they would soon return. This time however, it wasn't the same. The mood was different. The road ahead was murky. This was unknown territory. During the breakup of a relationship, even bereavement, Nick knew that his personality would invite laughter along, just to make the situation more bearable. This time, there was no glimmer of light, no spark of optimism, just darkness, uncertainty and definitely no enjoyment waving on the horizon. There was a genuine concern that high jinks may never return.

He woke at 11.58 that night and instantly re-established his association with the darkness. He made the decision to go to bed around 10.30 after watching, or more to the point, gazing through the TV for a few hours. Becky had nipped out earlier and purchased some herbal sleeping tablets, knowing that he needed rest and hoped that these may help. Initially, they did a reasonable job as he found himself drifting away, half an hour after taking them. However, the nocturnal gloom was much stronger than any plant-based medication and it woke him abruptly after initially allowing him to rest for a while.

It was a vicious two-pronged attack as well, with despondency making the first move, ordering him out of his slumber like an army officer waking his troops at the crack of dawn. The second aspect that then hit him was the terrifying bleakness of the room. The night before it was dark and shadowy, although there was a trace of light and the faintest slither of optimism that the diagnoses wasn't the one that they were dreading. Fifteen hours later and in possession of all the facts, everything was all just dark. It was Jet black, blacker than Cilla Black drinking a black Russian whilst singing Back to Black, at the Black Bull Pub, in the middle of the black country. So, in summary, it was all a bit gloomy to say the least.

There was no winner in the staring contest on this occasion either. Nick gazed deep into the heart of the night; night-time just glared right back. Unlike the evening before though, he didn't flinch, and peered right back into the soul of the darkness. Instead of it taking pity on him and letting him win just this once, it simply grew bigger and stronger. Then, without making a sound, Nick noticed that silence had crept into the room and was quietly standing alongside his sinister associate. He was subtle with his work initially, with peace and tranquillity gently suffocating the room. The leniency didn't last long and within minutes, he was pounding Nick's brain, wave after wave of ear-splitting stillness pulsating his eardrums. Enough was enough and Nick hastily switched on the bedside lamp. Darkness swiftly hid as light embraced the room and silence also made a quick departure as Beck stirred.

"Y..you ok" she said in a sleepy but sympathetic voice. He didn't respond, but gently shook his head.

Becky moved over and snuggled up next to him.

"You been sleep?" she asked, wiping a tear away from his check with the corner of the duvet.

Nick shook his head again.

"Fancy a cup of tea or something?" she asked, praying that the answer would be no, as the thought of getting out of bed wasn't very appealing.

He again moved his head slightly from side to side and took a deep breath.

"It's so dark" he said, letting out a shaky breath of air at the end of the comment.

"Do you want to sleep with the light on? "I don't mind" confirmed Beck. "Do you need or want to talk about it?" she added.

Nick got his neck movement hattrick with ease and simply shook his head yet again.

A minute or two passed before the hush was interrupted.

"I will switch the light off in a minute if that's ok" he whispered.

"ov cors itiz" mumbled Beck, who had again set off on her journey to sleepsville.

Deciding that he would replace the lamp light with the glare of the television, he pushed the button on the TV remote and the television toyed with the idea of turning itself on. It was giving the impression that being woken at this time of night, for the second evening running, simply wasn't on. It unwillingly displayed its contents a moment later after a firm, but influential press of the on button. Again, Nick found himself flicking through the channels, with even less purpose than the night before. The channel hopping continued till he stumbled across a re-run of "Only Fools and Horses", the one where Del Boy painted the local Chinese restaurant, as well as his mother's gravestone, in luminous yellow paint. There was something reassuring about watching a programme from the eighties and for a while, it gave him some brief comfort. Reminiscing being back at home, staring up at the TV from the floor surrounded by his mum, dad and siblings provided him with a much-needed distraction. That was his place when he was growing up, the floor!

There were six kids, plus his mum and dad, so seating was limited in the Dean household. It wasn't even a first come first served setting either, as he would be unceremoniously moved from sofa to single chair, to foot stool, to floor, by whoever came in. Only when the room filled up was it clear that there wasn't enough seating for everyone, and a full room meant one thing, he would be demoted to the carpet. If truth be told, he quite liked it down there. It was near the fire, so he was nice and snug, looking up at the TV, playing with his toys.

The Trotters did a reasonable job on getting him back to sleep, as he drifted off just before Trigger informed Del where he had been stealing the paint from. He woke again at 5.22 and although he tried to replicate the scenario by watching another classic sitcom from the eighties, Open All Hours, although it couldn't quite conjure up the same drowsy atmosphere as the boys from Mandela house did hours earlier.

He decided instead to go downstairs, allowing Beck to get a few hours of sleep, without a stuttering Arkwright playing in the background. His attempt to sneak out the room failed dramatically, as he stepped on a plastic coat hanger that was half under the bed, half in the walkway. The crack was like a branch breaking during an autumn storm; however, Becky was so tired it could have been a falling silver birch, smashing through the ceiling roof, and she still wouldn't have opened her eyes. He gently carried on with his mission and began descending the stairway, careful not to wake Maddy and Archie from their innocent slumber. Every creak, groan and squeak on the stairs was met with a grimace and an instant need to stand still in some rubbish game of staircase statues. He eventually reached the bottom and if he was in a better place mentally, would have internally high fived himself for a job well done.

The kettle light appeared as he flicked the switch and gave out a massive yawn. Looking outside the kitchen window, he could see the sun attempting to heave itself above the skyline. It wasn't doing a great job in all honesty and mirrored an overweight man trying out pullup bars for the first time. Nick stood for a while, just watching the liberation building in front of his eyes as the day slowly began to push night-time aside. There was an ashamed realisation that this happens every day and that it seemed it only took moments of massive significance in a life to embrace and acknowledge what a spectacular show it really is. He was only snapped out of his inspirational thought process by the kettle turning itself off, again failing to fulfil its own small electrical appliance fantasy, the one where he literally blows his own lid, and pushes hot steaming water into the air, in a Krakatoa type moment.

Nick gently lobbed a teabag in the direction of the cup that was approximately 7 centimetres away. It hit the rim and bounced the wrong side coming to rest on the sideboard.

"Typical" he muttered to himself and beginning to think even Tetley had it in for him.

He picked up the bag, shook it slightly and threw it again in the direction of the cup, this time reducing the distance by half, between mug and toss. This throw was a success, but the fact that a small, limbless chimp would have also successfully completed the same task, meant there was little self-praise going on for this brew-tiful achievement. The boiling water spluttered and gurgled as it hit the mug, picking up the circular tea bag, viciously tossing it from side to side. To add to poor leafy's woes, sugar and milk decided to join the unjust pummelling, swarming, and smothering the defenceless mites wafer thin armour. Only then, after the transparent sachet had submissively released its wares, was its battered and bruised body, brutally discarded in the waste bin, bleeding generously as the heat began to gently slip away from its crumpled shell.

Nick picked up his cup and moved into the lounge, carefully ensuring the door didn't bring any undue attention to the proceedings. Doors are one of the wonders on the world, as they do have a bit of a habit of speaking out at unwanted moments. In the middle of the day for example, when it doesn't really matter if they voiced their opinions, they remain silent. However, when you find yourself creeping out the room when your child has finally fell sleep, after you've spent thirty uncomfortable minutes laying on the floor, tenderly holding their hand, they do tend to chirp up with an unwanted, whistleblowing "Eeeeeeeeeeekk". If they were capable of using letters other than E and K they would surely add, "and where do you think you're off too?".

On this occasion, the door was either asleep or couldn't be bothered to comment, so it allowed him through with minimal fuss. He slumped into the L shaped sofa and placed the cup of hot tea on the floor adjacent to the settee. He took a deep breath that was immediately followed by another enormous yawn, large enough to force both of his eyes to close tight. He was shattered and two nights with limited sleep were starting to take its toll. Put it this way, his legs wanted to sleep, his arms wanted to sleep, his eyes, mouth, little toe and armpit all wanted to sleep. His mind however, refused. It simply couldn't, due to the quantity of questions that were playing in a constant loop.

What next?

How soon will it be before something happens?

Is it too late?

How far has it spread?

Will I need chemotherapy?

Will I die before I see my children grow up?

Becky gently pushed open the door to the lounge and was greeted with an "hello, who the devil is this?", type creaking noise.

"shush" she whispered, partly to herself but mostly aimed at the door for offering its opinion on her entering.

"How are you?" she mouthed in the direction of Nick, pausing momentarily between each word.

She mooched over and slid next to him on the sofa.

"Not great if truth be told" he murmured, his eyes blinking slightly after drifting off moments earlier.

"Do you want tea?" she added, moving the TV remote to one side.

"I'm ok...got one already" pointing to the floor.

Becky moved over and felt the cup.

"I will get you a fresh one as this one's a tad cold".

She stroked his head with her right hand as she clasped the now, lukewarm, cup in the other. Sun light was now streaming through the gaps in the curtains like water through the cupped hands of a fingerless man. Nick reached over and reclaimed the TV remote and switched the TV on, illuminating the room even further. The room was instantly filled with the sound of a rather well to do lady, from Winchester, talking about increased fly tipping activity in the surrounding areas, so he frantically pressed the volume button and the conversation gradually disappeared.

With that early morning disaster averted, he pushed the red button and typed in the numbers that lead to the news pages on teletext. The fact he still looked at teletext bugged Becky big time. She had hoped that purchasing Amazon Alexa a year earlier, would have prompted him to move away from reading the news and sports pages on the telly and instead, get updates with regards daily goings on via the power of the internet.

That was an over optimistic dream as he was a little old fashioned, although reading the teletext pages when it first came out, was considered quite hi-tech. Granted this was back in the eighties, so time had well and truly moved on. However, back when Charles and Diana were a couple and the Rubik's cube was a sought-after gift, you were actually considered a bit of a trend setter if you booked your holidays through this media, or better still, was a regular player of Bamboozle.

For those unfamiliar with teletext-based puzzles, this, was a quiz game provided by channel 4 teletext, where you simply had multiple choice answers to a question. The aim was to get all 25 questions right in a row, but if you got one wrong, you had to go right back to the beginning and start again.

For those Boozlers who frequented the game, the enjoyment disappeared faster than that speedboat being hauled off the bullseye stage, (after a failed attempt at scoring one hundred and one or more, obviously), when it was discovered that you could cheat the system by simply checking the page number that was displayed in the bottom right-hand corner of the screen. An experienced player would have known that the correct answer was always identified by the same number, so if you had guessed incorrectly, you would have known the answer was wrong by simply checking the number that was displayed at the bottom of the television. With it so far ? No, don't worry, we are nearly done! So, with that knowledge safely tucked away in the "box of useless information that will have no significant impact on your life", Nick knew that if he had guessed wrongly, he could just try another option until the correct page number was displayed. In all fairness, there was an element of speed required before the page revealed itself, but ultimately, the amusement and challenge were lost, and it became more of an "impossible to loser" rather than any Bamboozler.

"Do you want some toast?" whispered Beck, poking her head around the door.

He thought about it briefly before shaking his head and returning his attention back to the TV. She leaned around the doorway to see what he was watching.

"You and bloody teletext!" she announced, throwing an embellished tut in for good measure.

If nothing, he was a stickler for routine when it came to reviewing the information on the BBC red button. He always started with the news pages and over the past week, had started to take an unnatural interest in famous people that had died. The first thing he would look for was the age of the person who had passed, and this had become a familiar starting point. The second, and most important part of the analysis, was how they had left the planet. There was always a sick sense of relief when he discovered that they had taken their own life, either through the classic overdose or the more elaborate, suffobation technique. He was specifically looking for people who had succumbed to cancer and had even started back tracking on a few famous people who were in the forties or early fifties, just to check on the reason for their demise.

"What's your thoughts about today's appointment?" enquired Beck, walking into the lounge, impressively balancing two cups and a small plate with two slices of toast on it.

"Not too sure" he replied, "I just hope we get more answers on what happens now than yesterday".

"Yeah… we both need that" she agreed, offering the plate in his direction.

"Nah" he said, continuing the game of pass the remote, placing it next to her thigh.

"I'm going to compile a list of questions before hand" exclaimed Becky, munching on some undercooked bread whose dream of one day being toasted had been ruined.

"That makes sense, I think I will go and get ready and will take a look later and add anything you have missed." he added. " To be honest, I just want to get there; this waiting around is killing me".

He paused to realise the paradox within the last comment.

"It's just frustrating waiting, that's what I meant to say!" correcting himself, before quietly making his way upstairs, this time giving no credence to the moans and groans being made by the staircase.

Chapter 18 — Sperminomas.

The drive down to the hospital was quiet to say the least. Becky, who had unsuccessfully tried on a couple of occasions to engage in futile conversations about nearby houses that were up for sale and inadequate drivers, had given up the ghost and realised that for now, it was best to leave him with his thoughts. The journey was short, a brief 5-minute drive down a quiet country road completed sixty five percent of the trek, as the private hospital where the appointment had been made was the right side of the city for them. Unlike public hospitals, parking was also a doddle, and they found a space with ease, and that was even with a whole row of bays being reserved for surgeons and specialists. There was even the luxury of parking in an area where there were spaces either side, thus avoiding the dreaded door kissing and the Houdini type contortionist act of exiting the vehicle. Becky reached out to hold his hand as they completed the short walk from car to building and squeezed it ever so slightly as the automatic doors opened and they walked through the reception entrance.

It was surprisingly busy although he didn't really have much experience in this environment, so his internal gauge in relation to the busy versus quiet debate was extremely limited. The lack of cars in the car park had given the impression that there wasn't that many poorly people who were willing to pay the extortionate prices that private hospitals demanded. However, upon entering the rather plush yet still clinically constructed building, there was a hum of activity, with people flitting here and there. Like most, he had always thought private hospitals were simply for the over privileged and just a way the upper class could avoid mingling with the riff raff. On this occasion, exclusive or not, having the opportunity to speak to a specialist twenty-four hours after seeing an NHS doctor was an option that he was glad he could engage in. There was still a question on how much the session would cost though and the fact it would be funded through his work was irrelevant. Regardless that he would give his right arm, or in this case his right testicle, to get some reassurance from a specialist, his mother had done a sturdy job over the years of ensuring value for money was always an item that appeared on the agenda. In fairness, it was way down the picking order of questions to ask and sat in between, "will I still be able to play golf" and "will I walk slightly off balance after the operation". Nevertheless, costings of going private was a query that would gently chip away until an invoice had been received.

The pair of them stood behind a well-dressed lady who was queuing at the "out of respect for the patient in front of you, please wait here" sign. This seemed pretty pointless as there was about a 5 feet distance between the banner and the reception desk, so it was difficult not to hear the conversation going on just a couple of metres away. The lady floated forward graciously and advised that she was there for a blood test. In all honesty, you didn't need to be a few feet away to know this, as she was one of those individuals who somewhere along the line, had lost the concept of whispering. Patients walking through the entrance would have been aware of the reason for her visit, patients in the car park would have been aware and people in the surrounding postcodes would also now be aware that Charlotte Biggleston was at the hospital that morning. The reception politely acknowledged Ms Bellow and offered her a seat in the waiting area.

"THANK YOU" barked out the lady, nearly perforating the poor receptionist ear drums in the process.

Nick stepped up to the desk, whilst Becky stood back slightly. "I'm here to see Dr Khan" he said quietly, somewhat out of respect for the poor receptionist but also because he didn't want anyone to know the reason why he found himself in the queue. There was an element of shame, an admittance that his body had let him down and that he was now in need of urgent medical help, something he had never experienced before. He was understandably eager to limit the amount of people who knew about his ailment.

The receptionist repeated the instructions she had given to Bellowing Biggleston moments earlier, and the pair scanned the room for an area where there were a few vacant seats. He wasn't in the right frame of mind for a game of "choose your seat right", so just plonked himself down in a chair near the coffee machine. Becky polity followed and sat next to him, brushing the seat slightly, prior to sitting down.

Do you want a tea or anything? asked Beck, pointing at the coffee machine for no other reason than to back up the fact she had noticed the vending apparatus.

"No, I'm good thanks" responded Nick. He just wanted to speak to this messiah, this testicular guru, this font of all knowledge on the scrotum front.

"It's busy in here isn't it" announced Becky, trying to break the black ice that was forming around her husband.

Nick nodded.

"Right, I have a list of questions so if you don't ask them, I will near the end...is that ok" she added.

Nick again nodded but avoided eye contact.

"Do you want to read them "she enquired?

"Nope... .I'm ok" he confirmed. Becky took a sharpe breath of air, sensing his apprehension.

"But it's a good idea" added Nick quickly...... realising that she was in the moment and wanted to ensure that they didn't leave without all the information.

Becky smiled and again squeezed his hand, this time with additional purpose.

"Right" she announced sharply "we get the answers to our questions and move on from there ... agreed".

Nick nodded yet again, this time though prolonging the head movement in gentle belligerence.

"And we remain strong together" she added with a defiant purpose, aiming it at Nick with assurance, although realistically, directing it at herself after the previous days break down at the surgery.

He glanced at Becky, smiled, and returned the hand squeeze, picking up on the intention but loving the contradiction within her statement.

In the few moments of calm that followed and reviewing his current surroundings, Nick found that his opinion, that Bupa was for the upper class and was simply designed for those who had done rather well for themselves, was not only being supported by his first impressions, but also the people he had already experienced in the seven minutes since he had set foot inside the building. For one, all the other patients were, well, being patient basically. There were no single mums with five screaming children running around the chairs. There weren't any middle-aged men wearing shorts, showing off the tattooed names of the two children, that they see for a couple of hours every other weekend, and there was definitely no sixty-five-year-old women calling everyone "darlin" and modelling that well known fragrance "stale smoke with a hint of urine".

Although nervous, anxious, and frightened, he took comfort in the fact that he wasn't mingling with the riffraff. Although he knew this was elitist, he couldn't help breathing in the moment that was devoid of the impolite, the uneducated, and the basic low life that he had seen grow like a disease over the past twenty years. He had finally entered into the world of the highbrow and although extremely upset with the fact he had cancer; he was comfortable that he found himself in a more privileged surrounding.

"Mr Dean" called a rather dashing Asian doctor who mirrored a younger version of Omar Sharif

They both jumped up like a couple of greyhounds, snapping out of the traps after seeing the hare whizz past. Although on this occasion, you could say it was more Om-hare that caused the snap reaction. He provided them both with a reassuring smile and requested that they followed him to his office, which as they soon discovered, was just around the corner. Upon entering the room, he offered them a seat, repeating the smile and offered them a drink of water, which they both declined politely. Realising that they just wanted to get on with the Q and A section, Dr Khan decided to kick off proceedings.

"So, my secretary advises me that your GP has confirmed a recent CT scan has highlighted a growth within the testicle and the expectation is that it is cancerous".

"Well that about summed it up "thought Nick….. nodding in the doctor's direction, realising that the medical profession uses words like cancer, terminal, and death just in the same way he used words such as customer, enquiry, and complaint.

"So, what are the next steps?" he enquired, in a timid, childlike manner.

"Well…. we remove the testicle and hopefully that resolves the issue" advised the doctor confidently.

Let's just clarify at this point, Dr Khan was cool. If he was in a bar at that moment, Omar would have ordered a martini, shaken not stirred, grabbed the nearest girl and engaged in one of those passionate kisses, the one where the girls back is arched in the process.

Nick glanced at Becky with a slightly puzzled look before quickly turning his attention back to Dr Khan.

"So, you don't do a biopsy first then?" he questioned, producing a massive frown in the centre of his forehead in the process.

"No" confirmed the Doctor, shaking his head slightly in a "why on earth would we do that" manner.

"It's easier to remove the testicle" he added, "The operation itself is called an Orchiectomy and it is carried out under a general anaesthetic". Nick felt that he was using the medical terminology just to emphasise he knew what he was talking about, and to prove that he wasn't the cleaner.

"I have performed this operation on numerous occasions, so I am really familiar with the procedure. We then send the testicle that has been removed for analysis. This will confirm the type of cancer we are dealing with. There are two main types, Seminomas, and non-seminomas. The first is more common and less aggressive but both of these cancers respond well to treatment, although it's important to note that most of the time removing the testicle resolves the problem, depending on how long the growth has been there obviously, and how much it has spread of course."

Nick again looked at Becky and this time the puzzled look was replaced by a positive glint in both of their eyes. Not only was the news positive, but they had also stumbled across Clarke Kent of the Bupa Planet. He was taking time to inform them of the situation, he was the surgeon so knew exactly what he was talking about, he was ultra-optimistic to the point of it not being an issue at all, and the icing on the kryptonite cake, he was so bloody smooth. Although it was still early days in the conversation, it was already a far cry from the day before, when they left the doctors with a pocket full of unanswered questions and a genuine fear that he might have brain cancer.

"So, when you say most of the time, what percentage of operations are successful?" enquired Becky, beating Nick to the very same question he was about to ask.

"It depends. Look, this type of cancer is very treatable. Even if it has spread, it's a very curable cancer, and the prognosis is good. It responds really well to the treatment and basically melts away, but as I say, in a lot of cases, removing the testicle resolves the issue and you can carry on with the rest of your life as normal".

"O-kay" said Nick measuredly, simply because he had nothing more to give than that specific two syllable word at that junction in time.

"Do you mind if I take a quick look" asked the doctor politely.

As he wasn't really in any position to say, "no thank you, I am all good", he stood up dutifully. Guessing that he didn't want him to drop his denims there and then, he made the sideward motion over towards the examination table and clumsily, clambered on board. As the doctor began closing the curtain that surrounded the examination area, Nick sheepishly started pushing his pants and jeans towards his shoes, slightly bemused with the fact that Becky was being excluded from the peep show. It was also a bit pointless anyway and she could easily have highlighted several reasons for the needless piece of sheeting that was now omitting her from the inspection. One, she had seen it all before, so nothing down there was going to be a surprise. Two, she knew exactly what was going on because the doctor had just told the entire room that he wanted to feel Nicks scrotum, and last but not least, the combination of curtain and light left little to the imagination, so she was left watching a rather silhouetted version, which in all fairness, looked far worse than what was actually happening.

In a tweak of a foreskin, the doctor had felt what he wanted to feel and was instructing Nick to get himself dressed. The curtain was pushed back seconds before he had managed to pull his jeans up properly, meaning that Becky managed to get to see the encore of the show. If she was being totally honest, she wasn't overly impressed with what she managed to see of the main feature, so would have been more than happy to give the, and again, excuse the pun, curtain call a miss.

"So, does that feel larger than it should" asked Nick, realising the innuendo in the question but also acknowledging that Finnbar Saunders and his double entendres was in another room, so carried on regardless without the need for any kind of "oo eeer missus" comment.

"It appears normal for what we would expect at this point" confirmed Dr Khan, washing his hands in the process.

Nick sat back down and reached out briefly to hold Becky's hand, partially as a comfort mechanism but also as an apology for her having to sit through the shadow examination that had taken place only a few feet away.

"So, what now Dr?" he enquired, releasing Beck's hand and then resting his own on his knee?

"We operate. Simple as that. It then takes between 10-14 days to get the results back. At that point, we then discuss and review what further treatment may be required".

"Further treatment?" questioned Becky.

"Yes, sometimes the patient may require radio or chemotherapy, depending on the results of the biopsy….. but again, let me stress that the prognosis is good with this particular strain of cancer…. it's in the high 90 percent" He paused briefly before continuing, picking up on the fact that there were now two rabbits sitting in front of him and he was currently doing a damn good impression of a set of headlights.

"As I keep saying" looking at the pair of them knowingly "a lot of the time the operation itself solves the problem".

The pair of them were merciful that he hadn't chosen to go down the "if you are going to get any type of cancer, this is the one to get" towpath. Unfortunately for them, Dr Khan hadn't quite finished. This was mainly because he hadn't seen much encouragement on the faces of the two terrified looking cottontails that sat in front of him, and therefore, felt obliged to continue with the positive reinforcement surfboard he was currently riding.

"And if you are going to get any type of cancer at all, this is the one to get" announced Dr Khan proudly.

Ding ding ding ding ding, jack pot. Doc Khan didn't disappoint by reiterating Mr Aggarwal's much maligned statement of the previous day. Well, when it was said that it didn't disappoint, it was the polar opposite.

He quickly decided to move the conversation along.

"Have you got children?" he asked.

"Eh yes, two" they both said in unison, "Maddison and Archie" added Beck.

"Err…why do you ask? Enquired a puzzled looking Nick, mainly due to the fact that his mind had raced ahead and was now interpreting that the question was something to do with telling the children about the illness.

"It's just in case you were thinking of having a family or adding to the family, as we can take and freeze semen prior to the operation. Were you thinking of having more children?" added Dr Khan.

"Err..No..... we are finished in that department" announced Nick confidently.

He turned expecting to see his wife reluctantly nodding in agreement, however, he was startled to be greeted, yet again, by a sobbing individual, unable to speak, dabbing at her eyes with the smallest piece of tissue paper you would ever see. This incidentally was a skill, and she had a knack of finding the tiniest piece of tissue at opportune moments.

He was tempted to say, "is this you being strong again??", but decided against it, and instead held her hand and asked gently "what's up?"

She composed herself briefly before gesticulating with her hand to "move on".

"We have talked about it but with Archie now being eight, going back to crying babies and sleepless nights just seems the wrong thing to do" he added.

"No that's fine" said the Dr, passing over a fresh box of tissues in Beck's direction. "it's just an option that is available and you don't have to decide here and now "

"Its ...just..... so final" sniffled Becky, wiping another tear away from her left eye with an ample sized tissue that she had gently taken from the box.

"He is right" she continued "we have decided to not have any more children. It's just so decisive when you hear it out loud".

Nick squeezed her hand tighter for a few seconds.

"Well as I say, you don't have to make that decision today" declared Dr Khan, wishing now that he had never brought up the whole sperm conversation in the first place.

"So how long will it be before the operation" asked Nick, somewhat wanting the response to be tomorrow but at the same time, wanting it to be the 24th of never.

"To be honest, it's just as quick going through the NHS" he advised, "when it comes to cancer, they have a fast-track programme, so it's normally within a couple of weeks".

"oh" he responded, this time changing to a one syllabled response, but still sounding a bit on the dozy side.

"But is there the option of having it done private?" Interjected Beck, picking up that "oh" was filled with multiple questions that had cleverly masked themselves into the two-letter response.

"You can……but again, the likelihood of it being done any sooner is unlikely….and they really do FastTrack anyone with a cancer diagnosis".

"And what are the consequences of leaving the lump for two more weeks…. how fast will it grow?" enquired Nick, pulling one of the most significant questions from the numerous cumulus clouds that had formed in his mind over the past few days.

"Two weeks won't make any difference at all" announced Dr Khan confidently.

"oh" he declared once more, again struggling to find a relevant reply to the information he had just received.

He looked over at Beck and asked if there was anything else that they needed to check. She shook her head slightly and confirmed that they had all they needed for now.

Dr Khan stood up again shook both of their hands. He reassured them again that the prognosis was good in this type of cancer and wished them well. The pair of them shuffled their way back to the automatic doors near reception slightly stunned but ultimately in a better position when they arrived. On the unlikely off chance of them seeing someone they knew in the reception waiting area, they both looked directly at the floor as they left the building, picking up the place ever so slightly as the electronic doors began to open.

"Well, that was way better than yesterday's experience" declared Beck, completely forgetting to acknowledge the kind, elderly driver, who had stopped at the pedestrian crossing to let them cross.

"There are still a lot of ifs and buts though" replied Nick.

"Yeah, I know, but yesterday's meeting compared to todays is a world apart" she added with a smile.

"I'm a bit worried about the operation part. I've never had general anaesthetic before" he announced, pressing the car keypad, which in turn made the lights wink in an almost "good to see you...thank god you are alright" manner.

"Of course, it's not ideal but have the operation, remove the lump and it solves the problem. You then get on with your life of bugging the hell out of me and the kids!"

"It MIGHT solve the problem...might" reiterated Nick, shutting the door and reaching over to pull the seat belt that was now catching slightly on the loop section at the top.

"WILL cure the problem" responded Beck firmly, I've got a good feeling about this".

At this point in the proceedings, he was tempted to mention to her that she had a "good feeling" about the scan, as well as a "good feeling" that there was nothing wrong when he advised that there was blood in his sperm. He rightfully decided against telling her, and instead spent the journey home introducing the newly found upbeat information, dispensed by Dr Dashing, to the cloud forms of doom that were circulating in his head. This did cause a bit of friction internally, as the moody bastards, who had set up residence a couple of days earlier, were unwilling to listen to anything positive, and instead, just ignored the new arrivals, continuing to paint the interior of his mind with their favourite colour, which of course, was grim grey. Without a doubt, if these negative thoughts possessed imaginary fingers, they would have put them in their puffy drab ears and started chanting "la la la we can't hear you".

While they may have refused to listen, and although muffled, Nick could just about hear the faint assuring whispers of the constructive cirrus clouds, high above the disconcerted rumblings of the cold and angry nimbus and the stormy cumulonimbus clusters. On the internal positivity scale, it was still a decent nine point five on the scared shitless gauge, but there was a slither of light that was absent, prior to that morning's meeting. Maybe, just maybe, he might be one of those that after the operation, the problem would be fixed.

Chapter 19 – That's private.

The next few days dragged. They dragged slower than a drag queen, in a broken-down drag car, being dragged by a draconian dragon called Draggy.

Nothing really happened, nothing happened at all. All that he could do was wait...and wait. He continued to have internal discussions with himself, which at points turned into blazing rows. As the days passed, anxiety and doubt steadily increased and the positive message that Dr Khan had delivered days before, had drifted away into the distance. The thought that this disease was expanding, spreading itself like some overweight, pie munching individual, slobbing out on the sofa was a concern that just like that character, just wasn't shifting.

Doing nothing didn't seem the right thing to do. The reassuring words of "two weeks not making a difference" had now been beaten into submission, so much so, they had been completely modified and now the sentence that was being repeated in his mind was "two weeks could be critical".

The weekend had disappeared as soon as it arrived, leaving him hopeful of a letter arriving, if not on the Monday morning, by Tuesday at the latest. He messaged Beck from work around 10.30am, allowing the postman ample time to ring three times, let alone the standardised twice. She replied back almost instantaneously with, "nothing...sorry", accompanied by a sad emoji face. Beck had recently entered the world of adding emoji pictures to text messages, something which was a bit of a bug bear for him if truth be told.

At 10.32am, he rang.

"Hiya, what do you reckon?" he asked.

"Why don't you call them... it can't do any harm" responded Beck.

"Yeah ...yeah... I should call them shouldn't I?" he said, still seeking additional reassurance.

"Err...yeah..." responded Beck" with an unsubtle hint of "dur" in her voice tone.

"kk.... I will call them and let you know".

"Yeah, let me know...see you later" and with that, she disappeared.

He pulled out the pamphlet that had been well and truly tom thumbed over the past few weeks and tapped in the "help line" number that was on the back page. He cleared his throat slightly, which was optimistic to say the least, as the likelihood of him speaking to someone in the next five minutes was as probable as England winning a penalty shoot-out in a world cup tournament. However, he entered into the telephonic options game in good spirit and although apprehensive, the fact he was actually doing something proactive, made him feel better about the situation.

In all fairness to the NHS, his call was answered pretty fast compared to other organisations he had tried to contact in the past. Amanda greeted Nick with a compassionate but friendly voice tone. This was appreciated and made him realise how difficult a job Mandy had dealing with cancer patients from dusk 'til dawn. She took all the relevant personal details and before too long, had his case on the computer in front of her.

"I see you visited your GP last Tuesday and was advised that you would need an orchiectomy, is that right?"

"Yes, that's right" he confirmed.

"And were you given information about the next steps?" enquired Amanda, maintaining her empathic approach.

"Yes, I was given a few leaflets. It also mentioned that there is a fast-track programme for cancer patients, normally a two–four-week programme it says".

"Yes, that's correct Mr Dean" she confirmed politely, although slightly robotic.

"Looking at availability, I can get you in next Tuesday to see the consultant" she advised buoyantly.

"Great, will I need to come in before then, for a pre op assessment?" he questioned knowingly, feeling confident in the process after his meeting the week before.

"No, this is for an assessment to go over your case in more detail and to discuss next steps. An operation will then be scheduled after that meeting" Amanda confirmed, definitely giving the impression that he should be grateful that he was in the system, and things were moving forwards.

"Well, I spoke to the consultant last Thursday, so I have already had my assessment" advised Nick, accepting that any initial optimism he had, that the NHS system was going to compete with the private option, had departed. "We did discuss going private" he continued "but we were advised that operations are normally performed by the same surgeons and that going private, wouldn't really speed the process up".

"How soon is the operation normally scheduled after the initial assessment". He added.

"It is difficult to say for sure, but it's around a month afterwards" she advised, now distinctly giving the impression she was getting tired of the telephone Q and A session she was engaged in.

"For shits sake" is exactly what Nick wanted to say down the telephone. However, and credit to him, he managed to just filter his response so that it came out as "Oh that's disappointing". The main reason for him not giving Amanda a volley of abuse was twofold really, one, she had been really calm and supportive throughout the conversation and two, he wasn't really surprised that the Nonstop Horseshit System, NHS for short, looked again, like it was going to let him down.

"So, are you considering going private Mr Dean? enquired Mandy, deciding to now join in with the questioning.

"Well, I wasn't initially, but if it's going to take five weeks from now Amanda, I might call them to discuss options. I just feel like I need to do something now, rather than waiting around."

"I totally understand" she said in agreement, partly because her training had taught her to concur with the patient in these situations but also because she was pretty much done with the call and wanted to squeeze in another caller, who may have wanted to take up the support being offered by the national health service.

"Have you had your bloods done?" she added, picking up on his need to be doing something proactive.

"No...should I have?" he asked.

"Well, we will need the blood markers before the operation so we can always get these done for you?." she suggested helpfully.

He thought momentarily before responding.

"Yes, let's do that" announced Nick positively, "can these be done today?"

He guessed that Lorraine wouldn't have a problem with him nipping out, as she had been supportive throughout. He was confident she wouldn't stand in his way if there was a chance that he could restart the treatment ball rolling again.

"I am finishing my shift shortly" replied Amanda. "What I can do though, is leave an envelope with all the necessary paperwork and you can pick it up from the neurology department. Would that be ok?"

"Yes" he responded instantaneously, "I can be there in about an hour if that's okay?"

"Of course, Mr Dean. I will get the blood forms completed now and leave them in the reception area. Do you know where you need to come?" she enquired, picking up the pace in her voice tone slightly, as she realised that there was no time for any more calls, and she had her own appointment to attend immediately after her shift finished.

"I know where the hospital is but not familiar with the layout" he confirmed.

"Not a problem. Just head for car park 5. As you enter you will see an emergency department on the left. Just drive past there and park as near as you can. Parking is limited so you may have to drive around for a spot. You can enter the building there and just head to the reception area. I will leave the paperwork there for you".

Nick thanked her sincerely for all her help and went straight over to Lorraine's desk. She was on a conference call and looked as if she was listening intently. As he got nearer, he spotted that she was clearing emails and was only partly taking note, so was only half listening, so being totally pedantic, she was just "list" to the conversation.

"Is it ok if I nip out to the hospital to………." Lorraine interrupted him mid-sentence.

"Go... Go now.....of course it is".

"I will be in as ..." she interrupted for the second time in as many seconds. "Just go and give me a call if you have any problems."

She smiled and gestured for him to go in a real crappy "agadoo, push pineapple" manner, before returning to the fascinating discussion regards the collection process for fragile items. Nick smiled and walked off in the direction of the door, glancing back just to double check that she wasn't actually now making shaking trees and grinding coffee gestures.

It was a nice autumnal day, so Nick bypassed the option of taking a coat. It briefly crossed his mind to pick it up, just in case, due to the simple fact that hospitals weren't renowned for their central heating. However, as the sun had his hat on, and was hip, hip, hipping to its hearts content, he decided to join in with the whole sunbeam scenario and ventured out in just his work shirt. It was the right decision in the end, as the morning sunshine was burning through the windscreen when he got in his car and decided that he should do the touch test on the steering wheel, just to ensure he didn't burn his palms on the leather by going all in, with a full-on grip.

Leicestershire had three main hospitals and it was genuinely regarded that the General, where he was heading, was in direct competition with the Royal Infirmary for the much coveted, shittiest hospital in the county award. Nick had been to the General once before, when he was a kid, when someone in the family had given birth there. As was the way of a youngster, he got dragged along, with his parents, to see the sprog, something that was about as interesting at that time as visiting the National Tapestry Museum.

As he began recalling the last time he visited, it became clearer who the patient at that time was. It was his brother's wife Wendy, who Nick had fallen out with in spectacular fashion. In all fairness to this individual, she would and could fall out with her own shadow...... if it hadn't already scared her half to death already.

It was safe to say that Nick never really clicked with Wendy, even before the fall out, the warmth between them, was like an unlit fireplace. After the event though, the relationship was like a watch-less man being asked what the hour was, as he simply had no time for her at all. The fall out itself, was nothing directly to do with her, but such was her way, she managed to turn it around, so it was all about her.

The events leading to the clash were quite childish if truth be told, as he had got himself invested in a tit for tat exchange with his ex-wife. This was during the height of when they were splitting up and he had made a comment over the telephone, that in all fairness was as nice as a rich tea biscuit, covered in shit. In turn, the ex then showed up that night where he used to play football, albeit not alone Her then new boyfriend was built like a Herefordshire Bull, but also gifted with the same sized brain has his bovine counterpart. Put it this way, he would have been in direct competition with a decapitated dung beetle when it came to intellect. As highlighted earlier, she wasn't blessed with that much class from the get-go either, so it was no surprise to find herself associating with similar low life after the split.

Unfortunately for Nick though, his idea of conversation was limited.   In his defence, only knowing a handful of words due to his extraordinary stupidity and astonishing level of ignorance, it would have made it difficult to hold a decent conversation, well one that didn't sound dissimilar to a Teletubby convention anyway. On reflection, it made complete sense that the only option for him was to hit first and then think about it later. The failure in this cunning plan though, was that he was unable to think, so this left him with just the option of hitting, which was a bit of a shame all-round. One can only hope that mercifully, like all crazed and sick animals, he was put out of his misery later in his sad, pathetic little life.

So, on that near fateful night, after following Nick down the small unlit road, that led to the secluded car park next to the pitch, the pair of them, initiated a car-jacking scene with a novel twist. Instead of the normal, run of the mill, "get out the car" scenario, as we want to steal your vehicle, their main objective was instead to remove the occupant and basically, beat the living shit out of him. Not putting too finer point on it, if "billy bull shit for brains" had successfully pulled Nick out of the car that night, it was safe to say that the extension that was still awaiting planning permission, would have almost certainly featured wheelchair access, as the beating would have been severe, bordering on fatal.

Thankfully, he had clocked the pair of them coming out of the shadows, just in the Nick Dean of time and managed to lock his car door, although this didn't stop buffalo bill trying to yank it open. Thicko Mcthickttwat and his equally stupid girlfriend, where left frantically pulling on a door handle, before being forced to turn their attention to trying to gain access through the less familiar, window route. With no success, Bully was now focusing on ripping the wing mirror off with his cloven hoof, presumably

138

because he needed to cause some kind of pain, and if that wasn't going to be the occupant, then the Astra was going to get it big time.

Nick hastily shifted the gears in to reverse, with the sole aim of getting out of the place as soon as driver-ley possible. Several of the football lads, who were already warming up, had moved over to the fence to see what was going on. "Warming up" was of course in its loosest form, as bending over from side to side, whilst talking about last night's football results, hadn't yet been adopted by many premier league coaching units.

Again, Nick frantically struggled with the gears before whacking it into first, eventually pulling off at speed. There was a split second when he thought about aiming the car in the pair's direction, but in that fleeting moment, he knew that nothing good would come his way if he and Vauxhall retaliated in that manner. Although correctly avoiding contact with the pair of them, spinning the wheels at pace did manage to kick up numerous stone chippings in the process and there was a hope that several of the bigger stones had gone in the direction of the two assailants. As he left, he glanced at the empty space that had recently been vacated where his nearside wing mirror would have lived. Sadly, it had succumbed and became a victim of the Battle of the Bull-ge. He quickly moved his gaze to his rear-view mirror, where he noticed his fallen soldier, guts an all, being unceremoniously discarded into a nearby bush. By now, bullock bollocks had shifted his attention onto Nicks teammates. They had moved into the car park to get a better view but quickly retreated as "you can't beat a bit of bully" turned his attention on them, and he was now threatening to take every mother f-ing one of them on. Apparently that very same person beat the shit out of Nicks ex-wife a few short weeks later. If only there had been warning signs in the initial stages of their romance to give her some indication on things to come.

Five minutes later, away from the battle ground and back on neutral territory, the realisation of what had happened hit him. It wasn't the fact that some overweight, thick, brainless animal had attempted to beat the living bejesus out of him. No, it was because he knew from that moment forward, getting access to see his children, was going to be a challenge that even Anneka would struggle to overcome. On returning home, he relayed the sorry story to Beck who instantly picked up her car keys and headed for the front door. The Irish blood that lay dormant most of the time, didn't need much of a tweak before ravaging through her veins, transforming her from a petite blonde angel into a psychotic banshee. He managed to grab her just before she opened the door and convinced her that there was no benefit in her knocking on his ex-wife's door. She reluctantly agreed and instead of traveling to the war zone with the sole aim of inflicting a revenge attack, she grudgingly settled on sending her a long, threatening email instead. He yet again advised that it was ill thought out, and they should sleep on it, but as a written message was the much better option of the two, he decided to let it slide, and left her alone to just get on with it.

Half an hour later after a strong cup of tea, he began to fret about what had happened after he had left. He had tried unsuccessfully to reach several of the lads who would normally attend the training session and was becoming increasingly concerned with the lack of response from all parties. At this point, the only real option left open was for him to call his brother's wife, Wendy, to ask if he had returned early. The conversation was brief, as Colin wasn't there, but still unsettled, he asked her if she could get him to call back, being ultra-careful not to provide her with any specifics on the evening's events. It was a well-known fact that she panicked more than Peter Pan, locked in a pantry in the height of a pandemic. It was past 11.00pm, which incidentally would have been the normal time he got back from training, when Colin finally called back.

"What happened when I left Col?" he asked.

"He was a proper thug!" declared Colin.

"He had a go at me Bish and Frankie...I reckon he was on drugs or something" he continued. "What on earth did you say to the pair of them?"

"Nothing!" professed Nick. "I said something earlier in the day, when she was refusing to let me speak to the kids, but she deserved that" he confirmed, slightly annoyed with the fact his brother was indicating that he had instigated the whole situation.

"I will just need you to go to the police Col……. Just to let them know what you saw" confirmed Nick.

"Err…. Yeah…. Err…… well" was the initial response to his reasonable and what he saw, straightforward request.

"We don't want to get involved!" was the voice that could be heard in the background at the other end of the phone.

"Hold on a minute" questioned Nick "what does she mean, YOU don't want to be involved…..I don't want you to go and beat the shit out of him….. I just need you to go to the police to back my story up, otherwise, it will be really difficult for me to see my kids" agitation from the nights events now starting to shine through in his voice tone.

Again, he could hear Wendy barking out that "THEY" didn't want to be involved. At this point agitation left the ring, high fived pure fury, and he entered the arena in its place.

"What is she shouting for anyway, don't want to be involved. She isn't! You aren't… you just need to back up the fact that tonight I nearly got the living shit kicked out of me by a couple of twunts …… Don't want to get involved…. who does she think she bloody well is?"

"You can't say that ……" Colin attempted to interject, but by now, Nick was in full flow.

"She's always been selfish, always will be …as long as she's alright, she doesn't give a shit about anyone else. It's bad enough that I nearly get dragged from my car and that I'm not going to see my kids for who knows how long, but now I have to put up with that twat saying, "I don't want to be involved!!". Nick was now well and truly on a roll. He would have continued with his rant but unfortunately, or fortunately, whichever way you look at it, was brought to an abrupt end with Colin simply interjecting

"You can't call her that…. in fact,… you're the twat!" which was accompanied with the phone line then going dead.

From that moment on, the relationship was strained more than overcooked rice. Days later, Nick did send a written apology for calling her a name but tried to put forward the dismay of not being able to see his children, hoping that being a mother herself, common ground would be found.

Sadly, it wasn't the case. Maybe selfishness, insecurity, revulsion, fear or simply dislike of Nick were the reasons for her not seemingly understanding the situation that he found himself in. Perhaps it was as simple as she disagreed with his decision to split up with his wife. Conceivably it may have been a multitude of things that only she would ever know. Ultimately though, it meant the apology fell on baron grounds and from that moment on, the two never really spoke. The same went for Colin really and as soon as he had retired from playing Sunday league football, he lost touch with him also. Over the years, Col had started distancing himself from his siblings anyway, so contact was already limited to just those times on a Sunday when they would play football in the same team.

Sadly, It does appear a common theme in many marriages, that the wife's relationships seem to take priority. It looked the case in this instance, but either way, Nick didn't see them, and it wasn't something that he was going to lose much sleep over.

Chapter 20 – Ology apology.

Nick entered the General Hospital car park with apprehension. There were several entrances, as well as exits, and as he approached, it wasn't clear which was which. He optimistically looked for the sign that read "Nick Dean...this way" but realising that this was as likely to appear as an empty parking space, he decided to instead, go with the more sensible approach, and keep his eyes out for the words "neurology department".

To be honest, he may as well have kept looking for his own name, such was the pointless exercise of actually trying to find the place where he needed to go to. He revisited in his mind the conversation with Amanda, the receptionist who arranged the appointment. He recalled something about an emergency exit but apart from that, she may as well have been giving him instructions on how to get to Timbuctoo. After two minutes of driving around the "staff only" carpark, he ended up pulling up in an emergency only spot, with the hope of asking a passing worker where the chuff he needed to go. He was just on the verge of asking some hi viz vested chap, who in all honesty probably didn't work there and was probably on his way to get the results from his overactive thyroid test, when he spotted a "neurology" sign, out the corner of his eye.

He quickly pulled out of the emergency bay, not only nearly taking out Thyroid Tony but almost clearing up a Peugeot 305, who appeared to be suffering the same car park conundrum as himself. Nick acknowledged the error by gesturing a hand in the air as he drove away. He glanced in his rear-view mirror to see the elderly driver, pointing and waving his hands in Nicks direction, obviously not happy that he had to apply the brakes in such a hurry. His long-suffering wife, who had already died or had decided to pull the "pretend to be asleep because of the journey" rouse, sat motionless next door.

Although feeling slightly guilty, his attention quickly returned to his own parking predicament and continued frantically looking for any emergency entrance that would indicate he was heading in the right direction. There was nothing, so he continued, turning a corner that led to an even larger car park, but that turned out to be even busier than the staff only car park. He then spent a further five minutes, desperately going around and around in the aim of hitting on a patient who was just on the way out. His luck wasn't in, and in the end, frustration got the better of him, and he decided to just park on the verge, along with several other cars that had given up the ghost of ever finding an available spot. As he locked his car, he looked at the sign that clearly said, "no parking". His current situation forced him, uncharacteristically it had to be said, to carry on with the blatant disregard of the rules, and therefore headed off in the direction of an entrance, already accepting there was a chance he would be greeted with a parking ticket on his return.

Finding access into the building, became more of a challenge than parking. There were several doors that appeared to be for deliveries only, whilst other potential entrances, looked as if they were for private access only. He walked up the length of the building, and then back down, twice, before deciding enough was enough and proceeded towards an open door that appeared to head directly into a storeroom. As he approached, he was greeted with the sight of some bedraggled patient heading out the exit. Although this left him with the awkward dilemma of whether to acknowledge the dishevelled individual or not, it did give him reassurance that he could at least find his way to the wing of wonders, unless of course the poor chap was in the same predicament and had been wandering outside for the past few years and that was the reason for his gaunt expression. The meet and greet decision was taken out of his hands, as the patient made a direct beeline for him in the hope of cadging a cigarette. Nick, apprehensive about the whole visit, pissed off with the parking, and proper fed up with the lack of clear direction, wasn't in the mood for pleasantries. Again, it was uncharacteristic for him, but he simply responded with a "nope", with about as much eye contact as a reprimanded dog, when coarsely quizzed, "you got a fag matey?". His normal response would have been more apologetic, but as he was at the end of his tether, the unshaven gowned man was greeted with the dismissive four-letter response.

As he entered the building, leaving fag-end frank muttering outside, it was clear that the room was indeed a storeroom, as there were boxes everywhere. He noticed a door at the far end of the room, so made a hasty shuffle in that direction, taking additional care not to knock any cartons in the process. Trespassing was bad enough, but adding criminal damage to the list, wasn't high on his agenda that morning. He squeezed his way through the packaging pathway and softly opened the door, partly because he wanted his entrance to be as discreet as possible, but also not wanting to take out a nurse, who was rushing to the aid a patient on a life support machine, in some dramatic "Casualty" type moment. Why did the door open outwards anyway, he thought to himself, as a main corridor began to reveal itself, as it started its journey from ajar to partially open. The health and safety officer had obviously overlooked that potential hazard when signing off the necessary documentation, probably focusing more attention on the problems being caused outside by a lack of parking and entrance signage.

The corridor walls were an off-white colour and looked deathly cold. If he didn't know any better, he wondered if the stock room that he had just slipped through was a time portal, and he had been transported back in time to the "Carry on Nurse" film set. All that was missing was a slender Kenneth Williams, strutting by, accompanied with the odd "ooo Matron" comment.

He walked a few steps so that he could clearly view a sign that was hanging over a junction in the passageway. Neurology was in the direction where he had just come from, so although admittance into the building had not been the leisurely arrival he would have liked, the fact he was more or less in the right area, gave him a slight sense of misguided achievement. He pivoted on his right foot and set off along the busy corridor, following the signs that appeared every 100 or so yards. A couple of turns and three minutes later, he found himself outside a room that had the plaque "Neurology" blazoned on it. At this moment in time, the hospital took on the comparison of a school classroom, and Nick was fully expecting a room full of students to be facing a blackboard as he entered the large wooden door.

Obviously, there wasn't, but the expectation was placed briefly on hold as behind the first access, was surprisingly, another wooden door. It appeared excessive doorage was definitely on the agenda for the planning team when they drew up the hospital layout. He momentarily considered

145

the benefits of this entrance overload. Was it so that patients had one last opportunity for another deep breath, before entering the main arena ? Was it designed as a hiding place for over worked nurses to get 5 minutes of shut eye ? He decided that the matter wasn't worth thinking about further, so elected to just push the door in front of him, hoping that there wasn't yet another door behind that one, with a Cheshire cat sitting on the handle, beaming arrogantly in his direction.

Thankfully, there was no tabby, just a plain old waiting room. He moved over to the reception area and stood patiently, as the receptionist, who was a young Asian gentleman, stood fiddling around in the filing cabinet. After a few moments, he turned around and was a little surprised to see Nick standing patiently behind the counter.

"Can I help?" he asked quietly.

"Yes, I hope you can, I believe an envelope has been left here for me...my names Dean.....Nick Dean".

"Oh...err....right" ermmed the slender receptionist.

"I can't see anything here" he added, half-heartedly shuffling various paperwork around the desk to prove that he was searching.

"Shall I call the person who I spoke to this morning?" enquired Nick, getting that sinking feeling that all wasn't going to plan.

"I think you may have to; I haven't been given anything and I'm afraid I can't see anything here for your attention" confirmed Ash, his name tag giving the game away.

Nick stepped back away from the desk slightly, even though there wasn't anyone else waiting, and looked back on his incoming call history. He dialled the number that he had called 45 minutes earlier and to his surprise, the call was answered swiftly. He began relaying the story to the lady at the other end of the phone, who of course was a different person to the one he had spoken to earlier. He would have thrown in the name of the original lady if he could have remembered it, but as he wasn't sure, he just stuck to the story line, and kept personnel to one side. Thankfully, either Amanda had relayed the information about his predicament to her colleagues upon leaving or, and this is where his money was, Elaine, who he was currently speaking to, had been doing a spot of ear wigging when he was talking on the telephone earlier that morning.

"Yes, Amanda did mention that she was leaving the paperwork in reception for you" fibbed a nosy, but polite Elaine.

"Well, I have asked the gentlemen on reception and he definitely doesnt have anything" confirmed a now more than puzzled Nick on the other end of the phone.

"I just don't get it" she queried, "she even said she was going to drop them off at the Urology Department on the way out".

"Well, I'm not sure what I need to ………. hold on…did you say Urology?" He questioned, halfway through his sentence.

"Yes...Urology, why?"

 "Well, I think I know what the problem is...I'm at the Neurology Department" established a sheepish Nick.

If he wasn't so preoccupied with the whole hospital drama, he would have made a quip about possibly being in the right room after all, so much was the ironic mistake he had just made. However, as he was in no mood for banter, he simply thanked Elaine for her help and returned his attention back to Ash, mainly for directional advise, who was again busy ferreting through the filing cabinet.

 It wasn't long before he left Ash and his Bisley organising unit behind, with the newfound and albeit rather disappointing knowledge that the Urology Department was on the other side of the hospital. Not only was it in a completely different section and a good 10-minute walk away, but it appeared to have a different postcode too.

It became quite apparent that the "General" was a little run down and was in much need of a bit of TLC. To be honest, a crash team couldn't spark life into some of the corridors, such was the deathly feel to them. In addition, he was genuinely surprised with how many people were in the corridors. There were groups plodding, people marching, folks brushing past one another, nurses rushing, doctors standing, patients sighing and relatives crying. There was everything apart from laughter, and as everyone carried on with their own objectives, the lack of smiles started to become slightly overpowering.

Nick, who was always one for holding doors open, soon found it astonishing the amount of people who didn't smile, or even acknowledge him, when he benevolently stood, arm outstretched, to let them through. Some of this, he felt, was simply due to the nature of the hospital and the clientele it attracted. It wasn't private, and most of the ignorant morons that visited wouldn't even know what kindness was, if it stroked their head, told them pleasant things about themselves and gave them a crisp ten-pound note for good measure. Some of it was simply due to the fact, that over the years, society had become selfish, self-obsessed, and common courtesy, was sadly becoming a thing of the past.

As the journey progressed, so did the feelings of hopelessness and despair. He climbed upstairs, he descended downstairs, he went the wrong way more than once, and on several occasions, sensed he was in restricted areas, feeling that at any minute a team of medics, fully equipped with chemical coveralls, would come rushing through with a trolley, with an ET type character murmuring the name El-i-ot.

Eventually, and to his utmost relief, he found himself standing outside a room that had a small but significant sign stating, "UROLOGY DEPARTMENT." He walked up to what appeared to be a reception desk but of course, it wasn't that simple, as the person standing behind it, was a cleaner, with a limited grasp of the English vocabulary. Even with a mix of recognisable words and frantic arm gestures, he just about managed to make out that the actual reception area was further down the corridor. Unenthusiastically and mainly out of politeness, he thanked the hospital worker and set off on the final leg of this epic voyage, passing by what appeared to be a cupboard in his final steps to reception eutopia . The assumption of it being a cupboard was purely based on its size and the lack of lighting that came from within. Only In the split second after he had completely passed by the doorway, did he realise that it was in fact an additional room, as out of the corner of his eye, he clocked at least four beds. Not only were these poor unfortunates recovering from whatever ailment they came in with, but they were also now suffering from a sever lack of vitamin D due to the brutal lack of sunlight that wasn't being allowed into that area.

He finally approached the actual desk like some great explorer, finding land after being at sea for several months. However, the joy turned to confusion when he noticed a few feet away from the reception area was an automatic door that led to the car park. The sudden realisation that this was the entrance Amanda had talked about an hour or so earlier, hit him like the hidden mass of an iceberg. The Shackleton type jubilation he felt on arriving in the Urology zone moments earlier, sank faster than the endurance, when he realised that his car was no more than a 30 second walk away from where he currently stood.

He was greeted with a smile from the receptionist and although Nick was tempted to tell the whole sorry saga, he decided to settle with the more reserved "I've come about a blood test" request instead. Half expecting them to say, "There is nothing here....you need to go to the made up-ology department", they simply asked, "Can I have your name please?". He duly obliged, and they handed over an envelope. It was as simple as that, well that's what he thought until he asked his next question.

"So do I have the bloods done here?" he enquired.

"No, that's down at the blood clinic near the main entrance" replied the cheerful individual manning the desk. DING DING.....all aboard the fun bus for another trek around the dilapidated infirmary.

He listened, in a fashion, to the directions being given, but the earlier enthusiasm "to do something proactive" had jumped in the back of an ambulance and was now rushing off to its next emergency, leaving Nick with about as much fervour as a dead squirrel with a case of chronic fatigue syndrome. With this newfound listlessness, he decided to call his local doctors' surgery, to see how soon they could do a blood test. The thought process was that this would surely be a better option, and the idea was that he would book himself in around 1.00 pm, immediately leave the hospital via the exit that was beckoning him a few feet to his right, pop home for a cup of tea and a chocolate hob knob, before nipping down to the quacks to have his bloods done. However, the news from the surgery was as encouraging as a silent spectator, as the earliest they would be able to fit him in would be a week on Wednesday, completely defeating the objective of "speeding things up". Reluctantly, he decided to continue with the course of action he had initially set off on an hour earlier and trudged off in the direction of the main entrance, hoping that there would be a clear sign for the blood clinic, simply because he had taken no notice to the instructions that had been provided moments earlier.

Thankfully, there were hardly any further dramas on the journey through the corridors. One old boy did stumble slightly as he passed by, but the nurse who was inching alongside, managed to hook her arm under his armpit just in time, saving Nick from the embarrassment of having to help pick the old boy up from the marbled floor.

Once at the clinic, the test itself was also uneventful, with the only surprising element being that there wasn't a queue. He took a ticket which indicated the order you were seen in, and before he could even sit down, the nurse called his name, and he was relieved of a few generous ounces of bright red plasma. There was a thought that they could just do away with the ticketing system and just provide Nurse Linda with a set of castors, so that she could wheel back and forth to see how many were waiting. However, the likelihood was that this empty room scenario was a complete one off, so in reality the ticketing system was probably relieved to find himself printing and ejecting his receipts at a leisurely pace.

Thanking the nurse for her attentiveness and knowing that fresh air was only moments away, he picked up the pace. Instead of heading for the main exit though, he went back on himself and headed towards the urology department, with the newfound knowledge that the exit door near reception, was freedom into the rear car park. The person who was still manning the reception desk, did a slight double take as he walked past, but he was just relieved to be heading out of the overcrowded, depressing, shabby old hospital. The fact that he got into his car, completely forgetting that he was expecting a ticket, clearly showed how the recent experience had affected him. He called Becky as he pulled out of the car park, the sun still shining gloriously in the sky.

"I can't do it Beck" he announced calmly, although there was a massive hint of agitation in his tone.

"Can't do what?" she queried.

"I can't have the operation at the General…. It's a shitpit"

"Come back home and let's call the Shires again" she announced comfortingly.

He arrived back home to an excited Beck who had already been on the case, such was her nature.

"I've called them and there is a possibility they can do the operation this Thursday!" she confirmed enthusiastically.

"That would be great if they could," declared Nick. "Honestly, I don't think I can have it done at the General. The fact they can't do it for at least another month anyway, says we should look at other options, but even if they could do it, I would prefer the Shires….it just appears to be a nicer experience".

The snobbery in his voice wasn't lost on himself, but if he was being totally honest, at this point in proceedings, he couldn't care less. He had found himself in a position whereby there was a chance he could have the operation done privately and was going to grasp that opportunity with both arms, and for the time being, both testicles.

Chapter 21 – Fat bloke wearing a tablecloth.

It was confirmed later that afternoon that the operation could take place on the Thursday. He needed to arrive at the hospital at 6.00pm, which he questioned, as there was an assumption that the operation would take place in the day, why wouldn't it? He soon found out that private hospitals worked slightly different, and they fell outside the constraints of the "normal" hour's regime. It was established that the majority of specialists needed to travel from the local infirmaries, after doing a day of standard surgery, to fulfil these duties and to claim the extortionate additional income. So, not only was he having to come to terms with this being his first procedure and subsequent, overnight stay, he had to accept that the surgeon could potentially pass out with exhaustion, mid-way through the operation.

The euphoria of arranging the appointment had now departed, and the reality of the forthcoming events were hitting home. Lorraine, his boss, had told him to take the Wednesday and Thursday off "to spend it with family". Although really appreciated, there was a hint of the "last rights" to the instruction, which made him think that she knew more about the operation than she was letting on, and maybe it wasn't quite as straight forward as he was being told.

Before he left the workplace on the Tuesday, he spent 15 minutes talking to his manager about her experiences with regards being put under the knife. He found out that she had undergone several procedures over the years, and this had put his mind at ease in relation to the aesthetic. She described it as the "best sleep ever" and put it in such a way, that a part of him was intrigued, bordering on eagerness, to experience this encounter. He said his farewells to his colleagues and was keen to keep it on the lowdown, as he knew that if there was too much emotion, there was a chance he would follow suit, and the last thing he wanted to do was to show sentiment on leaving the building. He remained unscathed until Fiona, a lovely lady who he had managed for years, insisted on a cuddle. Nick attempted to advise her that they would have a celebratory hug on his return, but she was having none of it and embraced him anyway. "I will be fine … be back before you know it". He said unsteadily to which Fiona smiled and confirmed "I know you will".

The next two days were taken up with watching TV, thanking people for their messages and counting down the hours. He declined the invitation from friends who wanted to meet up beforehand, simply because he was concentrating on getting the operation out the way and now wasn't really talking that much to anyone. He was genuinely appreciative of the authentic concerns but had moved into focus mode and was now just needing the time to pass. Pete, who had known Nick for over 10 years, was having none of it. As he put it, "I respect your decision…. but I gotta see you fella". It was everything you would expect from an emotional, blokedom, meeting. He popped round the day before the operation, instigated a quick man hug, said a few words of standardised encouragement, and then left as soon as he had arrived. Although the encounter was briefer than a very small man, with a very small penis, wearing his tightest budgie smugglers, it was treasured more than Pete would ever know.

Building work was still in full swing, and it was like Clapham junction at times, although he had never been to Clapham, or the junction, so the comparison was based purely on anecdotal phrasing her had heard through the years. The knock through, from the main house into the new extension, had just been completed, and although there was no door, just a big hole really, accessing the top floor, was now possible through a makeshift curtain, which had been erected mainly to try and limit the cold air flowing into the rest of the house. Although impressed with the build, he found it difficult to enjoy this newfound space, as his thoughts kept tapping him on his shoulder, gently suggesting that he might never get to see the new house in its full glory.

Thursday evening soon came around, and the past twenty-four hours was partly spent rehearsing what he was going to say to Maddison and Archie. He knew that if he pondered too long, the emotion would get the better of him. In the end, he settled on a goodbye, love you, see you later, approach. Becky had invented a back story about going to the hospital regarding, well his back, so it really was quite a fitting account all round. In all fairness, on the scales of lies, this was more of a vanilla-coloured fib, as spinal problems, as already established, had been a reality for the past few years.

Although he would point the finger fair and squarely at the feet of poor sleeping habits, the harsh reality was a lot less simple to explain, as a simple lack of exercise in recent years had caused his back to stiffen. Physical exercise hadn't so much taken a back seat, it was more a case of it hiding in the boot of the lengthiest limousine. Since he had stopped playing football, his fitness regime had gone from three-hour sessions a week, to several 30 second trips to the kitchen, to make a cup of tea or to grab a biscuit. There aren't that many fitness coaches that have implemented the Typhoo and Jaffa cake programme yet, and the likelihood of "couch to kettle" becoming the next craze, also looked extremely unlikely.

It wasn't as if he was oblivious to his posterior issues either, as two years previously he had been advised by the medical professional that he needed to exercise and stretch regularly, to avoid his back from seizing. Apart from the odd occasion in the shower, when he would bend down to pick up the soap, and the additional strain would prompt him to spend a further insignificant 30 seconds stretching it off, about summed up Nicks "regular" exercise routine.

"Where are you going again Dad?" enquired Maddison.

"Just got to go to the doctors about my back remember?" he responded promptly, although adding a nonchalant twang to his tone towards the end of his reply.

"Is that right mum? She questioned, picking up on the fact that her dad was acting a little weird.

"Yes Maddy" smiled Beck reassuringly.

"Right... time to go Beck" declared Nick, partially aware of the time but also because he was getting emotional, so he wanting to leave before the kids pushed him over the edge.

"Love you...see you later" he said, softly, kissing Maddison and Archie on the tops of their heads in the process.

"Move out the way old man river" declared Archie, as the display of affection was getting in the way of some dire American kids programme he was currently engrossed in.

Ultimately, the kids were fine, and it appeared they had accepted the untruth with minimal curiosity. He took a glance back at the pair of them sprawled across the sofa and felt a wave of emotion rising inside.

"I'll meet you at the car" he shouted, leaving the house in a hurry in the hope of regaining his composure before Beck arrived. Moments later, after a couple of questions from Maddison in relation to what time they would be back, she jumped into the car.

"You ok?" she asked, giving him a reassuring smile and putting her hand over his.

Nick nodded.

"You got your overnight bag?" she questioned, stalling slightly with the seat belt, half prepared to jump back out to go and get it.

"Yep...packed it earlier this afternoon" he confirmed. "Well done you" she announced, synchronising the comment with the insertion sound of the seatbelt. "Now let's get this done" she added, opening the window slightly, allowing some of the stuffiness that had built up over the day to mingle with the fresh air outside.

The short drive to the hospital was relatively calm. Beck held her hand on top of Nicks, until it was time for him to change gears, but replaced it again once the car was moving freely. They pulled into the car park and due to it being later in the day, there were places aplenty. As normal, he started to park in one space but changed his mind at the last minute, meaning he had to straighten the car slightly to fit in the newfound spot, which was next to the original bay he had chosen. They both took a deep breath before exiting the car and headed towards the main entrance of the hospital. Rain was gently falling as they neared the automatic doors and he decided to first, take one last gulp of fresh air, and then paused briefly to look up to the heavens, which in hindsight was a pretty stupid thing to do, as a droplet of rainwater went straight into his right eye. He blinked a couple of times, in a woeful attempt to shift it, but this worked as much as a dole-ite, who had spent all his life signing on. Instead, he made the decision to just rub it away with his forefinger which worked like a dream, and turned his attention back to the task in hand, which was simply to enter into the building in front of him. He reached out, soggy finger and all, squeezed Beck's hand and together, they strode through the entrance that had just gracefully opened in front of them.

Inside, they were greeted by a smiley, yet professional individual, who took their details and asked if they could wait a moment, whilst the receptionist made a call to see if "they" were ready. His paranoid side watched closely as the telephonist held the handset to her mouth and began talking to the person on the other end. He was looking for signs, searching for fear, pity, sadness, any expression that may give the game away that she, and everyone else knew, that Nick Dean, a man with cancer in his right testicle, was in medical terms, well and truly buggered, and wouldn't be seeing the light of day ever again.

The person who met them on arrival and had returned from her visit to the receptionist area, then discreetly, started to explain what the next steps were. As they talked, she asked them to walk with her and she led them on a brief journey up one flight of stairs to their own private suite. She covered off the benefits of the facilities, which wasn't difficult as it basically consisted of bed, chair, window, and bathroom. It had the feel of some dodgy letting agent, selling a rat infested, dingy little flat with asbestos ceilings to some naïve first time buyers, before handing over the keys and scuttling off before they could ask any questions.

Although the room itself was basic, bordering rightfully, on the clinical side, it was ok and nothing like he had experienced before. That might have had something to do with the small fact that he hadn't really experienced hospitals that much before but comparing it to times when he had visited family members in the past, it was definitely a step up. He instantly compared it to a travel lodge, but a hell of a lot cleaner.

Upon dashing out, the smartly dressed lady had advised that the anaesthetist would be in shortly to discuss the procedure. Not knowing if this was going to be 5 minutes or 5 hours, Beck switched the TV on, knowing full well that's what Nick would have done if he was nearer to the remote. They sat quietly for a moment staring at the TV, neither of them actually watching it. The silence was shattered by a young girl barging through the door, announcing unceremoniously.

"SNATCH!"

Nick looked at Beck. Beck looked at Nick. They both turned to the girl and in unison questioned.

"Sorry, what did you say?"

"Schnacks…… what schnacks would you like for after the operaschion … sandschwiches…for exshample?"

The girl's impressive speech impediment briefly got them questioning what establishment they had entered.

"Ohhh" said the pair in harmony again…. Snacks !

"Erm…..I …I don't know?" responded Nick, slightly taken aback with the request so early into the evening's events. If truth be told and excusing the pun, eating was way down the pecking order.

"What do you have?" he asked politely, feeling that she wouldn't leave until he ordered something.

"Whatch wouldsch you like?" she responded.

The whole snatch situation was getting more difficult than was required.

"I will go for a sandwich I suppose?" he confirmed, but before he could offer any type of preference, he was rudely interrupted.

"Whatch type?" snapped the girl.

For the love of God!. Was this part of the procedure to make the actual operation seem less intrusive?

"Chicken? Ham? quizzed Nick, starting to wish he was in the toilet when Trolley McDolly came in.

"Yesch, whitsch one wouldsch you prefer?"

I don't even want a bastard sandwich you stupid girl. I'm sitting here, absolutely petrified about the next few hours and you are banging on about snacks like the demented sandwich police. That is exactly what he wanted to say, although his response wasn't quite as confrontational and less expressive.

"Chicken will be fine thank you"

"Drinksch?" she enquired.

"Tea, Tea…. a cup of tea would be great" he declared, instantly recognising the frustration in his voice, toning it down somewhat, as the sentence developed.

"Thanksch you" said the young girl, appearing just as disinterested the moment she left the room, as she did when she entered it.

"What the ….." announced Beck….. laughing as she made sure the girl was out of ear shot.

"I really thought she said snatch you know?" laughed Nick, turning his attention back to the TV that was now screening an episode of the Eggheads quiz show.

The room fell silent for a minute or so.

"How you feeling now? She enquired.

He gently nodded, forced a smile that could have been mistaken as a frown, and whispered the words "I'm okay". He was just about to comment on the generous size of the ensuite bathroom when a rather tubby, larger than life nurse, bounded into the room.

"Good evening Mr Dean…my names Dean….. well, that's a coincidence already isn't it ….. and I will be looking after you this evening".

"Hello" said Nick, followed a split second later by Beck, who gave a muffled "Hi".

"Wouldn't it be good if my surname was Nick...." added the bubbly character, who was busily readying the blood pressure equipment.

"Sorry, I don't get you" enquired Beck, who in all honesty was paying as much attention as a toddler crossing the road.

"Well then my name would be Dean Nick my dear......... and your husband is called Nick Dean......that would be hilarious wouldn't it?" proclaimed Nurse Dean, following the statement with theatrical, over the top laughter.

"Oh....right" said Beck, smiling politely. "What is your surname by the way?" she added, feeling that the conversation needed further clarity.

"Jones" he replied, diligently wrapping the blood pressure strap around Nicks arm, before switching the machine on, prompting it to make a delicate humming noise.

"Oh" repeated Becky, completely lost with where to now go with the conversation.

Nick felt the tightening off the strap around his arm and then a sudden release, as the blood pressure cuff, completed its niggling maltreatment.

"Right Mr Dean" announced Nurse Jones suddenly, "if you can just go and change into the gown in the bathroom, we will get you ready for the procedure".

"Uh...ok....now?" he questioned, realising that there wasn't going to be much waiting around, unlike what he imagined would be the experience at an NHS hospital.

"Yes indeed" the nurse announced in an upbeat fashion, "we don't mess around here you know!"

He slid into the ensuite that again mirrored a bathroom that you would find in some kind of budget hotel. The only clear differences were that this one was sparkling, contained complimentary soaps and had medical equipment hanging off most of the walls. So, when it came down to it, the word "mirrored" was dramatically incorrect.

"I take it I need to remove my underwear?" he shouted from the unblemished lavatory.

"Unless you want the surgeon to cut them off you, yes" was the chuckled response he got back from the nurse.

Nick looked at himself in the full-size mirror. The ill-fitting, round necked affair that he had just slipped into, didn't hold any prisoners. It also didn't hold his backside in either, so the question had to be asked, which clinical, clothing comedian, came up with that little medicinal chestnut. It was questionable, because at that very moment in a patient's life, when they are vulnerable, afraid, emotional and are looking for any crumb of support or comfort, do we provide them with a practical piece of clothing that is warm, provides them with an element of security, a sense of safety, but at the same time, retains their dignity ? Nah, let's give them something that is see through, doesn't retain any heat whatsoever, is ill fitting, and lets your arse fall out the back of it, classic.

He took one last look in the mirror, shook his head at the image in front of him and slowly opened the door, knowing at that point, it couldn't get any worse on the appearance front. Unfortunately, he was wronged more than a wrong un, taking a wrong turn, as Beck, upon seeing him, could barely contain herself. Although she desperately tried to bite her lip, the damage was done, as it was all too obvious that she wanted to laugh out loud. If it wasn't for the nurse, she would have told him what he really looked like, but she managed to hold onto those words of comfort until he had left.

The makeover however was still incomplete, as Nurse Jones, whilst Nick was busy dressing to un-impress, had provided him with the final, headlining addition to the outfit. He had gently placed on the bed, with the instructions to put them on before he left, a pair of what could only be described as, ladies see through stockings. Beck had questioned the need for these, whilst her husband was getting into his fairy feather operational gown, and apparently it was because they help with the blood flow and reduce the chance of deep vein thrombosis. So, five minutes later, with multiple huffs and puffs and several "do I really have too" looks in Beck's direction, reluctantly he pulled the leggings up and the getup was complete.

A fat bloke.. wearing a tablecloth... with silky nylons.....mmm niiiiiiice.

Chapter 22 – Well to do Nigel.

He didn't have long to brood over his appearance as the next medical professional entered into the affray. This was the one person that Lorraine advised that they needed to pay close attention to, as he was the one who as she put it, "holds your life in their hands".

It was the anaesthetist and the initial impression he gave was of an educated, well-spoken individual. Nick listened intently as Nigel, who gave off aristocratic vibes and was someone who you could imagine shooting pheasants on a bright Sunday morning, discussed the procedure. He was extremely reassuring, and if you were going to put your life in someone's hands, Nigel's mits would be well and truly in the mix.

Nick was concerned about the immediate aftermath of the operation and was more than aware that sickness was a distinct prospect. Recognising this and acknowledging that he had a phobia about vomiting from an early age, he was understandably keen to avoid this potential hazard, if there was at all any chance of it. His operational guru, Lorraine, had instructed him to ask for anti-sickness drugs.... and "don't spare the horses" was the parting instruction she had bestowed on him in relation to the topic. He waited for his opportunity before politely asking if anti sickness drugs were a possibility. Well-to-do Nige, was more than accommodating, making notes on his file and reassuring him that they had several different types and would ensure they provided him with the best cocktail to reduce the feelings of post operational nausea. Nick was visibly relieved with the news and although he looked like a proper Charlie in his current apparel, there was finally an element of relief.

Nigel finished off writing his notes on his document, either that or he was completing the bunny ears on his doodle. Whatever he was doing, he tapped the paperwork twice with the nib of his pen, before advising them that he was now setting off to go and get prepped for the operation, estimating that he would be ready for him in the next twenty, thirty minutes. With that, he shook both their hands, wished them well and made his way to the door.

"He was lovely, wasn't he?" smiled Beck, as the door closed slowly behind him.

"Yeah, really positive" replied Nick.

"I hope they don't forget the anti-sickness drugs?" he added, instantly reverting to type, and focusing on his glass being half empty again.

"Why would he you donut?" smiled Beck.

"He might just forget" continued Nick, attempting to justify his paranoia but failing like car brakes that have just had the pipe severed.

"Shut up and pull your tights up!" uttered Beck, getting up from the chair next to the bed, kissing the top of Nicks head before heading off in the direction of the bathroom.

Just as the lock to the toilet door clicked shut, a familiar face entered the room. It was Dr Khan. He shook Nicks hand confidently before picking up the clipboard that was attached to the bottom of the bed. As he scanned the document, he enquired about his current health. Nick obliged and began discussing his present wellbeing. However, he got the distinct impression that he was asking more out of standardisation and wasn't that interested in his response, so abruptly ended the discussion with the comment "but all in all I am feeling ok thanks".

"Chuckchick" went the bathroom lock and Beck greeted Dr Khan with a knowing smile. He held out his hand in the direction of hers and although she had just dried her hands on the electric hand dryer, she rubbed them discreetly across her jeans to ensure any excess water wasn't transferred in the palm-to-palm exchange. He began talking to them both about the procedure, and made it sound like a walk in the park. He made it sound so seamless and if he was in a Mary Poppins film, the images he created would have turned into an animated adventure, with wildlife skipping around the feet of a gowned patient, with butterflies and lady birds escorting Dawn to the canteen area.

He made the modus operandi sound so straight forward, that Nick, started to feel as if he had overthought the whole scenario. The operation that he had been dreading for the past week was going to be easy peasy, with an awful lot of lemon squeezy according to Dr Calm. He continued with the plan of attack, advising them that after the anaesthetic was administered, the right-hand side of his abdomen, just above the groin area, would be prepared for surgery. This was basically medical garnish, as the pair of them soon found out that this meant he would be shaved around the important area, which when they thought about it, made complete sense. The last thing the surgeon would want is a rogue hair intruding itself into the wound like some hirsute invader.

In Nicks ignorance, he thought that they would be cutting through his scrotum, whipping out the redundant said testicle, tossing it indiscriminately into some kind of surgical tray, before stitching the open scrote sack back together again, and maybe cupping the poor empty appendage in a specially made bollock bandage. In his defence, orchiectomy never came up as a conversational debate, when the lads got together on a Friday evening, so it was fair to let him off for his inexperience on this orchi-sion.

"How long does the operation take" he enquired, believing now that Dr Khan had made it so straight forward, that the short journey down to the operating theatre would possibly be the biggest drain on time.

"About an hour…maybe a bit more" nodded Dr Khan. Nicks animated world came to a sudden halt. The jolly holiday tune that had been blissfully playing in his mind screeched to a halt with a colossal scratching noise. The rabbits and birds looked at each other with an "oh no" type expression and quickly hid under the bed and behind the curtains.

"That's quite a long operation then?", quizzed Nick, realising that this wasn't going to be a zipadeedoodah moment after all.

"Not really" confirmed Dr Khan, " most operations take longer, so I would say it's quite a short operation compared to most. You will also be in the recovery room for about half an hour afterwards after we bring you round. So, you will be back up in here in around an hour and a half all told" he added.

"Any further questions on the operation?" he asked.

Beck and Nick shook their heads in a slight trance like state. "Okay then, the nurse will get you ready for the operation and I will see you shortly".

If this was a movie, Dr Khan would have thrown his jacket seductively over his shoulder, pulled down his shades and winked at the camera before exiting the room, obviously followed by a gushing blonde female nurse, swooning all over him as they left. However, it wasn't and his exit was a tad clumsy, as he bumped into the equipment when he turned to leave and then dropped his phone near the door, so more of a Jonny English moment than James Bond really.

"That sounds pretty straight forward doesn't it?" questioned Beck, still slightly star struck after choosing to ignore the awkward exodus.

"You have the operation then if you think it's that easy!" snapped Nick.

"I can't….I don't have the bollocks for it" she replied promptly, quite proud of her swift response.

"And neither will you in an hour and a half!" she added, knowing full well it was out of order but knowing that in any other situation, he would have said something similar.

"Unbelievable!" whispered Nick, secretly impressed with the sharpness of the comment.

Apart from the background noise coming from the TV, the room fell silent yet again. Nurse Jones re-entered the room to find Nick hiding the shameful operating theatre look with his own dressing gown, justifying the decision to pack the bulky, yet snug night time garment. The nurse was pushing a tray, like some type of clinical air steward, and asked Nick if he was righthanded, which he confirmed. He then proceeded to unceremoniously smear a blob of some dubious looking cream on the top of his left hand before carefully inserting a cannula. Although Nick had never experienced this before, he knew what it was used for, and recalled as a child, asking his father, when he was in hospital having a pacemaker fitted, what the "funny" contraption was sticking out his hand. Even at that tender age, it was clear, that these devices weren't designed for comfort.

"Ok Mr Dean, you ready?" announced the bespectacled nurse.

"What…now?" quizzed Nick, really surprised with how fast things had progressed?

"No time like the present!" added Nurse Jones, "just remove your dressing gown and get yourself comfortable in the bed".

"I thought we would be walking down to the theatre?" questioned Nick, now showing an ample amount of concern in both voice and expression.

"Not at all….. you get a ride down, so try and relax and we will do all the hard work"

He began removed his dressing gown, slowly, like some kid who had just been on the wrong end of a telling off, and gently peeled back the paper-thin bedsheets. Beck, sensing his discomfort, tried to lighten the mood with a comment about taking a photo of him in all his operating glory, just for the group in the village, before he got into bed. He declined in the politest way possible, by telling her to go and do one. It wasn't quite as pleasant as that, but she got the message, loud and clear, that he was no longer in the mood for jokes and graciously decided to replace her phone back into her pocket.

Nurse Jones, who was buzzing around being all medical, popped out and summoned support from a nearby porter. This guy strode into the room with reason and without standing on any ceremony, started unlocking the catches on the wheels with the toes of his boot. Beck scurried over and kissed Nick on his forehead and whispered "see you shortly" before quickly moving out of the way again to allow the bed to be manoeuvred out the room. Although she was a loving individual, public affection was never an area she felt comfortable in, so her recent display of warmth was as spicy as it would ever get. Nick glanced back in the room and gave a half-embarrassed wave as the bed gently bashed the door on its way out. The corridor, that only 45 minutes earlier was insignificant, was now a brightly lit tunnel that led to the unknown.

Down in the theatre area, he was greeted by a person that he initially, didn't recognise. Only when he started speaking did it click that it was the swashbuckling anaesthetist, although now in full operating regalia and no tweed jacket or flat cap in sight. "Right Mr Dean how are you feeling?" questioned Nigel.

"I'm okay" Nick muttered, feeling a bit of a fraudster for sponging a lift, when he was more than capable of walking the fifty yards to the lift and then the remain thirty to the room. The porter finished off shuffling the bed into position and diplomatically left the room.

"Good, good…. confirmed Nigel "just a quick overview of what is what. You are now in the pre-operative room. The theatre is through the double doors in front of you and the team are just prepping for the forthcoming procedure. It should take around 30-45 minutes to complete the operation but don't worry, I will be with you every step of the way, ensuring you are topped up with all the medicine that you need. Now, any questions?"

"That soon eh" queried Nick, "I thought there might be a queue or something".

"No" laughed Nigel, "we all want to get home…it's been a long old day!"

Nick looked around the pre op room from his prostrate position and, if truth be told, there wasn't much going for it. His private room had a modicum of personality, as the TV and the two pictures adorning either wall tried to give it a hotel feel. The pre operating room however didn't pretend to be anything other than a room that patients went through on their way for an operation. It was white, clean, and clinical.

" As I said before" continued the anaesthetist, "the operation itself will take around 45 minutes. The surgeon will make an incision in the lower abdomen and they will remove the testicle sack. Let me just check you have been marked on the right leg…… we don't want them removing the wrong one now, do we!"

Nick tried to raise a smile but was overcome with the whole scenario, so instead, just managed to utter the words "no we certainly don't".

"Once the operation is over, the team will wake you up slowly. You will be then kept in the recovery room for a further 20 – 30 minutes until we feel you are ok to go back to the ward….. questions?"

Nick was about to shake his head in confirmation but quickly blurted out "anti-sickness drugs….have you remembered the anti-sickness drugs?"

"Ha Ha yes, we have put a right cocktail together, as sometimes people react differently, but don't you worry, we have that well and truly covered".

Nigel nodded in the direction of an assistant who was busy doing what a good assistant should do.

"Righteo…. It looks as if we are ready to go" announced Nigel, moving around to the side of the bed.

Nick took a deep breath and closed his eyes.

"So, you will feel a cold feeling start to move up your arm as I inject the anaesthetic. After a couple of seconds, you should find yourself asleep and the next thing you know you will be waking up in the recovery room.."

He was a little disappointed if truth be told, as he was fully expecting to be told to count down from ten as the drugs were administered. He was confident that he could get to six, maybe five at a push. Friends and relatives had told him that it comes on that quick you will be lucky to get to eight. That was a challenge that he simply had to accept.

"Ok Mr Dean…in it goes" announced Nigel, faintly squeezing on the plunger that was now pushing the sleeping potion into the eye of the catheter.

"Oh yeah" thought Nick…. I can feel the cold sensation moving up my arm… that's amazing…ok let's do this ..ten, nine…………".

Lights out, he had gone! The optimistic goal was ruined in the space of two seconds.

Chapter 23 - Shouty Sharon.

"Mr Dean...Mr Dean, can you hear me" questioned a rather abrupt nurse, who by the sounds of things, had done her shift and was ready for her own bed. Nicks eyes flickered and through the disorientation, felt a sensation of someone pulling something from his mouth.

"Hello Mr Dean...... you just rest a moment whilst you come around", declared someone abruptly. "We will then take you back upstairs" said a different voice, who unlike the first nurse, didn't sound as if he had to be elsewhere. It was obviously a simple case of good cop, bad nurse.

He nodded sluggishly and slowly scanned the room. The first thing that he noticed was the clock on the far end of the wall. It was displaying 8.23pm. Well, if we were being ultra-factual, it wasn't displaying anything, due to it being an analogue clock face. This particular time piece hadn't moved with the modern times and all of the time telling had to be done by the individual, but even in his blurry state, Nick was able, in classic "play away" style, to make out that the big hand was pointing between the four and the five and the little hand was aimed ever so slightly past the eight.

The operation had taken over one hour but for him, it was like he had been asleep for seconds. Relief, happiness, confusion, liberation, elation where now busy partying alongside the cocktail of drugs that had been administered throughout the procedure. His brain was busy attempting to scan for signs of pain, but just kept getting dragged into the revelling that was going on. Eventually it gave in and just got stoned with all the other senses.

Glancing over, he could see there was a "recovery room friend", who didn't appear to be fairing as well as himself. He cunningly ruled out an orchiectomy straight away on the simple basis she was female, his sharpness and perception obviously unaffected by the medication he had received. The female nurse who initially woke him from his compulsory slumber, was now barking out her orders to "open your eyes" in the direction of this poor post-operative patient.

Unlike Nick who followed the instructions with ease, this lady was having none of Shouty Sharon and   instead of adhering, she simply moaned. Every time Shouty Sharon (or SS for short) commanded her to do something, the sleepy patient just increased the volume of the wailing. In the end it was a proper stand-off, so yet again, SS was packed off into a back room to do the pots, whilst good nurse took over with his reassuring prompts.

The overwhelming feeling of relief had now taken over Nick, and he lay there, contentedly staring at the ceiling. He could sense people busy milling around, behind and to the side of him, but their attention wasn't focused on him that much. To be honest, it didn't appear they were focused on the lady lying ten feet away either and gave the distinct impression that they were tidying up, similar to kitchen staff after a busy Sunday lunch. The clinking and jangling noises were intermingled, sporadically, with the groaning and whimpering that continued to come from the other side of the room. Although the surroundings and environment were totally alien to him, he felt surprisingly at peace, laying patiently, waiting for the green light to appear, so he could go back upstairs.

It wasn't too long, correction, it didn't seem that long, as a day could have passed by, and he wouldn't have been none the wiser. He was busy chasing Dougal, from the Magic roundabout, on his Raleigh chopper, when he heard one of the nurses announce that he was good to go. In strolled yet another porter, and again, began tampering with the wheels with the toe of his foot. Nick gave him a subtle smile, although due to the cocktail of drugs that where still doing the backstroke through his veins, he was essentially grinning at him like a teenager who had just experienced his first sexual encounter.

As he arrived back in his room, Beck gently placed the book she had been reading on the small table next to her and smiled in his direction. The porter, taking the normal "porters driving line" ensured that he bashed the doorway on the way in, after slightly misjudging the size of bed versus the access ratio. Nick was now sitting up and chatting to him like they were lifelong friends. He even suggested that they should "meet up for a drink" as the helper positioned the bed back into its correct spot. Carl, the name that Nick had probed out of him after he insistently repeated that he wouldn't allow him to escort him back if he didn't he supply his name, nodded sarcastically in his direction, although the subtlety of the head movement was lost on his patient, as he was already planning which nearby pub would be the benefit of his new found friendship.

"Hiya" he cheerfully announced to Beck, who had now come around to the side of the bed.

"Do you fancy something to eat and maybe a cup of tea?" enquired Nurse Jones, who was busy fussing around the bed, but in reality, doing very little. Nick nodded receptively and advised "tea with one sugar would be great"

"How you are feeling?" asked a concerned Beck, stroking his hand, relieved that he was back, but also thankful knowing that it wouldn't be that much longer before she could go back home .

"Feel really good....bit lighter down one side but good" he declared.

"I suppose it's a start with your weight loss!" she said, giving him a rueful smile in the process.

"Yeah, they are pretty much redundant these days anyway, so if they're still operating downstairs, get my mate Carlos to wheel me back down there, and they can whip the other one away as well!"

"Well, I don't think your balls will be partaking in much overtime over the next few weeks .... do you?" chirped Beck.

"BALL not balls, you are being pluralistic" replied Nick.

"Whatever" she said, "come on then...Lets have a look!"

"They haven't put it under my pillow for the bollock fairy to collect later you know" he announced, ruffling his bed sheets frantically in the process.

"Not your rotten old bollock, you silly tart, your operation....as you well know" tutted Beck.

He realised at this point that he hadn't looked either, so gingerly began the process of pulling the sheet back and shifting the gown to one side. To his disappointment, but after consideration, not really much of a surprise, a massive white bandage, with a congealed red blotch in the centre, covered his groin area.   The chances of a gaping wound being exposed to the world, was highly unlikely. It was a private hospital, not a ram shackled shed in the middle of two war torn countries.

"Well, that's unimpressive" she announced.

"Nothing new there then!" he quickly replied. "What were you expecting?" he added.

"Not sure to be honest" responded Beck, moving to one side, allowing Nurse Dean to glide past and off load the tea and biscuits he had just picked up.

"So, you will be quite sore for the next few days" announced the nurse, deciding to leave the cup on the side, as passing a mug of warm-ish fluid over the bandaged area, didn't seem the best of ideas.

"We will keep you topped up with painkillers throughout the night, but if all's well, you should be good to go tomorrow morning"

"Great" responded Nick " I can't feel anything at the moment" he announced buoyantly.   "I reckon I'm good to go now nurse….. pass my jeans Beck!"

"that's the drugs doing their job Mr Dean ……. a bit too well I might add!"
.

"Fair play doc….. stand down with the jeans Beck" he jovially announced, taking a sip of tea and removing a sizeable chunk out of one of the two biscuits.

Beck picked up the TV remote and pressed the on button. "I take it you want the TV on ? " she muttered, passing him the remote control mid conversation. He nodded and began flicking through the channels, pausing every now and again to sip his tea and munch on what was left of the biscuits.

Dr Khan, de-robed and back in civvy street clothes, swept into the room confidently.

"And how are you feeling Mr Dean?"

"Good thank you … how did it all go" he asked, squinting somewhat to soften the question slightly.

"The operation went very well. The testicle and surrounding tissue appeared to be intact which is a real positive. We won't know until the results come back from the lab, but it has gone as well as we could have expected".

As far as positive outcomes go, that was on the middle podium, flowers in one hand, medal round its neck, national anthem humming in the background, waving proudly at the crowd.

"How long does it take to get the result back Doctor?" enquired Beck, looking directly into the eyes of the dashing middle-aged medic.

"It can take anything up to two weeks but to be honest, they normally have them back within 10 days".

"What are the next steps?" questioned Nick.

"Well, we get the results back and you will then have a meeting with the oncologist, to discuss the way forward and review any potential treatment that might be required".

Suddenly, the waving medallist had been yanked off the podium with flower stems and petals cascading into the air during the mayhem. Potential treatment basically meant chemotherapy, and even the briefest suggestion of this method of medication had brought Nicks award ceremony to an almighty halt.

"I take it that means possible chemotherapy?" questioned Beck.

"Yes, it's a possibility, but that's not the only treatment available. It really does depend on the results, so let's focus on the positives. The operation has gone well, and it appears to have been contained within the testicle, which is really encouraging"

Dr Khan smiled at them both reassuringly before shaking Nicks hand and wishing him well

"See you in a few days then?" declared Nick.

" Possibly not" he stated. "To be honest, my work here is done really, the oncologist will go through the results with you, but if he does needs me for anything, I am sure he will get in touch"

And with that, he again said his farewells and left the room, tagging Nurse Jones on the way out.

"That's really good news", said Beck, again moving back to his bedside, sensing that as normal, his half empty pint glass was down to the dregs with regards positivity.

"Yeah …but the potential treatment aspect isn't good is it ….I really don't want chemo" he said, looking like someone who had just found a tenner but had his wallet stolen as he bent down to pick it up.

"Potentially is the key word here and remember, he also said that it looked like it was contained….so that's really good news " confirmed Beck, holding his hand as she clarified the information.

"Yeah…..yeah…. you are right …that is positive" although the words didn't match the manner in which they had been broadcasted.

"It does look positive" added Nurse Jones, picking up on the conversation and hoping that his little contribution to the discussion would help. He was wrong…. it didn't. Nick was way too busy focusing on the negative aspect of Dr Khans conversation, a skill that he had mastered over the years and credit to him, he was damn good when it came to him being pessimistic. He sat mulling over things for a few moments more, cunningly disguised as being engrossed in the TV. Yet again, another talent he had become skilled at over time.

"How do I go toilet by the way?" he asked, in the direction of the Nurse, changing the subject dramatically and breaking the dispirited thought process that was spinning around his head

"As you would normally" he replied, gently shaking his head and giving Nick a look as if he had just won the accolade for the most stupid question ever asked of someone medically trained.

"The bladder and the testicles work separately" he continued, still looking at Nick as if he wanted to add the word "you thick get" to the end of his remark.

"No, I know that!" snapped Nick, now questioning if Nurse Jones was the offspring of two very short and very thick planks.

"I meant, do I just get up and go loo or do I need something to do it into?". The nurse, still looking at Nick as if he was a few people short of a crowd, advised "No, you just go to the toilet as normal. You might be a bit unstable on your legs, but you should be fine".

"Ok, thanks" confirmed Nick, now shaking his head a little, as the conversation was a hell of a lot tougher than he had expected.

After removing the covers and swinging his feet slowly out of the bed, he stood up with a gentle quivering motion and headed off in the direction of the toilet. To say the short walk took effort was an understatement. If a bystander was unaware of his recent operation, they could have thought he was doing a Julie Walters impersonation, with the only thing missing being a couple of bowls and the words "two soups", as he wobbled his way to the rest room. The whole trip was painful for more than one reason and for a man who was known for speed and efficiency when it came to the urination category, this excursion was pitiful. The whole episode took a good 5 minutes, which when placed alongside his personal best of nine seconds, acknowledgement had to be given that he was, to put it mildly, a little bit off form. The water was still refilling in the cistern when the bathroom door opened. "Well, that wasn't too difficult" he announced sarcastically and began the painful walk back to the comfort of his bed.

Nurse Jones finished off what he was doing and raised his eyebrows slightly before leaving the room. In all fairness to him, he would have seen some sights over the years and Nicks elongated toilet visit, was possibly the last straw after a long, long day at the office. Beck walked back over to the bed and began gently tucking him back in, although Nick instantly pulled the covers loose again, as the restriction wasn't favourable when it came to the discomfort he was now beginning to feel. The pair of them sat together, well one sat whilst the other lay, silently watching an episode of Outnumbered. Twenty minutes or so had passed before the silence was broken.

"I'm going to get going in a minute..... is that alright?" whispered Beck, picking her handbag up in the process and rooting through the contents in a vain attempt to find the car key.

"No worries, can you kiss the kids for me and tell them I will see them tomorrow after school. What are you looking for by the way?"

"The bloody car key" she replied determinedly, items now leaping out the bag like disgruntled lemmings.

"Good luck with that" he announced, mistakenly taking a sip of tea, which was now cold, but deciding to swallow it rather than spit it back out. He let Beck rummage around for a few seconds more before adding,

"The key is in my coat pocket by the way".

"Twat" she said, regathering the contents and in the process giving Nick a prod, dangerously close to wounded area.

"Easy tiger" squirmed Nick, kissing Beck on her check as she leant down to give him a hug.

"You got everything you need?" she asked, swinging the handbag round, enabling the final two handbag lemmings to make their leap of faith.

"All good I think" he confirmed, having a sneaky peak at his wife's backside as she bent down to scrape the pour unfortunates up off the tiled flooring.

Beck glanced back to see him smiling like a two-year-old. "Pervert" she mumbled, moving over to the wardrobe, before rummaging frantically through his coat.

"Which pocket is... don't worry, found it" she declared triumphantly. "Right, call me in the morning when you know what's what" she said, walking back over to give him another kiss good night.

"Love you" he smiled.

"Love you too...nan nite" whispered Bec " shall I switch the light off?"

Nick nodded and the room fell into partial darkness as the door closed behind her, with only the light of the TV providing a tunnel effect over the bed. He briefly contemplated switching the television off, in the bizarre hope of getting some much-needed rest. He realised that there was as much chance of him getting some kip as there was Shouty Sharon displaying genuine empathy to one of her patients, as he was still buzzing from the whole operation experience. He drifted in and out of thought and time passed by in a fuzzy fashion, as did most of an episode of "Allo Allo", which he found whilst channel hopping, moments after Bec had left. Intrigue had got the better of him, so he had decided to watch the 80s sitcom, to see if it had become outdated over the years. It was safe to say that Officer Crabtree "pissing by the door and hearing two shats" was dated more than a cheap escort girl, but that aside, it still generated the odd smile here and there.

He soon realised that there hadn't been much activity in or around his room for the past thirty minutes. The corridor outside appeared emptier than his right scrotum sack and no one had been in his room since Beck had left a good 20 minutes earlier. Although surprised with the lack of the attention he was receiving, he was quite content with his own company. In reality, he wasn't sure what, if any, attention was actually required, so although factually correct in his observation in relation to the limited attentiveness, due to the fact that he wasn't sure what attention was needed, this thought was flawed from the onset. Another 10 – 15 minutes passed by, as did half an episode of Bread, another 80s sitcom that Nick had forgotten existed, before Nurse Jones strolled in the room.

"Has Mrs Dean gone for the night?" he questioned.

"Yes" confirmed Nick, yawning almost at the same time as he began speaking so it was more of a yaaaaaaaas, then a yes.

"Well, I'm almost done for the night as well. I will be back tomorrow but there is a good chance you will be gone by then. If so, hope everything goes well for you".

"Thanks Dean…. me too.. thanks for all your help".

And with that, the door gently swung back, and their brief association came to an end. The next thing Nick knew was waking to see Compo from Last of the Summer Wine, rolling down the Yorkshire dales in a barrel.

"Sorry, did I wake you Mr Dean?" said a softly spoken nurse who had entered the room moments earlier.

Nick had begun to realise, especially since becoming a father, that he could sense when someone was in the same room. This was the case if he was dozing or if in a deep sleep. Even when one of the kids would glide into the room stealth like at 1.00am, with no sound whatsoever, he would spring into life with a "what's wrong??" comment, directly aimed at the shadowy figure, which most of the time would be standing in the doorway. Again, this was another self-created, yet flawed theory, because in reality, he didn't have the foggiest idea on the amount of times people had been in the same room, and he hadn't woken up. How would he know, he would have been asleep!! Anyhow, he felt that he had a Spidey sense when it came to somnus and no one could convince him otherwise.

"No, I was awake anyway, I think" he replied, slightly disorientated and taking a few moments to gather his bearings.

Nurse Kemp was her medical name, something Nick had discovered when she leant over him and he got an extreme close up of her badge.

"How are you feeling now?" she enquired, "can I get you anything?"

"Any chance of another cup of tea and maybe something to eat?" all of a sudden realising that the two biscuits he had eaten earlier, hadn't quite filled the void of not eating since mid-day.

"I will see what I can do for you" smiled the Nurse, heading off in the direction of the door.

Nick was now reliving the conversation with the abrupt kitchen assistant who screeched "snatch" at him 45 minutes prior to the operation. He was salivating at the thought of a chicken or ham sandwich, with a salad garnish, accompanied by a packet of cheese and onions crisps. In all honesty, if Nurse Kemp rocked up with a pig-shit bap, with norovirus vomit flavoured doritos, he still would have woofed it down, such was the hunger he was now feeling.

Thankfully, he didn't have to wait too long to uncover what culinary delight was waiting for him, as the dark haired, slightly maturing nurse, came flowing through the doors like some modern day, snack bearing, Nurse Nightingale. The halo that surrounded her on arrival, immediately disappeared, as Nick spied, much to his disappointment, two more, chocolate exempt, biscuits. He was seconds from asking what Snatch Girl had done with his order but Ms Kemps smile and obvious delight in being able to fulfil the needs of her patient, meant he just reluctantly smiled back. He thanked her politely and decided that he would have no choice, but to hold out until breakfast. This wasn't as easy as he thought it would be, as the night passed slower than a lifeless snail riding on the back of a deceased tortoise. Hunger, at around 2.30am, had been overtaken by a sickness feeling and however much he tried, he just couldn't sleep it off. He attempted to "gaze the feeling away" through concentrating on the TV but this had the adverse effect and the feeling just grew stronger. Due to the act of barfing not being a close friend of his, he hesitantly pressed the little orange buzzer that was gently glowing next to the bed. He wasn't sure if this act would be greeted by ignorance or a full crash team, bursting through the entrance, defibrillator at full charge with several nurses flicking syringes as they rushed in to assist.

He was wrong on both counts. Firstly, as this was a private hospital, there was little chance he would be ignored. Secondly, with regards a crash team making a dramatic entrance, a break from watching casualty was the only medication required.   Nurse Kemp popped her head round the door.

"Are you ok?" she asked serenely.

"I'm starting to feel really sick" whispered Nick, taking him back to his childhood when he used to say something similar to his parents, normally during a car journey to the coast.

"Your anti sickness drugs will be wearing off, let me top that up for you".

As good as her word, she arrived back moments later. "Unfortunately, this will have to be injected into your bottom" she announced," will that be alright?".

Nick nodded. The choice of having a needle shoved in his bum cheek, versus sickness, was a vomiting no brainer. He adjusted himself onto his side as Nurse Kemp lifted the sheets. Although tempted to blurt out "don't look at my balls…. Sorry, I mean ball" he decided that banter simply needed to be replaced by procedure on this occasion. She tucked him back in and left the room, advising to just buzz again if he needed anything else. Within minutes the sickness started to fade, and the rest of the night was taken up by what felt like 15-minute power catnaps, twinned with glimpses of mediocre, slightly racist, somewhat sexist, early 80's comedy shows.   As the clock trudged closer to 6.00 am, he could see a flicker of light given birth outside of the window. Euphoria of the night before, had jumped in a taxi with one of the late shift nurses and the overwhelming sense that was now spanking on the inner walls of his mind, was hunger. It had started as a murmur, shortly after the disappointing double biscuit scenario in the early hours. Nearly 5 long hours later, the craving sensation had matured into a full blown, cantankerous old bastard, who knew exactly what he wanted, and there was Leslie Townes Hope (Bob Hopes real name to save you the time googling it!) of changing his mind.

Every slight footstep in the corridor lifted his spirit, as well as raising the anticipation in his taste buds. Time however, still tip toed by like a 25 stone welder wearing moonboots, and before too long, another sixty minutes had plodded by. There was little sign of a dolly or her trolley, to satisfy his needs, or more to the point, the empty stomach that was aching to be reunited with sustenance. Finally, what must have been a good ninety minutes plus a massive slice of Fergie injury time later, in sashayed an angelic figure, pushing a trolley, laden with food. She was of course encircled by imaginary cherubs and seraphim's, with heavenly music resonating throughout the room. Well, maybe laden was a little excessive, as it basically had a plate with a cloche to keep it warm and a small carton of fresh fruit juice, smiling cheerfully next to it. He nearly cried, such was the relief in seeing this four-wheeled delight, gently bumbling its way over to his bed.

The food angel parked the trolley and departed the room, this time alone, as the heavenly entourage had dissolved into the skies, taking the divine music with them. He wasn't too sure what culinary delight lay waiting for him and was now well and truly under the impression that the midnight chicken sandwich, that he ordered on arrival, had done a vanishing act and his money was on Nurse Jones as the main culprit.

Nick vaguely remembered passing the breakfast menu, and the responsibility, to Beck and he recollected her mentioning a healthy option may be the way forward in the morning. At that moment in time, he would have agreed to an avocado and five bean wrap such was his need for food. In all fairness, he would have agreed to join the schools under 15s chess club, wear lilac pants every Thursday and offer to play the bassoon in the local salvation army, if it meant he could get some grub down him.

In childlike anticipation, he lifted the cover that was keeping his delicious scran slightly hotter than lukewarm. He wanted there to be mushrooms, he yearned to see bacon and longed for succulent sausages to be bathing seductively in bean juice. He got poached egg on toast. Not even plural. Singular.

Disappointment couldn't contain itself and he simply tutted and shook his head. However, such was his hunger, positivity sparked into life, did a couple of stretches, moved its head purposely from side to side and leapt into the ring. He smacked disillusionment theatrically around its face, got him in a choke hold, and glancing back at Nick, telling him to "bloody well dig in fella".

He didn't need telling twice. He picked up a slice of toast with a generous chunk of egg clinging to it and shovelled it into his mouth, at pace. The only visible evidence left of the ruthless assault, was a droplet of yoke, that was left bleeding down his chin.   The second onslaught wasn't long in coming and faired the same as the first. This time though, the bright yellow yolk managed to find its way onto the white hospital gown, giving as good as it got second time around.

It wasn't an understatement to say that it was the best poached egg he had ever tasted and as he lay there, pushing his finger into the plate to pick up the last few toast crumbs, he wished he could eat it all over again. He begrudgingly pushing the tray to one side moments later, after accepting that he was now just tasting porcelain and however much he pretended that he could still taste the food, he was basically just licking night time sap off his fingers.

Although a cup of tea had also been delivered, which in normal circumstances would be the go to choice, he opened the carton of juice instead, as somewhere within, a part of him was crying out for vitamin C. The OJ went the same way as the egg, although this time without leaving any tell-tale signs of its existence. Although refreshing, the squash fell into the same unfulfilled category as breakfast, as there simply wasn't enough. Nick therefore turned to his trusty companion, tea, and had just started sipping it when his mobile phone, began softly vibrating.

 It was Beck checking in. Some of the friends within the village had nicknamed her "checkwibeck", a playful name based on the fact that Nick often utilised her to confirm plans, approve nights out and generally get reassurance on what he was saying. They talked briefly, mostly about the lack of sleep they both had experienced, but mainly about what time he would be released. This had now become the main focus, now that his stomach had been partially silenced with the earlier massacre that will simply be remembered as the Battle of Oeuf.

He mentioned how surprised he was with the lack of pain that was coming from the area that, only hours earlier, had been sliced open like a plump watermelon on a hot summer's day. Due to the astonishing lack of discomfort, this had given them both optimism that they would consent to him being discharged at a reasonable time and with that thought process in place, they agreed that Beck would do the school run and then come down, in the hope he would be allowed to leave, shortly after ten . It was nine fifteen when she eventually turned up. This was fourteen hours since his operation, nearly eleven hours since she had left the room, but more importantly for Nick, it was a full three hours since he had last eaten. Hunger had become agitated and was starting to cause trouble again.

"How was the shower?" asked Beck, noticing his hair was wet and electing on the notion that it was due to water and not a night of heavy perspiration.

"Bit of a struggle to be honest" he replied, "keeping the dressing around the area dry proved a bit of a challenge. Have you brought any food with you?" he added optimistically

"I don't think so, isn't it waterproof?" questioned Beck, returning to the shower conversation, but rummaging through her bag at the same time, in the faint hope of finding any nourishment.

"I think so, but still didn't want to run the risk of soaking it" confirmed Nick, his eyes becoming a little too fixated on the hidden contents of her handbag.

"You really do complicate things at times don't you" she chirped, pulling out a breakfast bar that in all honesty, should have been thrown away weeks, if not months earlier.

His eyes immediately lit up, as if it was the last wonker bar containing the lucky golden ticket, although the ticket itself wasn't the desired objective and would have been mercilessly discarded, with the edible contents being the only scrumpdiddlyumptious winner on this occasion.

"Have you spoken to the nurse about leaving? she added, passing the squashed, battered, oatey treat in his direction.

"They said it would be sometime around nine thirty, as they needed to get my medication ready" Nick confirmed, busy peeling off half of the badly faded wrapping that was desperately still trying to cling on to its sugary companion. Those words were still ringing in their ears at nine fifty-eight when the nurse finally came in. The delightful, but food-shy Nurse Kemp, had been replaced by a younger, less smiley, less helpful individual. She drearily provided Nick with a paper parcel and some specific instructions that were in all fairness, received with as much enthusiasm as the way they were presented.

Within the bag were some strong painkillers, a type of tablet that he had never come across before, a replacement bandage and a new pair of compression stockings. The directions provided, although partially ignored, were quite simple. Wear the sexy stockings for a few days, or until he was moving around regularly again, take the painkillers as per the instructions on the box and do not hesitate in contacting them, if he, or they, had any further concerns or questions.

Everything seemed pretty straight forward until, out of the blue, she provided him with an appointment card and instructed that he would need to return for a chest x-ray, a week later. Nick had flunked his Biology exam years earlier, but even he knew that the chest area was a different ball game when it came to the testicles. However, before he even had a chance to question the thought process behind this prescheduled rendezvous, the nurse advised that this was an important part of the post-operative process and would establish if the cancer had spread to other parts of the body.

Although the news of this additional procedure floated his boat with the same level of success as an iceberg damaged titanic, the need to get out of the hospital was the main driving force at that moment in time, so he decided to parallel park his apprehension, and address that particular issue nearer the time. So, with his appointment card in one hand and his little paper bag of drugs in the other, he inconspicuously slid out the ward exit, leaving behind a removed appendage that they could slice, dice and basically dissect to their hearts content.

Chapter 24 – David Cuppafeel.

The automatic doors to the hospital whirred lightly as they opened, and he breathed in an enormous breath of fresh air. It actually turned out to be 50% oxygen, 50% vapour, as a rather hefty gentleman, standing just out of view, had decided to release a mouth full of grubby, fruity flavoured smoke, just as the doors opened. The daylight that shot through the fruit mist made Nick squint slightly as he stepped onto the pavement outside. Beck removed her hand that was covering her mouth and glared at the chap who had just seconds earlier, spewed his carbon monoxide fog package in her direction. The scowl was lost on him though, as the chap had just finished with his vaping and had turned away and was now too busy concentrating on picking his nose and inspecting the contents. After deciding it wasn't worthy of eating or further examination, he wiped it nonchalantly on his trouser leg, before sauntering over to stand in front of a squalid looking taxicab. It didn't take a private or an NHS brain surgeon, to work out that he was basically a …. well, a dirty excuse of a man really.

As they reached the car, as normal, Beck went around to the passenger side and jumped in.

"I'm driving then am I?" asked Nick, pointing at his groin area with a "really??" expression slapped all over his face.

"Oh God, of course you can't …old habits and all that" shrieked Beck, opening the door and climbing back out.

Nick shuffled around to the passenger side and gingerly climbed into the seat, probably being too cautious if one was being ultra-critical. The sunlight danced through the trees as Beck drove home through the country lanes. Although Nick had took this particular route many times before, today was different. He noticed the geometry within the fields, he noticed the precision of the hedgerows and even noticed the architecture of the housing estate in the distance. For the first time, all of them were a thing of beauty. This perfect view on life was aided significantly by the sunshine that was radiating everything it touched. Would he have felt the same way if drizzle was drooling over the whole shebang, probably not, but today was a new day and his glass was nearly three quarters full, something he rarely, if ever, experienced.

On arrival back home, after the obvious detour to say hello to Ronald and his arches of gold, the workmen who were fitting the flooring in the newly built bedroom, had nipped off to get more material. Nick took full advantage of this unforeseen break and took himself off to bed, as tiredness had starting to kick in. This was a combination of factors really, with the main issue being the lack of sleep from the night before, but the drowsiness was being nobly supported by the cocktail of painkillers he had been taking and the three sausage and egg McMuffins that he had managed to devour in the fifteen-minute journey home. To be honest, he didn't really want to get into dialogue with anyone anyway, especially the hired help, and he wasn't yet in the position to enter into the world of "lad banter", especially considering the sensitive nature of his recent night away.

Beck fussed for a few moments, checking he had everything he needed. Nick knew that this current care in the community programme was going to be short lived, as Beck and nursing went together like pickled onions and custard. It actually was briefer than he thought, as half an hour later he found himself ringing her on his mobile, to establish if she had indeed gone to India to get the tea for the cuppa he was promised 30 minutes earlier.

The day dawdled along and after several slight snoozes, most of them cut short by the floor guys thumping with an equal measure of bumping, it was nearly time for the kids to come home from school, and this was something that he had looked forward to since arriving home. Although he knew that the encounter between father and children would be shorter than a pair of Trevor Francis England shorts, the cuddle he would get from Maddison would be better than any medication a pharmacy could prescribe. The same however, couldn't be said for Archie, who did exactly what his dad thought he would do. He popped his head round the door, said "hiya" before disappearing into his world of PlayStation paradise.

As the hours progressed, he soon found it quite a challenge to just lie in bed. Although he liked time out to relax, eighteen years of being a dad had provided him with a tinge of guilt every time he found himself not actually doing anything. As a child, he didn't do much around the house. A bit of washing up here, a spot of tidying his room there, but in the main, he was free, to do what he wants, any old time. As a father though, it was quite the opposite, as he would find himself forever being busy, his head spinning, like a whirlpool, it never ends. (yes, I know the lyric is actually Dizzy but deal with it!!). So, in his current state of being advised to rest, guilt had found its way onto his shoulder and was now making him feel uneasy about doing sweet adams, of the fanny variety.

Two days of uneasiness drifted by with little to report. The tablets that had been prescribed by the hospital remained in the paper bag they were supplied in, as he was keen to just stick to paracetamol and Ibuprofen, the Ant and Dec equivalent of the painkiller world. He had also by now, discarded the stockings, mainly due to the fact that every time he glanced in the mirror, he found himself looking at a crossbreed of his late great grandmother and Ebenezer Scrooge. Although there was still an outside chance that this decision may have welcomed DVT to the party, the visions, every time he went to the toilet of "old man in flesh-coloured stockings", pushed the scales very much in thrombosis favour.

One thing that had started to change though, was his mood. The drug fuelled elation that was all too apparent hours after the surgery had been replaced with a more reflective, sombre disposition. The relief of having the rogue genital brutally removed, and most probably beheaded, had now been replaced by the realisation of the damage that it may have potentially already caused. Having the operation was only the beginning and there was an emerging, realisation that within a matter of days, he would need to start chemotherapy, to try and remove offspring that it had left behind.

The internet wasn't much help and again, in hindsight, he needed to steer clear of that particular channel, as the information on the world wide web was not only clinical, but also menacing with regards possible scenarios. Beck was as always, still focusing solely on the positives. The comment that the testicle appeared intact was enough for her to cel-er-brate good times, come on. When Nick started with his "but what if?" conversations, she sprung back immediately with "but that's not the case, I just know its ok".

The problem he had with that specific upbeat response was that she had said exactly the same thing when he first mentioned he was experiencing discomfort down below. She also revisited the very same comment when the doctor referred him for a scan. The jock strap on the cancerous cake came when the results of the scan came back, and that they had found something. Even then, her upbeat verdict found its way onto her lips. By now, he had understandably began dismissing her assured correspondence and had started to ask her not to say anything at all. He started to genuinely believe that she may well be just jinxing the whole situation.

Nick had started moving around a bit more on the third day and had said a fond farewell to the guilt bed he had been lying in for the past few days. Although he was more tender than a company bidding on a contract, he soon found himself being more active than he probably should have been. Simple tasks like loading and unloading the dishwasher were okay, as long as the bending and stretching was kept to a minimum. Hanging the washing out, again bordered on being okay, as long as he didn't reach too high. The boundaries, however, were well and truly tested when Beck advised that the electrician was coming around later that day and to do the work that was required, an internal wall, that was only partially demolished, needed the final rights being read to it.

As he was feeling physically fit, kind of, and doing nothing for the past three days had took its toll, he offered to assist. Beck initially declined his offer, although on reflection and realising that there was a strong chance the build would be delayed, she reluctantly took him up on his proposition, albeit with a warning to take it easy. He began almost immediately, such was the need to do something and began tapping away at the brick work, gently at first, with about as much gusto as a tap dancer wearing slippers. It became all too clear that the Fred Astaire approach wasn't going to get the wall down in any reasonable time period, so instead, decided on more of a diversity, all action, no holds barred dance routine to get the job done.

He replaced the claw hammer that he had been caressing the wall with, and pulled out a rather battered lump hammer, that had obviously been involved in one too many hammerings in his time. This brought instant rewards, as chunks of brick and mortar tumbled like a single sock on a 30-degree mixed fabric wash. He did heed Becks warning though and was extra cautious of falling debris, adopting a side on stance, which although looked un-gamely, did the job. The electrician, who had turned up and was working on his own task list , worked around Nick, stepping over bricks, plaster board and basically anything else that had been hiding within the wall cavity.

"What was the operation for?" asked the electrician, looking at the ceiling whilst twisting and manoeuvring wires into place.

Nick briefly considered creating a story, as there was an uneasiness discussing testicles with the building trade, unless of course you were boasting how big they were and how potent the jizz inside them was. In the end, he opted for the truth of telling him about having a testicle removed, as he couldn't think of a viable fabricated ailment in time.

"Bloody hell mate, for what reason?" enquired Doug, who had now stopped what he was doing and was looking at him from the top of the step ladder.

"For the fun of it" briefly skipped through Nicks mind but seeing as the conversation had been instigated by a proper, tattoo covered tradesman, he thought sarcasm should take a back seat on this particular occasion.

"Testicular Cancer Doug" he announced matter-of-factly, taking another big swipe at the lower part of the wall in the process.

"Bloody hell!" repeated Doug, now re-engaging with the wires, prodding them with his screwdriver in an attempt to persuade them to sit exactly where he wanted them too.

"You ok now though right?" he enquired, descending the ladder, given the impression that that particular task was ticked off the list of things to do.

"I don't know to be honest... I don't get my results for another few days" clarified Nick with a hint of despondency, now tapping like a demented woodpecker on a cluster of bricks that just weren't for budging.

"Bloody hell!" blurted out Doug yet again, claiming the match ball for the fastest hat trick of mild swear words ever. "You must be worried mate?", he added, taking a huge step over the stack of bricks that had just came second in a two-horse race with a lump hammer.

"Yeah…… if truth be told, I'm bricking it" quipped Nick….. adopting what he thought was a tradesman like phrase but realising the pun as the sentence developed.

"Yeah, I bet you are mate" responded Doug, the gag flying directly over his head, before forlornly setting off in the direction of the graveyard for missed and misunderstood jokes.

Within half an hour, Nick had finished off his demolishing job and began gently throwing bricks, rubble and plaster board into the back garden. He knew at some point he would need to move them to the skip around the front of the house, but today wasn't that day and he severely doubted that the task would be on the agenda the following day either. In preparation though, he decided to load several of the larger objects into an old wheelbarrow that in all honesty, had fought the rust and the rust won.

By now, the effects of bending and stretching were starting to take their toll and he rightfully made the decision to retire from the bulldozing business and instead, decided to revisit a familiar vocation of drinking tea and watching daytime TV. He was hoping that his cinephilia career change would be short lived and would only last until he was fully fit again, but due to the grey cancer cloud that was circling above, he wasn't sure what health and fitness looked like in the future and maybe his destiny was to end his days, peering forlornly at a forty-inch screen.

Beck had by now picked up on the fact that her supposedly comforting "it will be alright" comment, was now as redundant as a bank cashier. It was heavily assisted by Nick taken the decision to finally tell her that her positivity hadn't "faired that well so far", and maybe it would be pertinent to avoid further cliché comments for the time being. This helped significantly in changing her mindset.

The brutal reality was that her mystic meg, medically inspired predictions, had peaked at an impressive 100% failure rate. With this newfound wisdom, she instead opted for the more cautious "lets remain positive" approach, which was frequently supported with, "remember what the specialist said" affirmation, in relation to the testicle appearing intact.

It was five or so days after the operation when Nick decided it was time to remove the bandage and clean the lacerated area. It wasn't as if he had become "Stig of the dump", or hadn't showered since the operation, he just hadn't bathed with the bandage removed. Obviously, he had been careful not to drown the strapping when taking a shower, as no one endorses a soggy bandage, apart from the promotor of the grunge band with the same name.

In fact, showering had become a bit of a challenge for other reasons since the operation, as the whole missing testicle scenario had caused additional drama. Over the past few years, he had become accustomed to checking the two Ronnie's as part of his daily grooming and cleaning process. It just didn't feel right anymore, just seeing if Corbet was okay and accepting that Barker had gone to the great sperm bank in the sky. There was also a certain level of disappointment that the double act had been disbanded. Although he knew that thousands of men have experienced the same situation, many of them a lot younger, he felt betrayed by his own body and saddened that there would never be the "Its hello from me, and hello from him" scenario in the shower again.

It was all unfamiliar ground too. He wasn't sure if it would be sore ? If it would feel saggy ? He wasn't sure if the other ball would move into the vacated area like some kind of appendage cuckoo. He eventually built up the courage a day later to David Cuppafeel and the results were spectacularly dreary, as there was about as much going on down there as there was a coned off area of the M6. However, the tentative fumbling that Nick had instigated, resembled more of a curious window shopper, rather than a full-on fanatic, who had camped out at the store two nights early. When all was said and done though, full on grope or tender caress, there was little, if anything of interest to report.

Due to this, he briefly began questioning if a testicle had been removed at all, as this first, brief examination, got him thinking that there wasn't anything different to his scrotal area, post operation. There was an expectation that the first feel would be the same sensation as picking up a deflated balloon, albeit a bit hairier and possibly more wrinkled.

Disappointingly, or more surprisingly, everything felt the same. He could still feel something occupying the area and seeing that he turned down the opportunity to have a prosthetic ball, he ruled that one out straight away. He was truly taken aback with how normal THEY felt, even though he knew, like a dissolved marriage, it wasn't us, them or they anymore, it was simply "it".

With the initial inspection over, he decided that was enough examination for that day and called off the Colombo style investigation there and then. He would have loved it if it was a slick review of the case, like Sherlock Holmes, mind mapping the evidence to come up with the obvious conclusion, that it was of course Moriarty, who had stolen the testicle in a daring midnight heist. Sadly, the findings were that of a bumbling detective in a trench coat, although give Frank Columbo credit, his clumsy "just one more thing" technique, always got to the killer in the end, so there was hope that an answer to this particular riddle would eventually be found.

The following day, again during his daily shower, he mustered up the courage for part deux of the "Mystère de la connerie absente" (or mystery of the absent bollock…..why does the French language make everything a touch classier?). This time, he knew that further serious questioning was required and there was a good chance that his fingers may have to result to good hand, bad hand if the answers weren't forthcoming. He was more determined than the previous day and this time, his persistent, hard-nosed handling of the case paid off, as he could feel that there was indeed, just the one testicle swimming around in its newfound freedom.

It must have been a similar sensation to being in the middle seat of the plane and the person on the aisle seat gets up to go to the toilet. That glorious feeling of additional space, allowing you to extend, stretch and trespass onto unknown territory. The main difference on this occasion, was that unlike the travelling companion who would inevitably return moments later, forcing you back into the Ryanair foetal position, old testy didn't have to gather in all its limbs and offer an embarrassed apology in the process. Nope, he could continue lounging to his spermy heart's content. Nick again decided that it had been prodded enough for one day, and with added reassurance that everything seemed to be in order, he left it alone to snooze, feeling that further provocation would only lead to more discomfort and insecurity for the lonely old sod.

The early morning ritual of waiting for the rattle of the letterbox, had yet again, offered less letters than a one vowel acronym. A week had passed since the operation and waiting for information was becoming the one and only focus in his life. The thought of having to undergo Chemotherapy was becoming the scariest situation he had ever found himself in. The previous time, when he was truly terrified, was a completely different situation but also boasted potential life changing consequences.

In his early twenties, he found himself walking alone, down a scantily lit side road, after attending a match at a local football stadium. Although rocking a "don't mess with me" leather jacket, he acknowledged that his build and appearance at that time was slender, with a strong hint of Rodney Trotter. Not the best combination it has to be said, when you are on your own in a dark alleyway. Nick had spotted the two would be assailants on the opposite side of the road and as he approached, they split into a lion ambush formation, making their way across the road, with him being the lanky Impala that had been singled out.

This prompted the young mister dean into one of the most over exaggerated walks he, or anyone else, had, or would ever, perform again. The reason behind this was at that split second, he revisited one of his rather sad and foolish bosses, who talked so much crap, that even his whispers where flatulent. However, for all the rubbish advice that he had provided over the two years he had worked for him, the one piece of counsel that jumped into his head was, "Remember to always make yourself big when walking". He briefly recalled seeing James, his old boss, walking down one of the warehouse gangways in a manner that resembled a cross between Frankenstein and an Orangutan. It was stiff, with exaggerated arm movements, an Oranganstein or the preferable name that Nick christened it, the Frankutan.

Moments before the two assailants split, one moving in front of Nick, and one going to the rear, he pushed out his chest, pulled back his shoulders, found an extra two inches in height, and started swaying his arms with more aggression needed by anyone taking a stroll. As one of the animals disappeared behind him, Nick improvised with a massive clearing of his throat. This wasn't on the list of bullshit recommendations provided by faeces features , but at that moment in time, he felt he needed some kind of audio to go with the visual effects he had shaped. The attacker to the front, who was still visible, intentionally strolled directly across his path, so much so, it mirrored one of those circus acts when horses or bikes, cross over each other's path with impeccable timing. To his credit, Nick didn't break stride, and if anything, managed to push his leather jacket out even more as he stomped past, like some demented, arm swinging, Arthur Fonzarelli from the 70's sitcom Happy Days.

As he strode past, bracing himself for the two-pronged attack, absolutely nothing. A stride later, still nothing. The temptation to look back was compelling but he felt that this was the weakness the hunters were waiting for and therefore deciding against it. He was now well and truly in full Frankutan mode, so continued for a few more steps, still awaiting the fateful first strike. Still nothing. That was the exact moment when his brain told the shoulders to drop slightly, to quicken the stride pattern a touch and for the arms to transform from aggressive flailing, to a more streamlined, by the side of the body, ready to run type action, which is exactly what he did after a few more moments had passed.

When reflecting on the event years later, Nick wasn't sure if he had just misread the whole situation and in fact, the hooded assassins were just a couple of lads who had moments earlier, been called in by their mums, as it was way past their bedtime. The reason why they split was simply due to the fact they lived in different houses that were three doors apart. Over time and with the memory of the event fading, he played it down, but James Davidson, his old absurd boss, most likely saved him from a kicking that night.

Chapter 25 - Hide and Seek, radiology style.

Mugging aside, and twenty-eight years on, he was now faced with a completely alien situation that terrified him. He couldn't move forward mentally and was totally reliant on the medical information that was still not finding its way to his door. The excitement of the build, which was at last nearing completion, was for Nick, as thrilling as sitting in a tailback. He found it difficult picturing himself looking out of the newly built bedroom window on a crisp, February morning, as he wasn't sure what the situation would be in three months' time. Although only 30 sleeps away, he did not, or could not, even contemplate thinking about Christmas. How on earth could he anticipate seeing the joy on Maddison and Archies faces, as they woke on the most wonderful day of the year, knowing full well that there was a chance that he would be visiting an hospital ward a few days later, to be pumped full of cytotoxic medicine. Medical appointments during the festive season are crap at the best of times, but the thought of trotting along, with cranberry sauce stains still on his jumper, to be injected with the terminator of all drugs, a potion so ruthless that it attacks anything standing in its way, certainly wasn't even near the top thousand things to do during the yuletide period.

As the days progressed, the cloud grew darker and became more menacing. The dreamy images of the post man passing him a letter, advising that the specialists had it all wrong and the lump was in fact a small snooker ball that he swallowed as a child, had evaporated. As had the fantasies of him and the said postie, skipping up the road, hand in hand in a Morecombe and Wise style, laughing at how the medical profession were so silly, had now been returned to sender, address unknown.

The picture that now replayed on a regular basis was a bleak, colourless room, with a faceless man, advising that the cancer, that started out the same size as a garden pea a few months prior, had now spread to his brain and although they would give chemotherapy a bloody good go, prepare for the worst.

To add to his woes, he had to also revisit the hospital for his x-ray. He vaguely remembered having one of these as a child, when twisting his ankle during the previously aforementioned, backfire buckaroo on his friends back scenario. He recalled at the time, sitting in the waiting room, with people milling around one moment, his mum included, then the next second, everyone disappeared in the shittiest game of hospital hide and seek ever played. The reason why the contest was so bad, was twofold. One, no one told him that they were playing and two, Nick could see them all huddled together in a room, staring back at him through the glass window. At the time he thought they must have been just discussing the injury and didn't want to upset the patient with the news that his leg would need to be amputated from below the knee. Only a year or so later, after watching a TV programme when it showed someone having an x-ray on a broken leg, did he realise the radiation reasoning for the fast exodus. In adult life, he knew that dentists and their technicians, still hid when taking a scan of your teeth. He felt that was surely due to the size of the room as they do tend to be a bit on the pokey side. He was confident that with incredible progress in modern science, since that day, thirty-plus years ago, he would encounter a completely new experience on arrival at the radiology department.

Sadly, it was safe to say that science had moved on with about as much success as the Sinclair C5, as yet again, he found himself playing shitty hide and seek, this time with just the one person. The whole visit was a bit of a mess if truth be told, although, as this was now the third time in a matter of weeks that he had visited, he was beginning to feel more comfortable with the surroundings and the whole experience was becoming less daunting.

Seeing as there was no queue, he strolled up to the "please wait here" sign with indulgent optimism, so much was his confidence, he was sure he wouldn't even have to break stride and would be immediately beckoned over to where one of the vacant receptionists were sitting. Nope, that would have been far too easy as none of the administrators appeared ready for him. Instead, he came to an abrupt halt, inducing the top half of his body to lurch forward in a slightly spasmodic, living dead, type movement.

Nick patiently stood looking at the three staff and guessed which one of them would have the honour of pointing him in the direction of the Radiology Department. The more mature lady on the left of the three, was either looking for a file in the cabinet or had decided she needed a break and was pitifully pretending to file something away. The lady in the middle seat had her head down and appeared to be busy writing something that simply had to be done at that point, regardless of whether it was Nick, or St Nick standing in front of her.

The last of the three amigos was the chap on the right-hand side desk, who was looking so deep into his screen, it was as if he had been hypnotised by his own booking in system. Cynically, Nick decided that he was faking it and had a distinct feeling that he just was waiting for one of the other two to say, "next please".

Thankfully, he didn't have to wait long for his answer and the winner, who was now the lucky beneficiary of being able to converse with a man with one testicle, was the lady in the middle. A split second later, hypno-boy lifted his head, justifying the cynicism that had been aimed in his direction moments earlier.

"How can I help you today?" she enquired, orchestrating beautifully with trance man next to her, who had just at that very point, fell under the spell of the spreadsheet yet again, as he clocked another patient making their way to the waiting point.

"I have been asked to come for an X-ray" Nick announced, consciously picking up on the fact his voice had carried further than he would have ideally wanted it to have done.

 The assistant, after gathering all the relevant information, shuffled over to the cabinet where her colleague had finally finished her rummaging, although, instead of returning to her desk, the mature lady set off down one of the corridors with a piece of paper firmly in hand, leaving the two of them to cover reception between them. Nick noticed out the corner of his eye that sleepy Sid had, albeit reluctantly, lifted his head and beckoned over the person who had stood in exactly the same spot as him moments earlier.

"Hope he gets someone with a severe case of halitosis " he thought, as he stood watching the lady elegantly flick though a row of files.

"Right Mr Dean" said the returning Margaret, a mid to late thirties lady who gave the impression she had been doing the job for a while.

"It looks like you also have a blood test booked in with us today" she proclaimed with a manner of authority.

"Oh, I wasn't aware" Nick stated, momentarily thinking about making up an excuse as to why he shouldn't have it done. "Do you know what it is for?" he added, still mulling over the possibility of advising Margaret that he was on a tight schedule and another day would suit better.

"Sorry Mr Dean, it doesn't say why. Where you not given prior notice?".

"Yes, I completely knew about it, that is why I advised you that I didn't know I was having it. I often spend my time having pointless conversations just for the fun of it Margaret." Was exactly what he wanted to say at that moment in time.

"No, I wasn't advised" was his actual response.

"I am sorry about that Mr Dean, but I am sure it will be needed for something. If you take this form with you, take a seat, one of the nurses will come and get you. Once that is done, please pop back here and I will point you in the direction of the scanning area. I will let them know you are here though".

Nick took the few steps to the waiting area and royally plonked himself down. There was absolutely no need to" play your chairs right" on this occasion, as there was more than enough seating available. In fact, the likelihood of the room filling up, which would have needed a major incident to occur right outside the doors, was extremely unlikely, seeing that the hospital wasn't on a main bus route, there was not a train track for miles and there wasn't a flight path above where he was currently sitting. Saying that, he still plumped for the old "cloakroom" option and placed his coat on the seat next to him, old habits and all that.

He was still feeling a little out of sorts, after what he felt, was being railroaded into having a blood test, when the nurse appeared and joylessly shouted out his name. He immediately rose and set off following, like some sheep, being shepherded back into its pen. The only thing that was missing was a couple of border collies scampering around the waiting room and the nurse bellowing "Come-Bye" in their direction. Unlike Baa

Baa black ewe and co, who would have merrily trip trapped up the corridor, he did a brief U-turn, swiping his coat from the vacant chair to the right of where he was sat only ten seconds earlier. He half-heartedly raised it in the air, like some crappy fabric trophy, just to indicate the reason why he was still more or less in the same place as when she entered the room.

The nurse was suitably unimpressed and just waited for him to catch up.

"Sorry about that" confirmed Nick, just as he reached the area where she was standing.

"That's okay" confirmed the nurse, who in all fairness seemed quite nice and maybe she just couldn't see what he was actually doing.

"I believe we are doing your bloods today Mr Dean" she questioned, opening the door to a vacant room in the process.

"Yes, I believe so" he advised "although I wasn't aware it was getting done today" he quickly added, guessing it would have instigated further discussions. It didn't.

Can you confirm your full name, Date of Birth and first line of your address please", she stated, whilst mooching around looking for what he assumed was a needle and sample bottles? Nick duly obliged and the nurse, dutifully checked off the details against the form she was holding in her hand.

"Can you roll your sleeve up please?" requested the nurse, placing the form on a tray Infront of her and picking up a needle pack and two rather small, plastic bottles.

"Any preference which arm?" he asked, pushing the hoodie sleeve up to and just beyond the elbow joint.

"Whichever one is better" she added.

At this point, he wanted to just clarify to the nurse, Michelle, that his role in this procedure was purely as a reluctant contributor, and that the limited medical knowledge that he possessed, didn't go much further than knowing it was important not to exceed the stated dose on a pack of paracetamol.

"I am not sure if I have a best side" he confirmed, adding "and in the past, it has seemed a bit of a struggle to find a good vein regardless of which arm it is".

"Let me take a look" she said, placing the strap around his left arm and choking his bicep within an inch of its life. This thinly veiled abuse (or thinly veined in his case) wasn't over, as she then began rigorously tapping on the reverse side of his forearm. This maltreatment was accompanied with assertive instructions for him to squeeze the palm of his hand together like an indecisive pugilist.

"It's a good job I am not called Nick Stone" he announced out the blue, still tensing his hand, but now losing any rhythm he had, so it just looked like he was now trying to catch an imaginary insect.

"Why is that?" announced Michelle, who was half listening and half focusing on the feeble blood channels that she was having to work with.

"Then it would be like getting blood out of a stone" declared Nick, pleased with the fact he had just set up the punchline and then delivered it with dad joke precision.

"Yes, that would be about right" she said, acknowledging the pun with the smallest of head movements. "Right, let's try this one" she said with nominal enthusiasm. "Slight scratch" she added.

Nick looked away yet again as the needle pierced his skin, causing his cheek to flinch ever so slightly.

"Success?" he questioned optimistically.

"Not sure yet" responded Michelle hesitantly, followed by "nope, that's not worked" a few moments later.

Three attempts on, feeling like a pin cushion, looking like a puncture repaired inner tube and carrying the additional advice to drink water next time he had his bloods done, he vacated the room. He thanked Michelle for her help and for the pack of round plasters she had used on him, and set off again, back in the direction of the reception.

He was however side-tracked slightly as he noticed a sign immediately after he stepped into acupuncture ally. It clearly stated that the Radiology Department was to the right, whereas the reception was straight on. He made the call to head in the direction of his next appointment, rather than go back to the main entrance and start the process again. It certainly couldn't be said that this decision was made in a rush of blood, as Nurse Michelle had haemorrhaged that option for him. The simple fact was that he was just a bit fed up of walking down corridors, to walk back up them again.

It was the correct decision as it happens, as the X-Ray area was just around the corner. This rebellious instinct gave him a modicum of self-satisfaction, and probably saved him a whole three minutes in time and 0.005ml of tread on his trainers. Margaret, the receptionist he had met on arrival, had done exactly what she said she would do and had informed the Radiology team that he was in the building. When he provided his name, they welcomed him with open arms, like he was a long-lost explorer. They offered him a seat in the waiting area, after ensuring he had confirmed his date of birth and first line of address as well, obviously.

The Radiology waiting area was a poor distant cousin of the main waiting arena. That could seat a hundred plus people on a good day, or bad day if you were of the unfortunate visitors. The one that Nick found himself in, sat a maximum of six, potentially seven if they did a bit of hospital feng shui and moved the water dispenser alongside one of the corridor walls. It wouldn't be a shock to anyone's system if that idea had been batted away by the Health and Safety committee as a potential walkway hazard though.

It was also much darker than the main reception. This wasn't really a surprise as there was way more lighting due to the size and the additional bonus of natural light coming in from the entrance area. Radiology was situated in the belly of the hospital, so there was zero sunshine, minimal amount of tube lighting and all in all, the lux level was low to say the least. That aside, he was the only one waiting so he was optimistic that he might be up and out within the matter of minutes, although as he didn't really know what a chest x-ray entailed, his thought process could have been shattered if he found out that it takes an hour for the machine to do its business.

It wasn't long before he had his answer, as out from one of the examination theatres came a burly looking chap who looked as if he probably did most of his shopping at Jacamo. Once in the room, Nick was instructed to take off his shirt and await further instructions. He did this with minimal fuss and glanced at his half naked reflection in the mirror. Even the past few weeks of minimal alcohol had not made much of an inroad into his alcho-pot belly, but as this wasn't the time or the place to be body conscious, he turned his attention to Big Ben, who with precision timing, had just re-entered after reappearing from the magic hiding booth toward the back of the room.

"Right Mr Dean, have you had one of these before?" he quizzed.

Nick shook his head and confirmed "nope" in a manner that tried to say, "I'm cool, confident and have this". Unfortunately, it actually sounded like Homer Simpson and if he took another glance in the mirror, the cap didn't just fit, it was well and truly snug in this instance.

"Don't worry" continued Ben " it's really easy. If you can just step up to the machine, put your chin on the rest plate in front of you, place the back of your hands on your hips and push your shoulders forwards please".

Easy was switching the light on. Simple was scratching your head. Effortless was blinking. The instructions just given by Benjamin were not far short from creating a dance move that Michael Jackson would have been proud of in his heyday, Shamone. Nicks lack of creativity within the world of disco enabled him to get every single part of it wrong. Firstly, he put his chin too far back on the metal plate, so that needed to be adjusted. Secondly, putting the back of his hands on his hips was so alien to him, he kept doing a double teapot handle, such was the utter confusion of having to turn his hands 180 degrees. If Ben would have said, pretend you are Mick Jagger dancing, but without the lip action, he would have had more success in knowing what was required.

The last part of pushing his shoulders forward, whilst keeping chin on the plate, and keeping ducky hands in place, was bordering on impossible. Ben, whose patience was obviously one of his stronger points, managed to get him in a place, that maybe, just about stood a chance of getting a half decent image.

"Right, hold it there!" he announced, dashing off to the Nuclear bomb shelter at the rear of the room. "Breath in" came a voice on a speaker in the unsafe room that Nick now found himself standing, rather obviously it has to be said, alone.

"Breath out" it said calmly.

"Breath in again and hold your breath" it announced moments later.

Although Nick did this, he suddenly began to realise that when you are told to hold your breath, it all of a sudden becomes ten times harder than when you just do it of your own accord.

"Breath out and you are finished" said the voice, which seemed like minutes later, but in fact, was no more than five seconds.

Mistakenly at this point, Nick decided to just turn his head back towards the mirror and could not ignore the reflection staring back at him. It was definitely Jaggeresque, although during his porky years, but with the added campness of Larry Grayson. Even Larry would have said "Ooo that's too much, shut that door!."

"Right, let's take a look at what we have then" said Ben, entering the safety zone, now that the self-implemented ceasefire had been put in place.

Stepping back from the machine, Nick was about to say "well I think we have an effeminate chap who needs a running machine" but decided against it, realising that Ben was talking about the X ray itself and at the same time, swiftly acknowledging that said chap may be slightly offended, thinking that he was directing the comment at him. This was a distinct possibility, especially taking into account that Benjamin probably found himself queueing down the chip shop most Friday nights.

The image took no more than half a minute to appear and was placed on the screen for all to proudly see. This was potentially a mistake as Nick instantly picked up on the darker areas of the image.

"Does that look normal?" he questioned, doing a good impression of a concerned patient.

"Couldn't tell you" said Ben instantly, "I am only trained in creating the images, I couldn't tell you if its good or bad. All I know is we have all the things we need on the image so from my aspect, it's a job well done."

Nick didn't quite believe him, but in all fairness, what could the Radiologist actually say? "Oh my, have you got plans for the weekend, if so, I would scrap them!".

With the scan in the bag, or at least it being sent to someone to download it onto the computer system, he thanked him and left the room, along with yet another slice of doubt to place alongside all the other pieces of paranoia he had collected over the past few weeks.

Chapter 26 - Deathwillbe Avenue.

The voices in his head paired with the lack of information coming his way, finally pushed him over the edge and he finally decided to call Dr Khan for an update. He knew full well that he would need to go through his receptionist, who in all fairness, was as warm as an unlit fire, but it was a step he had to take. Initially, he was taken aback upon hearing her voice, as she appeared to be coming across as what could only be described as "pleasant", and sounded as if she was actually happy to take his call.

Due to the sensitive nature of his request, she needed to refer the call to Dr khan which in all fairness, made perfect sense. Unlike a conventional call to a hardware store, where the operator can have a bit of a stab at a "will No Nails glue work on wood?" type question, the more specialised request of "can you give me an update relating to the cancerous growth that was caught breeding within my right testicle" was a little more exclusive.

The outcome was that she would call him back later that day. Although disappointed that he was no further forward and limbo was still the main event, he was pleased that he wasn't forced to arch his back for long as Michelle, Dr Khans miserable-turned nice secretary, as promised, rang back within the hour.

"Good afternoon Mr Dean" she announced, with more than a hint of positivity in her tone.

"I have managed to speak to Dr Khan, and he will need to talk to you with reference to the results".

Nicks expression, that only seconds earlier was filled with promise, dropped faster than a failed facelift.

"That doesn't sound good?" he enquired hesitantly, hoping that the response to this question was going to be something along the lines of "there is nothing to worry about, its standard protocol"

Sadly, it wasn't forthcoming.

Michelle continued with a severe shortage of compassion, returning to her old ways of not reading the audience and basically being pretty crap at her job.

"Unfortunately, he is going into surgery shortly, so he will not be able discuss this in detail until later this evening. He did however say that he needed to talk to you, so I am sure he will be in touch"

"Wow, that really doesn't sound good at all" repeated Nick, desperately casting his line to the furthest point of Lake Wish, hoping to catch the tiddliest slice of empathy. Regrettably, there had obviously been a severe drought and the creek must had been dragged of any benevolent emotions earlier in the day as again, miserable Michelle, dismissed the bait with distain, and swam back to the cold, murky depths off indifference with her comment "well, I can't tell you anymore, you will have to wait for the call from Dr Khan."

There was not a "sorry" in sight, no hint of an "I understand" lingering on the horizon and there was definitely an absence of "this must be a difficult time for you" running towards him with open arms. It was just a cold, sharp, dismissive "you have cancer of the brain, deal with it" type response. At this point Beck, who had gathered it was Miserachelle on the phone, was gesturing to Nick "what's wrong?" in a younger, yet equally theatrical, Una Stubbs charade type style.

"Can't you tell me anything at all?" he questioned, now just waiting for the words "spread", "riddled" and "months left" to come bounding down the phone.

"I simply can't Mr Dean" replied the receptionist, "You will just have to wait for Dr Khans call" she agitatedly repeated.

"So, there is nothing at all you can tell me now .....nothing.... not one thing......zilch" announced a visibly shaken Nick.

"No...No, I can't ....you know what you have, so I am not sure what you want me to say" declared Michelle, at this point not only winning the regional award for the most unsympathetic quote of the year, but also stealing the National Award for being the shit-iest receptionist of the decade accolade.

Beck, picking up on his distress, gently took the phone out of his hand.

"Good afternoon Michelle" she said in an authoritative, slightly pissed off manner.

"This is Rebecca Dean, Nicks wife" she added calmly. "Can you just explain to me what has happened. My husband is obviously upset with the information that has just been provided, so can I ask what the call later from Dr Khan is for?"

"well, I don't know why he is upset?" declared Michelle, now focusing on justification rather than information. "I simply advised that Dr Khan will need to speak to him later. I am not medically trained so cannot provide the level of information required. I have said too much already. Sorry I have to go, as I have another call coming in", and with that, Becky was left standing in the middle of the living room, with a silent mobile and a bemused expression on her face.

Nick by now, had gone into the back room that had recently been built, providing him with a much-needed view of the garden. If he stood on his toes, he could have seen the fields and woodland a mile or so away, but although agoraphobia was patiently waiting in the wings, the view of the backyard, which was a mix between a poorly maintained playpark and a miniature building site, was sufficient in allowing him to take a few deep breaths.

"She was helpful then!" announced Beck, walking up to Nick barefooted and realising that the newly laid concrete floor was not just cold, it was bloody freezing.

"What did she actually say to you?" she added

Nick took a moment before responding.

"Well, she said something along the lines that Dr Khan needs to talk to me which doesn't sound good. She also told me that I knew what I had, so wasn't sure why I was getting upset. I was hoping they had removed it, but it sounds like it's still there and that's what he needs to talk to me about…… this is the worst…. I was just hoping that it might, for once, be good news, but it looks like it's again, shit news!"

"She's a twat!" fumed Beck, "I'm ringing her back."

"Leave it" he sighed "there is no point, it will just make the situation more awkward …………and ultimately I will have to wait for the Dr to call me anyway".

"I know…" she said, "but that's just awful service and she shouldn't talk to you like that. You would have thought with the money they get paid; they would put a little aside for basic training."

"I will just wait for the inevitable" he shrugged, looking out the window again and letting out a sigh that well and truly fitted the mood that was now skulking around the place.

The next few hours where like a fun house, but with only the second word of the comparison being present. Nick hid himself away for the majority of it and even when the kids came home from school, Beck made an excuse that he was tired, so he could be at one with his own thoughts. It was around 5.30pm when the sleepy atmosphere was woken.

"Nick….its you're phone!" shouted Beck up the stairs frantically.

"Is it Dr Khan?" shouted Nick, who had just moved from the bedroom into the toilet.

Now back in the day, that would have been a totally futile question. Way before mobile mania had taken hold, knowing who was calling before you answered was a "tomorrows world" dream. Pre Nokia, it actually took around half an hour to dial someone, so knowing who was on the end of an incoming call back in the day, was like believing there would be a time when there were more than 3 channels to choose from on your TV.

There was no telephone keypad back in the seventies, so to dial, you would have to pop your finger in the relevant number slot on the telephone dialling pad and draw it around to a specific point. If the number you were dialling had higher numbers, like an eight or a nine, you would have to drag it round nearly 360 degrees. You then had to wait for it to chug its way back to the starting point, before repeating the process with the next number. Chug was probably the ideal word as well, as it did a kind of chugging or stuttering movement as it clomped its way back to complete its cumbersome task. Master Alexander Bell certainly didn't build the technology for those people having affairs or for folks who wanted to call dodgy phone lines. The mechanical stammering sound effect that went with the dialling movement meant discretion didn't have a chance, and everyone in the house, possible even next door, knew when someone was making an outbound call.

In addition, you did need to put a bit of effort into hauling the finger pad around, so that was potentially one of the reasons there wasn't any of your Jo Wicks workouts going on, back in those days. All you had to do was ring a few close friends and fifteen minutes later you were well and truly knackered. Crime was lower back in those days too. It didn't have anything to do with policing, poverty, schooling, or general respect, it was simply that people gave up waiting for the phone to dial 999, so crime just didn't get logged. It was also typical of the UK to choose the most time-consuming number to dial for the emergency services. Sometimes it just appears that forward planning and the United Kingdom just don't see eye to eye.

"Unknown number" shouted Beck, slightly out of breath after dashing into the kitchen to find the phone.

"Here we go" commented Nick nervously, meeting her halfway down the stairs.

"Stay nearby" he added, as he swiped the accept button.

"Hello Mr Dean, its Dr Khan from the Shires Hospital. My secretary advised you have asked for a call back".

"Yes, I did" he confirmed cautiously. "It's been nearly two weeks since the operation and I was hoping I might have heard more regarding the results of the biopsy. Do you have any further information?" he added.

"I fully understand Mr Dean. It can be a very stressful time waiting for the outcome and I fully understand your frustration. I have had a quick review of your case and from what I can see so far, is that it has been confirmed that the lump was malignant and was identified as seminoma, which as I probably mentioned before the operation, is quite common in testicular cancer. More importantly Mr Dean, this strain is less aggressive than other types of cancer."

"Well, that sounds positive. Is it?" questioned Nick, his emotion, briefly bordering on being optimistic.

"Yes, it is, and it is certainly more treatable than other forms of testicular cancer. Early indication also points to the cancer being contained within the testicle, but further scans and blood tests will clarify how far the disease has spread".

Nick instantaneously stepped back off the optimistic bus he was just about to board. He found himself yet again feeling very alone as the coach pulled away, crammed to the rafters of healthy people laughing and smiling as it disappeared into the distance.

"Have you had a chance to see the scans and the results of the blood tests?" asked Nick hesitantly.

"No" confirmed the doctor. "All of that side will now be handled by your oncologist".

Disappointingly, this didn't give him any reassurance and the shaded areas that he had noticed when, for want of a better expression, he was scanning the scans, were in fact parts of his body that would and should appear greyed out on an X Ray image.

"So, what are the next steps Dr Khan regarding further treatment?" he asked hesitantly, now sitting halfway down the stairs, doing a damn good impression of a desolate Robin the frog.

"Well, again, it is something your oncologist will go through when they have had a chance to review all of the results. Only then will they know what further treatment will be required"?

The line went silent for a few seconds.

"Are there any other questions you have Mr Dean?" asked Dr Khan, obviously nearing the end of his information providing session and now wanting to move into the goodbye, farewell, adieu, auf wiedersehen, aspect of the call.

"Er....No...." Nick muttered, looking at Beck questioningly just to ensure she didn't have anything she wanted to add.

"Well good luck Mr Dean. I hope everything goes well" announced the Doc, ticking another task off his list, whilst also earning a further £50 in the process for the two-minute consultancy session.

"Thank you, Dr Khan, thank you for all your help" said a downbeat but appreciative Nick and with that the call had gone.

"Well, that's good news Nick" said Beck, with more than an ounce of bounce in her voice.

"Is it??" said Nick, looking as if he'd been punched several times in his stomach and finding a decent breath was proving to be reasonably challenging.

"Yes it is!!" she exclaimed. " You heard him....he said it was contained...that's good news Nick...really good news. We should party!"

A shindig was the last thing on his mind. The only thing he was focusing on now was what "further treatment" looked like. In the 24 days since his diagnosis, he had gone through several emotions, with the thought of his potential demise, pretty much floating around ominously since day one. He had tried to manage the process mentally by dividing the whole situation into manageable, or less damaging sections.

The first step was getting confirmation of the diagnosis nearly a month ago, although that pretty much happened from the first telephone call from the doctor, even though the medic played a game of "I can't really tell you but have just kind of told you". The step before that was having the testicle scanned by the mouse wizard and his faithful companion, pervalot, although this wasn't included on the "managing cancer" checklist because at that point, Nick was naively still convinced that he had pulled a muscle somewhere close to the groin region. The second official action on the listing, was focusing on the operation or more notably, removing the disease that was growing within. Thirdly, and the final step on his imaginary register was something that he hadn't really focused on that much, until now. This was the aftermath caused by his substandard appendage.

What was accompanying Nicks chemotherapy fear, was sickening, literally. Just as Peter Cushing and Dracula went hand in hand, sickness, hair loss and feeling shit snuggled right alongside chemotherapy. It wasn't as if this hype was driven by the media either, as he had seen first-hand with his sister the true effects the life prolonging drug had on people. On those days when she was receiving the Angelic demon, he intentionally stayed clear, as the reality of what she was going through wasn't something he was able to, or capable of, witnessing. Just a few short years later, he was now standing at the entrance to the same cul-de-sac she found herself at, and was now squarely looking down the bleak, unlit Deathwillby Avenue. Unlike his sister, who wretchedly became a fully-fledged resident on that street, before eventually succumbing to the uninvited bastard, Nick, for the moment, was standing firm, just staring at a road ahead.

Insecurity, fear, and doubt were prodding, nudging, and cajoling him in an attempt to push him onto the pathway, just like some tubby, bespectacled kid being bullied in the playground. He searched desperately for an alley that led away from the gloomy highway, away from that fateful trek that seldom returned. A small narrow trail would suffice, one that was overgrown, covered waste high with wild grass and littered with stinging nettles. That would be a welcome option, anything that took him in the complete opposite direction and led onto Secondchance Crescent or Lifesprecious Lane. Although a voice from within desperately shouted out "the testicle was contained!", it had the similar, limited impact, as a loan supporter, chanting for the away team at a packed Wembley stadium. For the time being though and until further news of his pending doom was confirmed, he was officially just a window shopper, although he felt there was a distinct chance that he would be forced to make an unwanted purchase in the next few weeks.

He finally received a letter the day after, from the receptionist of a Dr Gavin Kirby, and it became clear that he was the oncologist who had been allocated his case. A date had been set, the following Wednesday, for Nick to see him to discuss the results and the dreaded "next steps". Within the correspondence there was a piece of advice, that where possible, you should attend the appointment accompanied. Even in his current state of despair, he could see that this was standard practice, even with the devil on his shoulder trying to convince him otherwise. Beck had already invited herself anyway, so the supportive recommendation had already been considered, accepted, and implemented before the envelope and been, licked, addressed and shoved in the overnight post tray. Although he wasn't surprised in the slightest with her decision, he was secretly delighted he wouldn't be entering the unknown world on oncology alone.

The next few days passed slowly. Becks upbeat mood wasn't being reciprocated in any shape or form. Nick was still withdrawn and was constantly staring into the shadowy future, desperately looking for that glimmer of hope. The harsh reality was that even with the sharpest pair of eyes, the strongest telescope or the most elite search team in the world, the only possible way to find what he was looking for, was for Dr Gavin Kirby to tell him the news that he was longing to hear.

Wednesday eventually lumbered into play, pushing an uninteresting Tuesday to one side. Nick was up early, so early in fact, Dawns crack hadn't even considered making an appearance yet. He had made five cups of tea and drank about 2 of them. The television had been playing non- stop since 5.00am but he had only taken notice of maybe fifteen minutes, twenty-five tops. Beck was still fast asleep, as the half hourly local news came on the TV, repeating the same information that had played thirty minutes earlier. Nevertheless, the newsreader still delivered the information with the same emotion, perfectly subdued on the sad and down beat articles and adequately smiley when it came to the news about the pet rabbit that found its way back to its new home after going missing during a house move.

Nick wasn't paying any attention to any of it and was just gazing out the window. Light had started to stretch itself out across the skyline and for the briefest of moments, he was again in awe with the glory of it all. He was so engrossed, he wasn't even aware that Maddison had dragged herself down the stairs and was now turning the TV channel over, regardless of if her father was watching it or not. Beck closely followed and although her early morning conversation was normally on par with that of a mute monk, halfway through a 10-year sponsored silence challenge, she placed her hand on his shoulder and whispered.

"Morning... it will be fine...trust me".

Fifteen minutes later, Archie made his entrance, and it wasn't long before the pre-school, morning mayhem was in full flow. The kids were on top form, and if there was an Olympic medal for "dragging your heels", both would have been gold medallists in their respected age group. Tasks were quickly allocated, and Nick was burdened with the kids pack up , whilst Beck reluctantly plumped for the "trying to find the PE kit" game, closely followed by the "hunt the homework that Archie had chucked to one side the week before" contest. To be fair, preparing the kids packed lunch did briefly take his mind off the pending results, with the "does Maddison prefer penguins or a fruit flavoured club?" dilemma, taking up a valuable 5 seconds. He eventually took a stab in the dark and decided to p.p.p.p.p pick up a club and with that, he snapped the lunch box lid into place and stood back, admiring the mini picnic he had just prepared. Ten minutes later and with forceful encouragement, the kids were out the door and on the short walk to school, Beck marching ahead like some demented explorer, excitedly beckoning her team to catch up, waving her arm in a "this way chaps" manner.

Nick smiled briefly. The sight of this trio disappearing up the hill made him realise how much he wanted the results to be good. No, he didn't just want them to be good, he wanted them to be spectacular...... as in, "Mr Dean, the great news is that it hasn't spread one bit. You have a tungsten testicle and it managed to contain the cancer in the same manner that Sellafield contains nuclear waste".

His dreaming was interrupted as Becky reappeared in the distance, no more than two minutes after disappearing around the corner. She was doing a kind of a run/walk that from the waist up, with arms a pumping, gave the impression that she was running, or in the least, jogging. From the waist down however, the effort wasn't being reciprocated. He quickly concluded that she just wanted to give the effect of rushing but wasn't in any haste at all, although, in her defence, they had time to kill as the appointment wasn't for another hour.

Half an hour trundled by before they both agreed it was time to set off. Although the journey time to the hospital was about eight minutes long, it was felt that parking time and getting to the right department needed to be factored in. Taking all of this into account and even allowing for the potential hazard of being stuck behind a tractor, they decided that it was worth it on this occasion, breaking their own code of conduct and decided they should arrive early to an appointment.

Nick, with the medically induced, two week driving ban completed, drove, and although the journey took a similar pattern to when they travelled together for the operation, there were a few differences. The silence between the two of them was identical. The radio channel, joyfully playing current songs that Nick had no idea who was singing them, was the same. The roads were alike in relation to the volume of traffic and surprisingly, no pointless temporary traffic lights had been erected, using up some of the annual council wear and tear budget.

The weather however wasn't the same, as the sun was shining, whereas the time before, they drove in darkness. The fact that he hadn't required to pack an overnight bag was also different, in all fairness, if they had told him to consider taking a spare pair of clothes and his toiletry bag, the edge that he had been delicately balanced on, would have surely tipped. All of these were subtle differences from the previous journey. The biggest transformation over the past two days was with the person sitting next to him. Beck, who had misplaced optimism throughout the whole process, and had only taken the gas off the positive pedal when Nick pointed out that she had been a little off the mark with her confidence, was now well and truly back in the "everything is hunky dory" room.

Ever since the call with Dr Khan days earlier, she had been basking in the comment "it appears the cancer was contained", whereas Nick, would only focus on the forthcoming treatment that would be clearly heading his way. Although he occasionally dared to dream that this specific cloud had a golden lining, those hopes were fleeting at best, whereas she was utterly convinced that the results were going to be encouraging. They did have the briefest of conversations about "the next steps" but these fizzled out as soon as they started, as she would immediately get on , get on, get on, get on, get on the upbeat train and cheerfully speed through Dooms Ville station, ensuring that this particular intercity wasn't planning on stopping at Woe-is-Me by the sea either.

He got out the car and looked at the building that was now becoming all too familiar. Beck was a little slower getting out the car, as she was traditionally finishing off her makeup using the small little mirror that was discreetly hidden on the inside of the passenger sun visor.

"Come on!" he snapped impatiently.

"Patience young Nick" she responded "looking this good comes with a price" she added with a smile.

The reality of her comment was ironic anyway. She was naturally attractive, as the multiple boxing analogies that had been directed at Nick clarified that over the years. She liked to look her best and took pride in her appearance, so much to the point that she wouldn't even go to the door to accept a parcel unless she had done her daily blusher and eye shadow ablutions.

He shook his head ever so slightly, although the moment was lost on her. She was still inside the car and wouldn't have taken note if he had been kidnapped at gunpoint, therefore making the small motion of his head that he had just mustered, well and truly redundant.

"Ready" she announced, climbing out the car like some Royalty on a visit to open a new state of the art stadium.

"Come on will you?" he repeated, reaching out his hand to meet hers.

"How are you feeling?" she questioned.

"Ok-ish" he replied.

"It will be fine" she said, squeezing his hand and giving him one of her best reassuring faces, blissfully unaware that she had given the same comforting smile on at least five occasions over the past month.

They strolled through the automatic doors with humbled confidence and unlike a couple of hospital virgins, who would cautiously make their way to the receptionist desk, they marched passed the greeting area, instructing that they were heading to the Chemotherapy Department , gesturing if they "should just go up?" in the process. The receptionist smiled and advised them that would be fine, just politely checking that they knew the way. It was only one flight of stairs which was a blessing as his knee had also started to play up over the past week. In hindsight, it wasn't helped by his wall demolishing exploits a week ago. At the top of the stairs, Nick pushed open the door that had a modest plaque with the words "Chemotherapy Suite" upon it.

That in itself was literary garnish of the upmost level, and adding the word "suite", at the end of the word, didn't fool anyone. The fact that the poor unfortunates who found themselves frequenting that particular hotel, would surely jump at the chance to not have to book themselves in on a regular basis. "Chemotherapy suite" was as ironic as a compassionate executioner or a luxurious sewer.

"It all seems a bit surreal" said Nick, squeezing some alcohol gel on his hands, unsure of the protocol, but seeing as the gel was there, with a sign advising to use it, he thought he'd better comply.

"Yeah, it does seem strange, doesn't it?" confirmed Beck, also gelling her hands, and giving them a good once over.

He took a deep breath and recalled back to the time, a couple of weeks earlier, when they arrived for the operation. The pair of them did, from time to time, do the "this time last week" game, when they would sarcastically reminisce about what they were doing days, weeks, or months before. To be honest, it was more of a Nick thing than Beck, but she half-heartedly played along on most occasions. Although it briefly crossed his mind to recycle the gag again, he thought better of it and instead just wiped the remaining gel from the back of his hands onto his jeans.

"So, we go left this time then?" Beck queried, remembering that last time they went right, which led to the patient recovery rooms.

Nick shrugged his shoulder whilst moving his head like the Churchill dog and they set off hand in hand, in the direction of Cancer Central Plaza's front desk.

Chapter 27 - So Dr Kirby.

"Good morning, how can I help you?" questioned yet another very smart, extremely polished, sunny receptionist.

He was slightly taken aback with her cheerful demeanour, although wasn't totally sure what he was actually expecting. Did he think that the person greeting him would be all sombre looking, dressed like a Scottish widow, whilst quietly asking him to confirm his name, so that no one knew that he was diseased, unclean, and not to put a finer point on it, a bit of a let down to the community all round. No, she was the total opposite. She was buoyant, colourful, cheery and although unexpected, he quite liked the welcoming.

"Take a seat and Dr Kirby will be with you shortly" advised Little Miss Sunshine.

He was still bemused by the time he had taken his seat. The preconceived idea that he had of the chemotherapy suite was well and truly being washed away by cheery staff, sweet smelling corridors and a sea of books, papers and magazines. The pair had glided past an elderly-ish couple and one single gentleman, who was so engrossed in the magazine he was reading, that even if a cure for cancer had been invented that morning, he would have been none the wiser

"You ok?" checked Beck, shuffling slightly in her seat with the aim of finding a comfortable spot. "Yep" he nodded positively, although anxiety was merrily bouncing around his head on a space hopper.

Unlike in private, where he would settle for more of an introvert behaviour, in social settings and a way to mask his nervousness, he did tend to go more the other way, hence the confident response and the slightly excited mannerisms. It was simply him getting into character as he wanted to come across as assured, even though inside he was that six-year-old who was scared of everything.

Nick contemplated taking his mind off the forthcoming results with one of the many magazines that were available. The thought was quickly dismissed after he discovered that the only material on offer, either related to women in their sixties or focused purely on what celebrities were wearing, with most of them seemingly unaware that they were being photographed, looking somewhat dishevelled, coming out of Marks and Spencer's on a Saturday morning.

"Why isn't there a Man's Weekly" he asked.

"Erm... not sure?" questioned Beck, who was now in the process of picking up the magazine with the headline "Little shopper of horrors".

"I know there are lads' mags that specialise on stuff like fitness, football and good-looking girls, but why isn't there a publication that just deals with more mature blokes stuff?" he questioned.

"It's one to consider" responded Beck, who wasn't really paying that much attention and had already flicked her way through the first ten or so pages.

"It could have sections on what age it's ok to use "Just for men", or techniques on how to remove random ear and nose hair. It could also include a section where it asks, *"Is it okay to yearn for a cup of tea instead of that last pint on a night out?".*

Beck offered nothing this time and carried on thumbing her way through the magazine with wanton extravagance.

"It could have one of those self-help sections as well" continued Nick, steam rolling ahead regardless of if she was listening or not. "You know, when it offers support for those men who realise that they no longer look lustfully at scantily clad girls waiting at the bus stop on a cold Friday night, and instead, just have a genuine concern on how cold they must be".

He glanced across at Beck, knowing that his previous comments and been brushed aside faster that an army of cleaners, sweeping the sweets of London on New Year's Day.

"It's a good idea isn't it?" nudged Nick.

"what's a good idea? she questioned.

"Doesn't matter!" he said smiling slightly, pleased with the nonsense he had just spouted and the fact that she hadn't listened to any of it.

While we are on the subject of not paying attention, this was quite a common theme in the Dean household. Normally though, it was the reverse, with Beck pointing the finger in his direction with regards not listening. His argument with regards this topic was simple. According to him, the majority of his working day, consisted of listening to people's problems and without putting a finer point on it, having to put up with them "banging on" about their run of the mill existence, day in, day out. This, he felt, gave justification for the fact that he may, just switch off a little, every now and again and the last thing that he wanted to do when he got home, was to go into extra time, with a distinct possibility of a penalty shootout at the end of it. There was also an issue with regards finding the right moment to engage in a conversation. Although she knew that it was about as successful as preventing a tub of "Ben and Jerrys" melting in a microwave, she would still frequently attempt the cardinal sin of any relationship, by trying to engage in a conversation during a live Manchester United game. Justifiable grounds for divorce in anyone's eyes.

The door to Dr Kirby's office opened and out came a casually dressed gentleman.

"Will be with you in a moment" he announced, reaching out a reassuring, outstretched arm in Nicks direction, giving some authenticity to the statement but realistically, having no real desire to make any physical connection. This enchanting gesture initially put Nick at ease, which was obviously the Dr's intention. Seconds later though, this thoughtful action was being internally grilled by the person it was intended for, as the devil on his shoulder, that had recently appeared all too often for Nicks liking, had climbed over mount scapular, and now sat there, throwing his unwanted opinion into the metaphorical ring, yet again.

"He's putting you at ease because there is bad news ahead" whispered Dev menacingly.

"Do you think he's putting me at ease because of bad news Beck?" asked Nick, a disturbed look appearing on his face.

"Don't be daft ....he's just saying he will be with you in a minute because..... he's going to be with you in a minute !"

Nick took a deep breath, gave a subtle shrug like motion before brushing his right shoulder twice, with a dismissive sweeping action. As there was no sign of the returning oncologist, he scanned the other people in the room and wondered where they were on the "pathway".

At a glance, he found it near on impossible to categorise, as there were no real tell-tale signs. In all fairness, if they were doing the same to him, they would have certainly said something similar, as he had also left his "Testicular Tumour Removed - Awaiting Results" cap, on the dining room table.

Such was the difficulty in exposing the truth, it became a near on impossible task, one that would only be potentially clarified, if he was still in the waiting room when they finally got called in. The elderly couple for example, who were probably in their mid-seventies, who sat directly opposite, both appeared healthy and fairly fit, so establishing which one of them was the actual patient, was hopeless. The single chap, still engrossed in his reading material, (or as Nick now thought, had picked up the wrong piece of reading literature and not wanting to bring unnecessary attention to himself in the whole magazine melee, continued to stare at "Knitting Monthly"), also showed no signs of illness either.

This gave Nick a modicum of reassurance and he began to think that they may allocate certain days or times to more healthier patients. So, with that reasoning, Friday must be "Fit Friday". He started to convince himself that if his appointments fell on that day, then he would be on the right track. From that moment, the aim was to avoid at all costs "More treatment Monday", "Touch and go Tuesday" and most definitely, steer clear of "Won't be long now Wednesday".

"Do you want to come through Mr Dean" smiled Dr Kirby, walking back into the waiting room and breaking Nicks pointless and grossly inaccurate thought process. Beck again squeezed his hand tightly, gave him her thirteenth comforting smile of the day and whispered, "it will be fine...trust me". He mouthed back "let's do this" and returned the compliment on the hand squeezing front, with significant interest.

"Please both, do take a seat" announced the casual, but smartly dressed bespectacled gentleman, as they shuffled hesitantly into the room.

Dr Kirby was a small chap, and he looked a little bit like Morocco mole, Secret Squirrels trusted sidekick. The only thing that was missing was the fez, although due to the extremely easy-going atmosphere that had been created within this specific part of the hospital, no one would have batted an eyelid if he pulled one out of his deskside drawer, plonked it on his head and broke into a rather embarrassing Tommy Cooper tribute.

"So, good morning both" announced the specialist, siting himself down in a rather plush looking office chair, after closing the door behind them.

"Just a quick introduction from me. So, you have been referred to me by Dr Khan and from your notes..." He paused briefly, spinning around in his chair to double check the accuracy of the information he was providing.

 "You are currently recovering from your recent orchidectomy that took place........ten days.... so, no, hold on.... just doing my maths..... so, two weeks ago...... well just over two weeks..... is that right?.....so the operation was on the 1st of November?..."

"Two weeks and 1 day" interrupted Nick, concerned with how long it was actually taking to work the date out.

"Yes... that's right...very good ...two weeks and a day..... so, fifteen days then...... just over a fortnight...not that long ago at all then really. So, as I was saying, I'm what's called an oncologist, which basically means I specialise in treating patients who have or have had cancer. So, tell me a bit about yourself Nick".

This in itself was another slight change to the norm for Nicholas. He was getting used to being addressed as Mr Dean in these types of settings, and being addressed by his first name, albeit natural, and fitted in perfectly with the cosy surroundings and introduction, it felt surprisingly informal. In addition to this, he had also picked up on the fact that Dr Kirby liked to use the word "so" an awful lot. He had a bad feeling that as things progressed and depending on how many times they would have to meet; this would possibly become a bit of an annoyance.

"So, my name is Nick" unaware of the irony in his choice of first word.

"Erm, I am a 48-year-old, married to Beck" pointing at the person next to him, who was still holding his hand tightly, "....and I am not too sure what else you need to know?"

"So, just tell me a bit more about yourself...do you smoke, drink, exercise, what are your interests?"

Although unsure in where the current Q and A was going, he continued.

"Well, I don't smoke, never have, I do like a glass or two of red wine though"

"Who doesn't!" interrupted Gavin, making notes on a rather fancy looking pad that sat on his lap, before placing it gently on the desk to the side of him. "So, that seems like a good time to give you a quick examination Nick. If you pop behind your screen, drop your trousers and pants to your knees, we will have a look at how things are progressing". Although slightly surprised a blood doctor was interested in his vacant testicle, he wasn't in the state of mind to question the worthiness of the invitation and did as requested.

Gavin or Dr Kirby given his official title, was being overly descriptive in relation to the word "screen". It was yet another flimsy curtain that may as well have been transparent, such was its weakness on the secrecy front. Nick reluctantly pulled the curtain over with the same enthusiasm shown by the worst ever McDonalds employee on a final written warning. The blind stopped woefully short of the length of the examination table, so this pointless piece of equipment took another step up on the list of most useless things ever invented.

Seeing though that it was only his wife and a medical professional who would benefit from the shittiest striptease ever, he started to undo his belt and began unbuttoning his jeans. He turned 180 degrees, so that he

225

was in a better position for the ascent onto the table and was met with the astounding realisation that the plastic see-through sheet was the least of his problems.

The examination table he was about to mount, was in the direct path of a window. Not only wasn't this window curtained, shuttered, or tinted, there was no obvious way he could see how the five-foot squared section of glass, could be curtained shuttered or tinted. It was becoming clear that the instruction of bringing someone with you was not for moral support, but to provide a star shape screen in front of the window. He was surprised that the advice on bringing an escort didn't stretch to state, bring a larger member of the family and someone with a big coat.

It wasn't as if the view was of fields or distant buildings, no, it overlooked Gladys from the payroll team. So not only would she be busily reconciling accounts that morning, she would be also having the joy of watching an overweight man, stripped from the waist down, having is damaged package, inspected by a bespectacled middle-aged man, who incidentally, would have looked good in a fez.

All of this would be done whilst his Beck desperately attempted to shield his manhood, by doing some crappy workout in the window frame. As it turned out, she wasn't required to do any Zumba moves, as the doctor pulled out a freestanding blind from behind one of the cabinets.

Thankfully, the examination was brief and within seconds, he was instructed to get himself dressed and to come and sit back down. Nick quickly adjusted himself and returned to the seat, giving Beck a sheepish look in the process. At this point, they both thought that finally, the news they had been waiting for, would be delivered. They held hands again and prepared themselves for the information that was coming their way.

No, that would have been all too simple. The doctor confirmed that everything seemed to be healing well, before continuing with his medical, twenty questions, game.

"So, what are your interests Nick?"

"Er, I like playing golf and I support Manchester United" confirmed Nick, forcing a confused smile to the surface of his face in the process.

"So, not a City fan then I see" smiled Dr Kirby. "I have never played golf myself, but always fancied it. Takes a few hours though doesn't it, something I don't seem to have in abundance".

"Yes, it can" confirmed Nick, now wondering if he was just completing a survey on hobbies and pastimes and the real medic would pop in at any time.

"Do you play as well Beck?" questioned Gavin, switching his attention on to her, but giving the impression he was still jotting the answers down.

"No, I did try it once, but was a little hungover, so don't feel I got the full experience. It's a good job because I know I would be better than him at it".

"In your dreams" replied Nick, falling for the bate and rising faster than a warm, moist, mass of dough.

"And what kind of exercise did you say you do Nick" questioned the Dr, pen and pad poised for the pending reply.

"Not as much as I used to, but still try and get a couple of runs in a week, and of course the golf".

"Good, good, yes, you will need to back off from running for a few more weeks, but you should try and keep that going as best as you can" nodded Dr Kirby, jotting a couple of additional points on the paper in front of him.

"So, do you have any children?" questioned the specialist, adding a more serious approach to his tone.

KAAAAABOOOOOOOOOOOOOOOOOOOOOOOOOOOOOOOOOOOOOOOOOO OOOOOOOOOOOOOOOOOMMMMMMMMMM

Here we go again, thought Nick. All the cosiness, the comfort and relaxing surroundings were designed solely to soften the bombshell. The inevitable "well you need to make the most of the time you have left with your loved ones" was shortly heading his way. They get my wife to come along to hold my hand, make me feel valued, ease me into their reassuring décor, before giving it to me with Lock, Stock and one massive smoking barrel. So, that's how "Mister So, So ,Sodding Kirby" wants to play it does he?

"Wh...wh..why do you ask?" questioned Nick sharply.

"No reason" responded Gavin, reverting back to his cheerful demeanour, focusing on his pad yet again, blissfully unaware of the shock that was being displayed all over his patients Chevy chase.

"We have two children" intervened a puzzled Becky, mouthing the words "what's up with you?" in her husband's direction, taking the opportunity to silently berate him and hijack the conversation at the same time.

"Yes" continued Becky proudly "we have Maddison who is ten and Archie whose eight. Nick also has two older children from a previous relationship".

"So, you have got your fair use out of the old testicles over the years then?" smiled Gavin, looking up this time, obviously proud of the comment he had just fashioned.

"Why do you ask about the kids Dr Kirby?" asked a concerned Nick, still convinced there was an ulterior motive behind the offspring interrogation.

"So, I normally ask just to get a picture of my patient, what they like to do, how they keep themselves busy..... I suppose I am just a bit nosy really .... especially if I am going to be treating you over the next few years".

"Treating ...what type of treatment?" asked the pair, paraphrasing slightly out of sync.

"So, treatment, yes. Now that seems like a good time to review your results" he announced, rotating once again in his chair, before finally coming to a stop in front of his computer screen.

"So, scoot yourselves over so you can see the screen" added Gavin, slightly shuffling up on his seat, which was completely pointless as there was no intention from anyone to park a bum cheek on the same chair.

"So, here are the results of the chest X-Ray" explained Gavin, pointing at the screen informatively.

Nick instantly renewed his acquaintance with the image he briefly scanned days earlier. The ghost grey had now turned into more of a charcoal shading, so his terror level instantly shot from moderate to severe in a matter of seconds.

"So, you can obviously see the spinal cord here" pointed the Dr knowledgably "and these here are the lungs, with the heart just hiding over this part of the scan" he added proudly, pointing freely at the screen in front of him.

"And what does it tell you?" squirmed Nick, squeezing Beck's hand a little too tight and taking a deep breath in preparation for the response.

"So, it tells me quite a lot Nick" he confirmed, appearing to drag out the suspense longer than anyone actually required.

"Firstly, it confirms that the cancer hasn't spread to the lungs which is great news".

"But" interrupted Nick, waiting for the part where he would be told that it had skipped the lungs and instead decided to head straight to the brain.

"There isn't a but at this moment in time" confirmed the oncologist, giving a reassuring smile in the process.

"The blood markers have also come back negative" he added, "so at this moment in time, it appears Dr Khans assumption that the cancer had been contained in the testicle, was correct".

Both Nick and Beck let out a breath that they were impatiently holding. "Do you know what treatment is required now?" questioned Beck, smiling in Nicks direction, rubbing his hand reassuringly in the process.

"So, I think the best course of action is to monitor things now closely over the forthcoming weeks. We will look at getting you back in about three months for a CT scan and to check your blood and then we will look at doing another chest x-ray a few months later".

"What?..... and no chemotherapy or radiation required at all?" questioned Nick.

"So, I think you mean Radiotherapy", corrected Dr Kirby "but no, at this present moment, it very much looks like we captured it before it had a chance to spread. We do need to keep an eye on it for the next few years, but fingers crossed, you won't need chemotherapy moving forwards."

In danced a mariachi band, with several colourfully dressed performers, prancing, and skipping around the room, Ole-ing and whooping to their hearts content.

"So that's it ?" expressed Nick, accompanied by a smile that although familiar, had not been seen for a few weeks and had just decided to pay his face an unexpected but very much welcomed visit.

"that's it!" confirmed the doctor, repaying the smile with an equal amount of delight.

"Thank you so much" chirped Becky, who by now had joined the smiling party and the three of them continued for a few moments more in the cheery bubble they had just inflated.

"So, we will be in touch with regards the scans in a couple of months but for now, carry on looking after those children of yours and get yourself ready for Christmas" announced Dr Kirby, getting out of his seat before making his way to the door to let them out.

"Thanks again!" they both said with heartfelt appreciation as he led them to reception, before bidding them a final farewell and then turning his attention to a gaunt looking chap, who had been patiently waiting outside. "Come on through John" Nick heard him say, maintaining his upbeat and perky persona.

"Did you see that poor bloke?" he whispered to Beck, as they set off down the corridor.

"I didn't really notice him" she gently mouthed back.

"He looked in a bad way" confirmed a fretful looking Nick, beginning to comprehend the enormity of the bullet he appeared to have just side stepped.

As they walked out, down the corridor of the Chemotherapy suite, the reality of what cancer brings to the party was on full show. There were six "examination" rooms that they had to pass and not one of them was vacant. Every single one of them had someone occupying the bed, being intravenously drip fed the magic potion that would hopefully cure or in the least, prolong the wonder that is life.

Half of them had someone next to them, reading, talking or just being there, whilst the others were alone. They may have had someone accompanying them, maybe they had just nipped to the toilet, or popped to get a cuppa or were possibly running late, but ultimately, with or without supporting cast, every single one of them, who were the named person on the attendance rota that day, had started the journey.

How far down the line they were and how many of them had the chance to find their own Inremission Crescent was unknown. The simple fact was that unless Nick decided to hold his own Q and A session with them all, this would remain one of life's unsolved riddles.

The walk back through the hospital was reflective to say the least. The farewell to the cheerful receptionist was more of a "see you soon" rather than a "bon voyage". The corridor that led to the operating theatre were filled with blended recollections of a few weeks prior, when he was anxiously wheeled away, only to be triumphantly returned a couple of hours later in an adrenalin induced home coming. Passing by the room where he was butchered by a crazed nurse with a needle, prompted him to remind himself of the mantra to drink plenty of water, which he would inevitably forget, the next time he was required to have a blood test. Seeing the sign, further down the corridor, which pointed the way to the Imaging Department, all of a sudden impelled his mind to start playing "I can't get no, satisfaction", which in turn, flickered a smile that Mona Lisa would have been proud of.

Finally, they exited the department via reception, into a grey and joyless November morning that was possibly the brightest and warmest day that Nick had experienced in many a year. The reality that life is precious, was creeping its way onto his horizon. The fact that he had taken everything for granted for way too long, was being overtaken with the need to hold his children, to listen to them talk, to gaze at the overwhelming beauty of Beck, who was blissfully just being in the moment. To breath and acknowledge the air that he had breathed a million times before, to smell the world that he had at times ignored, to watch the birds do nothing and everything simultaneously. He vowed at that moment, to never abandon these thoughts and feelings again.

Arriving at the car, Beck again walked around to the passenger side. Nick this time followed and kissed her gently on her forehead. "I'm driving aren't I!" she declared, laughing as she made her way around the back of the car, heading towards the driver's side.

"You know what?" announced Nick, clicking his seat belt into place.

"What's that?" she quizzed, pulling off slowly, braking slightly to allow the elderly gentleman to cross in front of them.

"The past few weeks has just been a right old ball ache" proclaimed her husband proudly.

"No, you just didn't!!" cried Beck.

"I just did!" he confirmed. "Do you like the fact I got the words "right" and "old" in there as well….as it was on the right-hand side …. and it was an old bollock compared to the majority of people who get the disease".

"Yes, very good dear" she sighed "I don't know why I'm surprised" added Beck. "I'm used to you talking bollocks all the time anyway…sorry, I mean bollock" She said smiling, overlapping her hand on his before finally adding.

"Come on Uncle Bulgaria, Let's go home."